WET WORK

Dick Thornby Thriller #2

Donald J. Bingle

Cover Design by Juan Villar Padron
Base Cover Image by Marianne Nowicki

This book is published by
54°40' Orphyte, Inc.
St. Charles, Illinois

54°40'
ORPHYTE,
INC.

ISBN 13: 978-1-7323434-3-6

May 2018

For Randall Lemon and Steve Glimpse,

top gamers and Top Secret spies,

for generations to come.

Prologue

Jerry hated his wife's car. He loved the hybrid's gas mileage, and he didn't mind saving the planet for future generations, but he was six foot two and husky. Squeezing behind the wheel practically let him steer with his beer belly.

Worse yet, his claustrophobia was heightened by a smoke-belching stream of growling Mack trucks hemming him in as they hauled gravel down the double black diamond sloped street plummeting to the intersection at the entrance to the Joliet bridge. The rusting, Erector Set style span crossed both the shallows of the Des Plaines River and, on the near side, the darker, deeper Sanitary & Ship Canal. With traffic moving, Jerry felt like he was running with the bulls at Pamplona as powerful behemoths thundered about him. When stopped for a red light, like now, he felt like a surfer caught in the break as he paddled out, praying a monstrous wave wouldn't crash down from above and pulverize him.

So Jerry kept his eyes glued to the rear view mirror ... just in case.

Today his watchful paranoia paid off. A fully-loaded dump truck crested the hill with the momentum of a tsunami, threatening to obliterate him like one of the splattered moths littering his windshield.

Damn.

Wet Work

Jerry manhandled the wheel hard left as he checked for oncoming traffic, then punched the accelerator to escape being rear-ended to death.

The subcompact whined like an overstressed golf cart, inching to the left until the gas motor kicked in, then trembled into stuttering acceleration. Jerry stared at the mirror, watching as gravel flew off the looming truck's payload and skittered across the roof of its cab. The unshaven driver inside braked hard, his eyes wide, a lit cigarette falling out of his surprised mouth, as his body lurched forward from the attempted emergency stop.

It was going to be close, closer than Jerry's morning shave with the quadruple blade razor the kids got him for Father's Day.

Jerry wasn't a religious guy, so no prayers whispered forth as he watched his ignominious death approaching, his grim reaper laying black rubber on the pavement and churning out white smoke as worn tires tried to overcome the momentum of tons of loose, shifting rock. Instead, a stream of invectives flowed from Jerry's lips as he imagined the huge tires of the gargantuan machine rolling atop his wife's mouse of a car and stomping it down, greasy, bloody, and flat. He was going to die a stupid, needless, painful death simply because his wife traded days for the neighborhood carpool to school.

He hoped she would feel guilty about it at his funeral.

Closed casket, of course.

But, then ... then the crappy automatic transmission shifted up. Jerry leaned forward instinctively, as if that could possibly save him. As he swerved farther into the open lane on the left, the truck driver jinked right toward the curb and the empty sidewalk, each action incrementally slowing the rate at which the gap between the vehicles was shrinking.

Maybe, just maybe ...

Suddenly, the hybrid farted forward, as if it had just seen what was about to happen via its reverse view camera. Jerry kept his foot on the floor—he didn't want to take any chances. He couldn't do the math to figure the angles and vectors, but his big, fat gut told him he was going to make it. His pursed lips turned up into a tight smile. But when he looked ahead he saw a lumbering garbage truck turning into the oncoming lane from Canal Street, which fronted the dark, murky waters of the commercial canal.

Jerry had snatched his life from the jaws of defeat only to thrust it into the jaws of a Browning-Ferris Industries garbage truck. He kept the steering wheel hard to the left, hoping to jump the opposite curb to the far sidewalk. With any luck he could stop before he reached the corner and t-boned the big, green machine with "BFI" blazoned on its side. He twitched his foot up and to the left, then stomped down on the brake as hard as he had flattened the accelerator only moments, yet an eternity, before.

Nothing happened.

Nothing fucking happened.

His foot ground the pedal against the floor, but the brakes did not engage. He searched frantically for the center-mounted emergency brake with his right hand as he gripped the wheel tight with his left, his eyes wide and forward, scrutinizing this new terror. Jerry's fingers grazed the emergency handle for a millisecond before the bump from bouncing over the curb flung them up and off, grasping at air. He jerked the wheel to the right now, straightening the car to avoid hitting the brick building flanking the sidewalk. At the same time, his foot stabbed repeatedly at the brake pedal. He gritted his teeth, bracing for the BFI, the Big Fucking Impact, to come. But somehow his lizard brain took over and he whipped the steering wheel back left again just at the correct moment, at the very edge of the corner.

Wet Work

The shitty car careened to the side, miraculously clearing the back of the garbage hauler by a whisker, avoiding the BFI.

There was a wondrous moment of sweet, sweet bliss before his still accelerating midget auto-coffin crossed the narrow breadth of Canal Street and rocketed up and off the grassy embankment. The toy car sailed into the air, defying gravity in glorious flight before arcing down and plunging into the stabbing cold, foul black waters of the Sanitary & Ship Canal. The windshield shattered upon impact, water enveloping him in a torrent as he sank deeper and deeper.

Fuck.

The only things he feared more than enclosed spaces were drowning and hypothermia.

Oh boy, a threesome; just not the kind he'd always craved.

The tiny car settled rear down from the weight of the batteries as Jerry—still trapped by the cold shock of the water, the heavy pressure of the deep, and an auto-tightened seatbelt—struggled for freedom. As the last wisps of faded gray-green light abandoned him, he watched in mounting terror as the air in the car rushed past him from behind, bubbling out through the broken windshield, seeking a sunny, warm freedom he would never know.

As his consciousness faded to match the cold black of the muddy bottom of the canal, one last thought flittered through his fading neurons.

He really, really hated his wife's car.

Chapter 1

Dick Thornby stepped off the pathway in Singapore's Jurong Bird Park and eased into the foliage near the hundred foot tall waterfall dominating the spacious confines of the African Aviary. He tugged at his cap, making sure it nestled low against his aviator-style sunglasses, then eased off his backpack, accessing a pocket and slipping on a pair of latex surgical gloves. He was taking a chance by sneaking into a prohibited area to find cover, but he figured waterfall maintenance was generally handled when the park was closed. A pair of scenic overlooks atop the falls normally provided tourists a panoramic view of the four acre aviary, as well as his chosen perch. But he'd dropped a couple of clapboard signs indicating the pathways to those lookouts were closed for maintenance, guaranteeing his privacy.

That the waterfall was one of the most picturesque and most photographed features in the sanctuary didn't help his tactical situation. But between his camouflaged clothing and his "act like you belong wherever you go" movements, he didn't think gawking tourists would raise any issue. A suppressor threaded onto the end of the rifle barrel would minimize any flash when the time came to take his shot, as well as lessening the rifle's normally booming report.

Escaping after the fact would be good, too, and taking up a position in the enormous bird sanctuary literally as far from the park entrance as one could get was tactically suspect. On the other hand, there was no denying the top of the falls was the best spot to pick off his target during a scheduled meet with a local thug seeking to up the quality and the quantity of his gang's armaments.

He was willing to take some risks to pop Pao Fen Smythe—the Hong Kong arms merchant who had indirectly caused the death of his last partner and been the moving force behind his son's crippling third-degree burns. Yeah, he'd risk a lot to take out Pao Fen Smythe.

5

Wet Work

He crouched low as he crested the top of the falls and crept into the ornamental plants covering the plumbing and water filter access. Finding an acceptable perch, he settled in and scanned for optimal sightlines for a clean, clear shot. No sense pulling out his disassembled MSG90A1 yet. He had more than an hour to go and he could assemble the weapon in less than thirteen seconds, even with surgical gloves on. No one but amateurs and movie thugs poked a barrel out of cover before the actual hit. Besides, many of the birders carried binoculars with prodigious magnification, though they were unnecessary in a park where the birds were enclosed in aviaries ... even one where the netting was more than a hundred and twenty feet above the ground. The African Aviary was so massive there was actually a station for the park's monorail system inside the netting. Of course, they'd closed the Panorail, as they called it, back in 2012. Apparently monorails weren't the transport of the future Walt Disney had thought they'd be.

Dick relaxed into surveillance mode as a small flock of Hildebrandt and Purple Glossy Starlings fluttered past, along with a pair of Whydahs. Birding was a good hobby for a spy. It reinforced skills needed for clandestine ops. Things like catching a flitter of movement out of the corner of your eye and being able to focus quickly on a precise spot to confirm the target location. Guys were better at detecting motion because the photoreceptors in their retinas boasted a higher proportion of rods to cones. Rods only required a few photons to fire, so they triggered in lousy light or from minimal movement. On the other hand, women were better at discerning color because their retinas included a higher proportion of cones, which triggered off of varying wave-lengths of light.

Spies trained to maximize both abilities. Dick could tell whether a distant avian sported a yellow eye ring like the Superb Starling poised nearby, its wings iridescent in the sunlight, or whether the

Livingstone's Turaco perched on the feeder well below him had a red beak (yes) or yellow spots on its black toes (no). He could also identify the make of a rifle pointing down from a rooftop by its profile and identify a Chinese assassin in Tiananmen Square when everyone else in the open, crowded location was wearing practically the same damn thing. You could tell women had no power in Communist China; they all wore identical drab olive pantsuits.

But Dick hadn't come to Jurong Bird Park to beef up his birding skills or test his eyesight. He'd come to kill. And that was okay with him, at least in this instance. He didn't ordinarily enjoy this aspect of his life as an agent for the Subsidiary, the worldwide clandestine organization devoted to keeping the planet safe when governments couldn't—or couldn't be trusted to—do the job themselves. It's just that he was, as HR recruiters always said, overqualified for the position. He was more than a trained killer. He was a trained spy— intelligent, resourceful, stealthy, clever, decisive, and skilled in surveillance, tracking, improvisation, and a hundred other disciplines used in the real world of espionage.

He hadn't used most of those skills in months, though, not since Denver International Airport. Luke Carroway, Dick's last partner, had died at DIA, helping Dick thwart one of Pao Fen's schemes. After narrowly escaping the DIA encounter himself, Dick had rushed home to New Jersey to find his college-aged kid, Seth, had been the target of an assassination attempt by way of arson. Seth made it out alive, barely, but suffered third-degree burns.

Retaliation was waiting in the wings.

Pao Fen Smythe was late, but that didn't worry Dick. Type-A personalities always tended to show up late for meetings. It was a way of demonstrating dominance, the whole "my-time-is-more-important-than-you-so-I'm-arriving-late-so-you-have-to-wait" macho bullshit. Big time arms dealers like Pao Fen also generally had bodyguards who, no doubt, would check the place out before the big guy entered the aviary.

Yep. Just as expected, two Chinese thugs arrived. Both had bulges under their jackets that weren't dancing pecs. They separated to scan both sides of the pathway as they made their way around the circuit in opposite directions. Tourists traveling as a group wouldn't do that. Of course, the fact they never looked up and their eyes never paused at the bird feeders or swarms of Carmine Bee-eaters or strutting Guinea Fowls made it crystal they didn't give a crap about birds.

Dick watched them as his thoughts drifted home. He blamed himself for his son's burns. Not just because Seth might have been safe if Dick had been home. No, Dick was at fault because Matt Lee, Pao Fen's favorite hitman, had set the fire. That meant Pao Fen had crossed the line between professional adversary and personal nemesis. And anybody who crossed that line shouldn't be surprised if Dick was willing to cross a few lines to retaliate.

He'd wanted his vengeance hot, but he couldn't rush things. Seth needed care and so did Dick's marriage. He couldn't devote his full time to his lethal quest and still pay Seth and Melanie both the attention they needed—they deserved. The powers-that-be at the Subsidiary weren't stupid, either. They knew Dick had a few things to work through and had limited him to local, low-level jobs for the most part since Denver. Lucky for him, one of those local jobs had involved a stateside arms dealer. That, in turn, led to information about Pao Fen's penchant for conducting his Singapore meetings at Jurong Bird Park. From there, it had been relatively easy to set up a fake meet for a specific date. He begged a few days off because of Seth's recovery and related "family issues," then booked a flight on his own dime and his own time to take care of business.

8

Dick crouched a tad lower behind the foliage, making sure to tilt his head so his sunglasses didn't glint toward the pathways. He hadn't provided any description of the mythical buyer Pao Fen was supposed to encounter when he'd set up this fictional rendezvous, so there was no way these guys would wave off their boss because his counterpart had yet to arrive. Instead, Dick had instructed Pao Fen to wait for his fellow gun aficionado to approach and identify himself by using the pass phrase "Excuse me, do you happen to have a piece of gum?" Given Singapore's draconian regulations about chewing gum in public, he had little worry someone would ask the question by accident. At the same time, the phrase was innocuous enough not to sound artificial.

Dick reached back and assembled his weapon, screwing a flash suppressor onto the threaded end of the muzzle.

He suspected the Subsidiary knew he was here, had tagged his international travel. Hell, they probably even knew why he was coming to Singapore. But the Subsidiary was a practical organization, not an idealistic one. They probably wouldn't mind if Pao Fen Smythe disappeared, as long as it didn't have any repercussions for them. They'd let this little frolic and lethal detour slide.

That didn't mean the Subsidiary would back him if his vendetta went sideways. The organization's first priority was to protect itself. Unilateral action was always risky. He could end up doing hard, long time in leg irons, breaking rocks in the hot sun by day and fighting off assaults by prisoners or guards at night. Asian prisons were anything but pleasant; choking down cockroaches was the best source of protein in most work camps. Yep, getting caught would suck, and he already had enough suckage in his life.

A few minutes after the Chinese mooks finished their woefully inadequate walk-through, Pao Fen sauntered into the aviary, wearing his usual Panama hat. At least the arms dealer's low-life muscle followed two steps behind their leader, so Dick didn't have to worry someone would pull a Timothy McCarthy and fling his body in front of his target like the Secret Service agent who leaped in front of President Reagan while Hinckley was unloading his Röhm RG-14 revolver. Most people didn't realize Hinckley never directly hit the President with any of his six shots. The crazed wannabe assassin had just gotten dumb-luck fortunate; the President had been hit with a glancing ricochet off the Presidential limousine.

Dick was a much better shot than Hinckley. Hell, he was a much better shot than Oswald, who missed with at least one bullet, too. That was important, because he wasn't just going to let loose with a spray of automatic fire until the clip was empty. He didn't take those kinds of risks with innocent civilians about, especially kids. He hadn't been a fan of collateral damage before he joined the Subsidiary, and he was even less of a fan of it now. No, this had to be clean and precise.

Dick steadied the barrel against a faux boulder, took aim at Pao Fen's center of mass, exhaled, and squeezed the trigger. The 7.62 round slammed into the target's chest at supersonic speed, exploding out of Pao Fen's back, spraying his goons with blood as Pao flew back. His Panama hat tumbled off as he fell. Dick followed the body through his scope, having anticipated the likely trajectory of his target when struck. He quickly zeroed in on Pao Fen's shocked, still face staring straight up into the air, which was already beginning to fill with hundreds of startled, squawking birds of African origin. Dick ignored the tumult below and above and centered his second shot. Another slow squeeze and Pao Fen's head exploded, further showering the bodyguards with blood, brains, and bone, sending them scurrying back toward the aviary entrance as their wide eyes searched for a target at which to return fire.

Chapter 2

Dick scrambled sideways, thrusting his left hand holding the MSG90A1 into the midst of the nearby waterfall and letting go. The sniper rifle disappeared into the spray and plummeted into the splash pool without a noticeable sound. It would be recovered, but not quickly. He hated wasting a good weapon, but it was hard to blend in with a crowd while carrying an unconcealed rifle, and he wasn't about to take even a few seconds to disassemble it. It was time he flew this coop.

He crouched low as he made his getaway. As he did, he stripped off his latex gloves, pocketing them as he headed to the nearest closed observation lookout, then ran along the walkway. He knew Security would not be on-site yet, and Pao Fen's troops had exited the field, so he wasn't too concerned about being identified by anyone with the ability and sworn duty to stop him. Soon he was back down to the level of the main pathways, joining the throng of startled tourists hastily exiting from the scene of the shooting. He slowed to match their speed and did his best to mimic their expressions of troubled panic. Thankfully, at five foot ten, he didn't tower over the crowd, even in height-challenged Asia. It helped, too, that Jurong attracted a large audience of Western tourists.

Of course, Pao Fen's guys and/or Singapore police—trained observers—could be waiting outside of the African Aviary, ready to corral, interrogate, arrest, or kill an escaping gunman. Dick needed another exit. He could cut the mesh enclosing the aviary and flee out the back of the park, but he'd discarded that idea when he'd first planned the hit. It wasn't just that the birder in him hated the notion of flocks of African birds escaping into the wilds of Southeast Asia, it simply wasn't practical. The mesh was built to be tough. Cutting it would be slow. Besides, the back of the park wasn't where he wanted to be; he couldn't blend in there. Instead, he stuck with the crowd thundering across the suspension bridge along the main path. Unlike the rest of the horde, however, he turned off at the Panorail station platform.

If he were in a James Bond movie, he would jump onto the top of a conveniently passing Panorail and somehow cling to the smooth roof as the train traveled considerably in excess of its rated high-end speed. Then he would simply stand, strip off his camouflage windbreaker to reveal a perfectly pressed tuxedo, and hop into a waiting Aston Martin. But he wasn't James Bond, the Panorail had stopped running in 2012, and he was definitely getting too old for that kind of shit.

All that, however, didn't mean the Panorail system wasn't useful. Cars might no longer hug the monorail as it swooped along giving panoramic views of all of the key aviary habitats, but the park had never torn down the elevated platform for the system. Instead it loomed above the exhibits in this section of the park, like the closed expressways in San Francisco pending repairs after partial collapse in the last big quake. Up here he could walk or run as fast as he wanted, with no tourists to get in his way and no adversaries to slow him.

He took off at a lope along the concrete path atop the flat, wide, magnetic, center rail, running clockwise, the shorter route to the main entrance. He breezed past Swan Lake, Pelican Cove, and the kid's area across from Flamingo Lake. It was almost too easy, but then, out of the corner of his eye, he saw someone pointing at him from one of the pedestrian pathways below. He ducked and swerved instinctively, adding a burst of speed as he focused in on the figure.

Damn, no luck at all. It was a local cop, now twisting to talk into his shoulder-mounted radio while he simultaneously struggled to unstrap and pull his sidearm.

The last thing Dick wanted was a firefight with anyone, but there was absolutely no way he would return fire on a policeman, especially in the midst of a throng of tourists and grade schoolers on field trips. The cop was just doing his job; he didn't deserve to die. He had a life and a family, no doubt. Mercenary thugs probably had families, too, but their career choices made them legit targets for spies like him. Offing them was a public service any day of the week.

Dick's tactical planning let him literally sidestep the nascent moral dilemma between capture and killing an innocent; he had other options. The Panorail system had, by this point, dipped close to ground level as it neared the main station. Dick kicked his run up a gear, then simply stepped off the monorail track as soon as he reached vegetative cover near the restrooms across from the wetlands display.

He ducked into the men's room for a moment to reverse his jacket, switch caps, and splash cold water against his face to ruddy up his cheeks. During the pit stop, he also flushed his used latex gloves down the crapper after slashing them to ensure trapped pockets of air wouldn't make them bob back up and clog the pipes or surface in the bowl later. His cover in wastewater treatment had taught him a few things.

Hope may spring eternal, but some shit simply floats.

Less than fifteen seconds after entering, Dick exited the facilities a changed man, a relaxed man.

A few minutes later, Dick was in the midst of what had become a mass exodus from the park as news and rumors about the shooting had spread via text, cell phone, and the panicked stampede of African Aviary patrons. He did his best to look irritated at having his day at the park ruined as he joined the exit queue to get his hand stamped for re-entry. Then he headed with the rest of the throng of disgruntled sightseers to the parking lot and joined the bus stop crowd.

Wet Work

He transferred twice and rode for more than an hour to get to his hotel near the airport. As he played bored commuter on the surprisingly tidy bus, he read the rules posted above the back exit door. No spitting, no smoking, no chewing gum, no jaywalking, no roller boarding, no music, no singing, no talking loudly, no eating, no drinking, and no pets. Fortunately for Dick, the sign didn't say "No revenge killing international terrorist scum who endangered your kid's life and ended your partner's," so he relaxed and enjoyed the ride.

Finally, he arrived at his hotel, checked out, and booked a seat on the next international terminal shuttle. Then he strolled into the dim, over-air-conditioned hotel bar to wait, hitting the john before sidling onto a barstool and seeking refreshment after a job well done. He ordered a non-alcoholic beer, getting a bottle of Asahi Dry Zero. Passable as beer, he guessed, but like drinking grape juice for communion.

More jolting was the price. Fifteen Singapore dollars. It was like dropping a ten spot at an eight-year-old's lemonade stand. The bartender, a kid who looked to be of mixed Asian descent, apparently noticed his eyebrows darting up when he saw the tab. "Not much demand at a bar for the alcohol-free stuff. I mean, what's the point?"

"Well," drawled Dick, "for one thing, the taste is sufficiently bland, you nurse it slowly, so you don't have to keep getting up to pee."

The bartender smirked.

"You laugh," Dick continued, "but having seen both the drink prices and unsanitary conditions in your restroom, drinking a lot here doesn't seem like a good idea."

The bartender's smirk morphed into a scowl and he stalked off to the other end of the bar to chat up a couple of German fräuleins. Hormones trump logic, Dick guessed, even in a dank, frigid, overpriced bar like this.

Nothing to do but kill time until his flight, now that the real killing was done. Since this was an off-the-books excursion, there would be no reports to file, no debriefing, and no need to check in with his bosses at the Subsidiary.

He did make one call, however, using a cheap, prepaid phone he'd picked up for the trip. As expected this time of night in the United States, the call went straight to voicemail: "Hey, Melanie. Just checking in, as promised. I'm still in Singapore, but heading back home, landing in Newark mid-morning day after tomorrow, your time. I'll stop at the hospital to see Seth on my way to the house, roughly thirty hours from now. Take care … love you, babe."

He always felt awkward about calling home to check in. It wasn't just that it felt childish and emasculating … he could live with that to save his marriage. But the operative in him knew it was bad spycraft … damn bad spycraft … he and Melanie might someday regret.

Still, he did what he had to do. And right now, he had to do this.

He sighed. Maybe he should just get out of the business now that this score was settled. It would certainly simplify reconciling with Melanie. It was a tough decision. He liked making a difference in the world, and he was getting too old for a major career-change at this point … assuming the Subsidiary would even allow that.

Maybe something in franchising? Shave ice, perhaps? He'd stopped over in Hawaii a few times on missions and had always been impressed by the smooth, snowy texture of true shave ice and the vibrant, fruity syrups poured on top. New Jersey had nothing like that. It could catch on.

He shook his head to clear his thoughts, but instead spied a couple in the back booth, nuzzling like a pair of Black-Masked Lovebirds he'd seen cuddling and cleaning one another in apparent romantic bliss at the Bird Park.

Wet Work

No, his chances of making a go out of a shave ice business in Jersey were the same as his chances of ever getting that cozy, that innocent and playful, with Melanie again—a snowcone's chance in hell.

Chapter 3

Glenn Swynton arrived at the Philadelphia headquarters of the Subsidiary with the dawn. His summer-weight bespoke suit was a light charcoal with micro-thin, pale gray pinstripes. The double-breasted cut highlighted his impeccable fashion sense and subtly accentuated his trim physique. A rose and burgundy silk tie knotted tightly flat against the stark, starched white of his tailored shirt complemented the polished garnets on the cufflinks fixing the French cuffs peeking out from the crisply defined sleeves of his jacket.

He knew some ... probably most ... of his colleagues at the Subsidiary found his meticulous attention to detail in his appearance a tad compulsive, even prissy. Certainly, his fastidious fashion-sense was one of the many subtle things that distanced his relationship with his putative boss, Deirdre Tammany, Director of the Subsidiary. Of course, no one, including Dee—as she so colonially insisted being called—had any complaint about his parallel level of attention to detail in his work. His clothes fetish, as he had heard one wag refer to it, was not an affectation or a quirk; it was a physical manifestation of his complete and utter devotion to make certain beyond doubt that everything everywhere he could control was proper and orderly and correct in every way. Far from a character flaw, it was outward evidence of an orderly and precise character.

He took the wood paneled private lift for Catalyst Crisis Consulting's executive level to the top floor and stepped out into the clean, modern offices. As befitted the Subsidiary's cover as a high-end consulting agency, the equipment was top-end and the decorating a mixture of rich hardwoods and Italian marbles. The furnishings were sufficiently opulent to make the Chief Executive Officer of a Fortune 500 company comfortable, but not so extravagant so as to make the

Wet Work

Chief Financial Officer of such a company worry the firm's services were overpriced.

Fixing a heavily-steeped spot of tea and honey with quick, efficient motions as he read the overnight intelligence reports, Glenn separated the wheat from the chaff and compiled the morning summary to be electronically transmitted for Dee to read during her short, chauffeured ride to HQ in a few hours.

The morning brief had been getting briefer in the past few months. He was concerned by the trend. It wasn't that he worried about his job security or wished there was more murder, mayhem, and strife perpetuated by evildoers in the world. There would always be enough to keep the Subsidiary busy. His concerns were, as befitted his function as the Operational Liaison of the Subsidiary, more operational.

Assuming the amount of evil and chaos in the world was either at a steady state or, more likely, increasing over time, a thin morning executive summary signified one of several things, all of them bad from an operational perspective.

First, and perhaps worst, the relative paucity of chatter could portend something really big was in the works—a sort of quiet before the storm. The bad guys knew that despite disposable cell phones and algorithmic-scrambling of signals, sophisticated anti-terrorist services were monitoring them. They, of course, couldn't be sure of what was and was not monitored, what was actually deciphered, and what communications actually made their way to someone's attention, rather than being lost in a mound of other data. Even if they did, they couldn't know whether that someone had the smarts to put the pieces together and the personal or bureaucratic clout to get the powers-that-be to pay attention. No, the safest thing when a really big event was imminent was to simply shut up—a silence that might speak volumes about an impending doom, but did little to identify the time, place, mechanism, or actors involved.

Second, intelligence gathering and analysis might simply be falling down on the job. Monitoring and deciphering techniques could be losing the technical battle—it was certainly more difficult to intercept a signal and decode it than it was to send an encrypted communication. Even worse, techniques like jamming, euphemisms to thwart key-word analysis, and utilizing the expanding scope and depth of the internet, which made every amateur YouTube video a potential mass-communication medium for spies, sleepers, and assorted evil minions, meant the good guys didn't always even know what to capture and decode, especially now that virtual worlds and online games could be used to pass information. The difficulty in keeping up with rapid change in means of secure electronic communication was why on-the-ground, human intelligence sources remained valuable. A lack of briefing material could simply mean the mix of human versus electronic intelligence was askew.

Third, the lack of information about new, large-scale threats could signify evil was simply becoming more widespread and more decentralized as the world simultaneously became more homogenized in its technology and fractionalized in its radicalism. Espionage had never been quite as spy-versus-spy simple as the ops-jockeys from the Cold War era liked to think, but the complexity of the world was definitely in the midst of a massive upswing. Not only, sad to say, did the sun set on the British Empire, but it set on an ever-increasing patchwork of countries, provinces, territories, and tribal enclaves. Every such sovereign power was beset by secessionist movements for every patch of land large enough to hold a rioting crowd and for every group of people who felt they or their distant ancestors had been downtrodden at one point or another in history.

Wet Work

And all that was before factoring in the gangs, criminal organizations, drug dealers, and religious cultists, who simply wanted what they wanted and thought they were divinely entitled to take it. Worse yet, you could never ignore the anarchists, who didn't even seem to know what they wanted besides anarchy, but were determined to create that by any means, often manipulating others to do their chaotic bidding. With the proliferation of communications, arms, and agendas, the world was more chaotic and less stable than ever. These under-the-radar threats were likely less than cataclysmic, but no one knew for certain. Small cabals were unknown, diverse, and difficult to penetrate with field assets.

Glenn picked a half-dozen mid-level reports which normally would not have made the cut and tossed them into the executive summary, just for flavor. Dee needed to know the world was not becoming all rainbows and kittens. Glenn had plenty of threats to the stability and peace of the world from which to pick.

Lots and lots of chaff, but little wheat. Yet the grain silo could still explode.

Thinking of explosions reminded Glenn he needed to have a chat with Dee about Dick Thornby. If Thornby's current side-trip to Singapore didn't work out the operative's obvious vengeance issues, the man would be of limited utility to the Subsidiary going forward. Not only did the organization not have enough pure "wet work" to justify keeping him on for that alone, it was unwise to retain someone who could not be relied upon to keep his cool in dangerous situations. Sure, the fellow had always been quick with an incendiary device, but Dick's operational decisions before the DIA caper had always been made with cool detachment. Since then, not so much. If Thornby couldn't or wouldn't get back into the operational groove, the

Subsidiary was likely to have one more piece of wet work to perform, and Thornby would be at the bloody, wet end of the stick.

#

Dick steered his aging Oldsmobile into the hospital lot and parked in an empty section well away from the entrance. It wasn't that he worried about getting a ding from someone opening their door in the adjacent spot—the powerful barge had enough scratches and dents that he never worried about someone trying to boost his ride—he just liked the car to be in the open, where it could be maneuvered in any direction if needed to make a quick exit. Given a choice, a good operative parked where no one could lurk, hidden by nearby vehicles, to ambush him or surreptitiously rig the car for explosives. Dick practiced good spycraft even when he was not on a mission.

He also figured it was nicer to the docs and nurses to leave spaces closer in for them to use. And he certainly didn't want to grab a spot someone in a real emergency might need.

Melanie, of course, had her own car, a Subaru. Seth had a scooter. The time had come, though, for Seth to get his own car. The kid was old enough to really need it and, God knows, Dick owed him at least a car for what he had put the kid through.

Dick added a bit of a jaunt to his step as he headed toward the hospital entrance. Maybe he'd tell Seth about upgrading his transportation today. They could go shopping as soon as the kid was released, or at least as soon as the physical therapy reached a point where he could safely drive. Seth probably expected to inherit the Oldsmobile someday when Dick got a new car, but there was no way Dick was going to let his big old boat go. Not only was it virtually thief-proof and nicely non-descript for surveillance and local missions,

21

it had a trunk so big you could fit two bodies and a shovel inside without a sweat.

Dick knew that for a fact.

Dick waved at Helen and Ornell at the third floor nurses' station and made his way down the hall to the burn unit. He heard a murmur of voices as he approached Seth's room and saw Melanie exit, facing away from him as she waved goodbye to Seth. He skidded to a stop to prevent a collision just as she turned and stepped toward him without looking.

"Oh," she said, obviously startled by his proximity. "It's you." A tone of irritation crept into her voice. "How long have you been lurking out here?" She glanced at her watch—the watch he had given her for their tenth anniversary. "You said you would be here earlier." Her lip twitched. "Or were you hoping to avoid me?"

Dick decided against telling her about his long series of connecting flights, a journey fueled by bitter, burnt coffee delivered in Styrofoam cups in the coach section of off-brand, discount airlines. Instead, he shrugged. "Had to stop for coffee so I didn't fall asleep while I was driving."

Her brow wrinkled and her eyes narrowed. "So, you really were in Singapore for work this week."

He pressed his lips together and stepped back against the drab green wall of the hallway. He glanced up and down the corridor as he gently pulled her toward him so they wouldn't be overheard by the nearby staff or, more importantly, Seth. He lowered his voice to a hoarse whisper. "Look, that was the deal. I've told you who I work for and what I do, at least in broad strokes, even though sharing such information is forbidden and dangerous. I can't and I won't tell you the details about precisely what I do or what the missions are about. But I promised to always call and let you know where I am."

She said nothing, as if waiting for him to go on. He turned his head and looked past her as he continued, staring down the empty hallway at the shining linoleum. "Even that much is risky, for both of us, but I want to save our marriage. I want you to know I trust you and I want you to trust me."

He shifted his gaze back to her face—beautiful to him, but tight with stress. He cursed himself for every worry line he had caused her. "I was in Singapore on a mission, though, as I told you, my cover story for any nosey neighbors was that I was in Uzbekistan working on a wastewater treatment facility. Now I'm here, like I promised." He avoided her slit-eyed glare by looking down as he finished talking and realized he was fidgeting with his hands, like a teenager at prom trying to screw up the courage to ask a girl to dance when there was no one on the floor yet. He dropped his hands to his sides and stared straight into her eyes. "Look, Melanie. I still have to lie to you about plenty of things, but I told you I would always let you know where I was, and I will. I love you. I love Seth. I won't lie about those things."

The wrinkles on Melanie's brow softened. "Sorry, Dick. It's just hard, you know ... taking it all in and ... Seth acts so brave, but the doctors say he still has a lot of pain ... and he's missed almost the whole year at school ... and now the summer session's about to start and he's going to miss his only chance to catch up ..."

He pulled her into his arms and held her tight, rocking gently in the embrace. "I know, babe. I know. But Seth, he's strong, stronger than you know. He'll be up and around soon, you'll see."

She pulled back from the embrace and looked at him, a tight smile competing with the unshed tears glistening in her eyes, refusing to fall. "You think?"

"Yeah, babe. I think." He smiled and her smile broadened in return. "I've been thinking about something else, too. When Seth gets out of the hospital, I've been thinking we could get him a car of his own, cuz, you know, he's growing up ..." Dick hesitated for just a moment as a flicker of concern flashed on Melanie's face. "... and it's way safer than a scooter."

The look of concern faded. "That would be good," she said. She nodded toward the door. "Why don't you tell him during your visit?" Now it was Melanie who gazed past Dick's shoulder, her eyes unfocused as she looked down the hallway. "He's having a rough day."

Dick nodded and stepped into Seth's room. "Hey there, champ," he boomed.

Chapter 4

Dee scanned the morning intelligence summary and stifled a snarl. The day had started out so well. Being an off-day for her regular exercise routine, she had slept in late after getting to bed at a reasonable hour for a change. She'd even gotten a bit of downtime during the evening, when Mitzi, her live-in house-sitter, free-spirit, and confidante, had pulled her away from reviewing personnel files to relax. Mitzi had insisted on introducing her via DVD to the first few episodes of a television horror series about brothers who secretly fight supernatural monsters in an effort to save the world from evil.

Despite the parallels to her own life as a never-ending struggle against evil, Dee had found the series entertaining. It didn't hurt that the guys were hunky and the monster of the week got defeated by the end of the hour—escapist fantasy on both scores there. She was a little surprised when Mitzi told her it had been on for twelve years already (adding, with a squeal, that the guys were even hunkier in season twelve). Dee had a tremendous impact on the real world, but she didn't really live in it herself. Mitzi was her only connection to pop culture and the day-to-day lives of regular folks—mundanes, she remembered Mitzi calling them. Dee's life was anything but mundane.

She flipped through the intelligence report a second time. All the usual hotspots were included: terrorist training camps in Yemen; tribal genocide in Africa; cyber-hacking of the energy grid by the Chinese (though the Chinese representative on the ten-nation oversight board for the Subsidiary strenuously denied his countrymen did anything of the sort); funneling of North Korean fissile material to radicals in Iran; and on and on.

But scattered between the stubborn troubles that beset the world on a grand scale were reports of more minor, but notably more bizarre, incidents. For example, animal rights activists had apparently stopped setting ablaze the vacation homes of meatpacking executives and had instead started disinterring recently deceased relatives of the same group of corporate villains, dropping the sometimes bloated and decomposing bodies on their doorsteps with signs saying things like "It's just meat. Why do you care?"

And, in the Philippines, the cadre of hackers who had long bedeviled modern society by creating viruses, Trojan horses, and data worms, were apparently shifting to infiltrating the software systems built into modern automobiles. Most such hacks scrambled the navigational GPS systems, not only sending clueless drivers astray, but rerouting vehicles to limited-capacity side streets and construction zones to deliberately snarl traffic. But in at least two instances, the hackers hijacked the auto-updating features of onboard computers monitoring things like tire pressure, fluid levels, and engine timing, reprogramming major operating components, introducing in one slew of recent cases a nine-second delay between pressing on the brakes and the brakes engaging. Nine seconds was a long time to wait when attempting to stop a car at speed, assuming your driving capabilities weren't as fast and furious as Vin Diesel's.

There were more odd reports. All flashy stuff to be sure, and some of it deadly and dangerous. But Dee didn't know what the Subsidiary could do about any of it. Small groups of true believers in a cause were notoriously difficult to locate and infiltrate. And anarchists—Dee counted hackers among their number—were worse. They didn't have enough organization to form groups that could be infiltrated; they just liked to cause mayhem to prove they could.

She was about to ask for Glenn Swynton to come explain his report, when he arrived at her doorway unbidden with a sly smile and arched eyebrow. She wasn't in the mood for either.

She scowled, holding up the sheaf of papers comprising the morning's briefing and shaking it. "This is supposed to be a summary of critical intelligence information ..." she snapped. She dropped the document onto her desk, "... not an issue of *World Weekly Weird*."

Glenn showed no visible reaction to her criticism. Not only was the man always on duty and always impeccably groomed and dressed, he was nigh unto unflappable. A part of her desperately wanted to see him "flapped," whatever that might mean.

Glenn simply looked languidly toward the report on her desk. "We may spend a lot of time worrying about the distribution of centrifuge parts as they relate to potential uranium enrichment in the Middle East, but the 'average Joe,' as you Yanks would so colorfully call him, worries more about whether his brakes are going to go out or his putrefied mother-in-law is going to show up on his doorstep." He blinked slowly, as if deliberately. "People need structure in their lives. These mid-level irritants are on the rise, and no one seems to be doing anything about them."

"Well, I'm not committing the resources of the Subsidiary to chasing after random grave robbers." Dee's thoughts flashed back to Mitzi's supernatural television show; those guys seemed to dig up a lot of graves to salt and burn the bones. She prayed there wasn't a connection. "Someone else will just have to handle that. And as for hackers, I'm not sure what we could do, short of vaporizing every island with functioning WiFi in the Philippines archipelago. I doubt our international oversight board would go for that."

Glenn did not respond. He simply stood there, irritatingly placid. She still didn't know how to flap him.

"Fine," she growled. "Pick a few of these 'irritants' that look like they might actually be solvable and assign a couple of the newer, low-level agents and a few of the burnouts we haven't retired yet to see what they might be able to do about them ... without nuking any countries out of existence."

"Done and done," replied Glenn. Dee didn't know if that meant he would do it or he had already done it without waiting for her permission. She decided not to ask. But she also noticed that Glenn hadn't moved.

"Something else?"

"Since we are talking about both nuclear weapons and employee burnouts, I thought I should tell you that, although Thornby obviously didn't report it, we do have confirmation Pao Fen Smythe was killed in Singapore."

"Is Thornby okay?"

"He's alive and functioning, if that's what you mean. His low-level insubordination continues to grow and he's yet to have a single pleasant interaction with the staff since Denver." He paused. "I've also scanned the transcripts of his communications with HQ from the field."

"And?"

Glenn sniffed. "Less formal and less precise than I'd like. He also swears more than he used to."

"Swearing's a classic indicator of stress," said Dee. "I wouldn't worry about a few extra f-bombs when he's calling in a SitRep. Thornby's stressed. He has good reason to be stressed."

Glenn's eyes narrowed. "Stress is part of the job; it's always been part of the job. Less-than-professional language isn't just an indicator of stress; it's also a classic indicator of not giving a flying fig about your job."

Dee gazed out the window at the plaza far below. Agents were expendable for the greater good, and not just while a mission was in progress. Yet she wanted to save Thornby if she could, even if he was rough and gruff and much too enamored with explosives. She looked back at Glenn. "He just had a few things to work out. Now that he's eliminated Pao Fen Smythe, let's give him a little bit more time to get back in sync."

"I thought you would say that," replied Glenn, a bit too smugly for Dee's taste.

Even though it was unclear whether Thornby's son, Seth, had been targeted at Pao Fen Smythe's order, rather than on the order of someone else seeking retaliation for Seth's own online activities assisting Chinese dissidents, Dee had let Thornby redeem his own self-image by taking Smythe out of the picture. Of course, letting him do it was Glenn's idea in the first place, but that didn't chafe. She wasn't such a controlling boss that she surrounded herself with yes-men and sycophants. No, she hired clever, competent people and took good, smart ideas when she got them, whatever the source.

"Let's work him into something simple. Something investigative, rather than action-oriented."

"Easy, enough," replied Glenn, "but he needs to have a new partner. He'll never integrate himself back with the staff if he keeps doing solo work."

"Good idea," Dee replied. "Tell him his prior experience is critical for the task and he needs to share it with whoever you assign to him." She sat at her desk, consulting her calendar for her next appointment. She noticed again, however, that Glenn was still standing at the door.

"What?"

"Shouldn't a highly-trained agent be able to see through that? If he can't, maybe we should be letting him go."

"Maybe he will see through it, but he'll do the job anyway. Don't underestimate the power of deceit. It's what makes the world go round. When you lie, just try to make the lie something the recipient wants to believe anyway."

Glenn put the toe of his right shoe behind his left, his usual indicator of an impending military-style spin and departure. "From your lips to my ears; words of wisdom, as always, Dee." His face betrayed no smirk to Dee's eyes as he spun and exited the room.

"Nice suit," called out Dee lightly as Glenn strode down the hall. "Nice work, too."

#

Taren Sykes finished skimming the after-action report detailing the results of his Filipino-outsourced hacking prank and tossed the file folder into the bin for shredding. Not as many deaths as he had expected, but the survivors were doing a great job of sowing panic across a wide swath of humanity—setting the worldwide news apparatus abuzz with their lurid tales of desperation and panic as their vehicles stopped obeying their operators and ... well ... failed to stop until they hit something solid or, in one case, submarined into a ship canal. No, a sanitary and ship canal, whatever that was. It sounded like a delightfully grisly and disgusting way to die.

Reporters speculated as to what might be the reasons behind the hacking attack—assuming without any evidence there had to be a logical motive. Stock manipulation, revenge, a fog of cover for one particular murder ... blah, blah, blah. Who benefits? Who reaps a windfall from the event? Did the manufacturer cut corners? Had a virus infected vehicles worldwide? A cacophony of choruses calculating the course of causation, instead of focusing on the serene beauty of pure chaos. Unexpected, dangerous things happening to innocent, random people, all for amusement. It's not that he minded

benefitting from even his lesser endeavors of malicious mayhem—
money is money—but anarchy was its own reward.

Did they learn nothing from the onslaught of computer viruses,
worms, and Trojan horses that emanated from disaffected youth,
particularly in third world countries, over the past decades? Hackers
slaved away for hours to create pranks, software-devouring worms,
hard-drive erasing viruses, and worse ... and for what? They never saw
their victims, never benefitted from their labor, other than in their
delight in knowing they had inflicted pain to their victims ... perhaps
thousands or millions of victims. They wreaked havoc for the sheer
delight of making others frustrated, miserable, and afraid.

Did no one in power ever give any thought to what chaos and
suffering could be wrought by a genius with more than a little time,
money, and power on his hands? After all, power corrupts. Brains and
money just grease the skids for a wild ride.

Chapter 5

Dick still felt the jetlag from his trip back from halfway across the world. It didn't help that he was also withdrawing cold turkey from the toxic brew of chemicals associated with the mission. Not just the caffeine load necessitated by having to stay awake, the lactic acid from the exertion of the past several days, and the adrenaline from the hit itself, but from his post-hit mindset. This wasn't like his normal wet work for the Subsidiary; this was personal. He'd gotten his revenge, but his mind had been fixed on that topic too long, putting him on edge, heightening his senses and his reactions as he sought to make his revenge reality. Now his emotions, his mindset, even his brain chemistry had altered. Serotonin levels and who knows what else were out of whack. The soup in which his brain simmered was so different that his thoughts were sluggish, his nerves frazzled.

Maybe he should eat some chocolate, the darker the better. That's what women did when they had trouble coping; at least, that's what Melanie had done when they were still together. Given all of his absences over the years—and the lies the Subsidiary had made him tell about those times—he should have invested Seth's college fund in stock of Godiva.

Fuck.

Now he was depressed on top of everything else.

At least the drive to the Philadelphia headquarters of the Subsidiary, which looked down on the "clothespin" sculpture on Centre Square downtown, required neither effort nor imagination. The route to the Subsidiary's front organization, Catalyst Crisis Consulting, LLC, was engrained muscle-memory by this point in his career. He wished he could have called in sick, but explaining why he needed to recover from his time off would have been an awkward and unnecessary lie.

He was fairly certain his boss, Glenn Swynton, knew exactly where he'd been and what he'd done during the past few days. Hell, for all he knew, Dee Tammany, head of the whole damn Subsidiary, was also in the know. But it was both good tradecraft and good manners to pretend it all never happened, that he'd just spent some extra time with his sick kid.

Best case, he was going to get sent out on another job, a sanctioned job, before he was fully recovered from the after-effects of his personal vendetta. Worse case, they were calling him in to can his ass face-to-face because of his little side job, or maybe because they found out he'd been telling Melanie where his missions took him. Worst case, the firing was going to be literal and they wanted to off him at HQ. At HQ there was no chance of third-party witnesses and no chance of any pesky law-enforcement using their cute spray bottles of Luminol and chic little UV flashlights to track down the minimal blood spatter from two shots in the back of the head.

If so, well, at least he'd gotten to see his kid first and tell him he was getting a car. That, and they'd let him whack Pao Fen; he knew they could have stopped him if they'd wanted. Hell, the powers that be at the Subsidiary could do a shitload of things if they really wanted. Fortunately, they were the good guys. He ... he was one of the good guys.

#

Dick arrived a few minutes early, but reception sent him straight through to Director Tammany's office as if he was late. Not a good sign.

He strode through her office door, stopping at a well-practiced parade rest about eight feet from her desk. Whatever was going to happen, he was going to hold his head high. He'd only done what he

33

needed to do; he wasn't about to apologize for anything. At least not to Dee Tammany. He'd done nothing but apologize to Melanie ever since Denver, but his wife still hadn't come back to their marriage, though she was at least talking to him.

Glenn Swynton was already in Dee's office. Dick had expected that. Dee was seated at her desk, with Glenn hovering nearby to her left. A striking woman sat on the couch along the wall to Dee's right. Mid-twenties, pixie-cut brunette, physically-fit, with a lithe build and enough toned and tanned leg showing he knew she'd be only a couple inches shorter than he if she stood, but she didn't. She just sat there, giving him a hard stare, her lips tight, her face giving no hint of emotion.

He didn't worry the mystery woman was there to kill him. They wouldn't create a mess in Dee's office. No, if he was going to disappear, he'd simply be sent down to human resources to update his insurance forms or to accounting for a chat with Pyotr Nerevsky in Internal Audit and never be heard of again. He hoped, at least, that if he did disappear forever, someone would tip off the geeks in the IT department he'd gotten vengeance on Pao Fen, not only for what Matt Lee did to Seth, but for Luke Calloway's death beneath the runways of DIA.

He didn't ask who the woman was. Espionage was all about need to know. If he needed to know, they'd tell him. Hell, they'd introduce him if *she* needed to know him, though he would bet Seth's car fund she'd already read his complete dossier before the meeting. He'd also bet Glenn had remarked on how thick the dossier was when he'd handed it to her to review.

"I trust you had a pleasant time off?" asked Dee by way of greeting.

"Spend a lot of time with your son?" chimed in Glenn before Dick could respond.

Dick smiled. "You can always trust me to enjoy time off," he replied, tilting his head toward Dee. He swiveled his face minutely toward Glenn. "My visits were extremely fulfilling. Thank you for asking."

Both Dee and Glenn were much too professional and, frankly, serious to smirk, but he noticed a twinkle in Dee's eye as she nodded toward the mystery Amazon. "I'd like you to meet Acacia Zyreb, newly transferred from our Eastern European Field Office in Prague."

The woman on the couch stood, striding toward him with her hand outstretched. "You may call me 'Ace,' Agent Thornby." Her accent was pure American, revealing no trace of her Eastern European origins. "I'm looking forward to working with you."

Dick forced a chuckle, "Well, at least you can lie with a straight face, so you're either a natural or you've been at this game longer than I would have guessed from your looks."

Glenn cleared his throat in typically British fashion: all condescension, no phlegm. "This is not a game, Thornby, and, if it was, you would not be winning at the moment. I suggest you dispense with any more attempts at witty banter and pay close attention."

God, he hated working for people younger than him, especially bureaucrats in suits, but he let his irritation slide. It wasn't difficult—a lifetime as an Army Ranger, then Chicago cop, gave him plenty of practice. Besides, the fact they were introducing him to a new partner meant he wasn't being fired, figuratively or literally, and that brightened his mood more than he'd thought it would have only minutes ago. Dick did his best to look serious, even stern, as he turned back toward Swynton. "You have my full attention, sir."

"That remains to be seen," grumbled Swynton. "Both your focus and your attitude have been lacking since ..." Swynton's eyes flicked toward Zyreb ... "the unfortunate death of your last partner. The question of concern here today is whether you are able and willing to go forward on a new project with a new partner ... and no more special requests for explosives."

Dick wanted to say he preferred to work alone and the damn explosives he had requested for DIA had saved everyone's ass, because God knows both were the truth. He also wanted to say Glenn was the one who had insisted Luke not survive the DIA mission, even if Dick had to do it himself. He knew, too, that Luke hadn't been a true partner in the typical sense, because he'd never been trained as an operative. He was just a bright computer geek whose expertise had been needed on a mission. Dick had been tasked to take Luke along against the better judgment of both of them. But he didn't say any of that.

Spies know when to shut up, even when they're not being tortured.

"I'm here to do what you tell me," he said with no edge to his voice.

"I'm glad to hear that." Swynton inclined his head toward Dee. "We both are."

"What's the job?"

"We don't need to take up the Director's time with details about a minor investigative matter," said Swynton.

"I just wanted to make sure you were amenable to moving forward with Agent Zyreb," said the Director. "Please keep us informed as to Seth's recovery, too."

"Will do, ma'am."

With that, Swynton ushered Dick and Ace out the door to a nearby conference room with glass walls looking over the document replication cubicles ... the forgery division. With the door closed, it was soundproof, though not exactly private. Much better, though, than a windowless room in Internal Audit by Dick's way of thinking.

Just like that night at DIA, maybe there was light at the end of the tunnel. Maybe things were getting better. He could do low-level investigative work, train the newbie from the Czech Republic, and have an almost regular life ... a life with his kid and his wife, if she'd have him.

Maybe, for a change, it wouldn't be up to him to save the world.

#

"Not exactly saving the world, here," Ace complained as she flopped down into an ergonomic chair after Swynton left at the end of their situational briefing. "Investigating random acts of chaos and suspicious chatter ... Bullocks! Like that's high priority."

Ace swiveled her chair to the left and looked over the table at her new partner. Fit, in a middle-aged, stocky kind of way, but not exactly Ryan Reynolds to her Blake Lively. She couldn't help but wonder who he'd killed—or not killed—to get assigned to break her in as a U.S.-based operative for the Subsidiary. Thornby ignored her as he casually leafed through the manila file folder of key word intercepts Swynton had dropped on the table during their briefing.

"Yo," she mock-shouted. "Ricky-Rick-Richard! I'm the newbie here, so I expect some low-level shit drudgework. Who'd you piss off to get stuck with it?"

Thornby's eyes darted up from the file to meet hers. "That's need to know," he growled. "And it's Dick. Unless we're undercover, it's always Dick."

Ace snorted. "If you're handling things under covers, it's probably dick then, too."

Dick rolled his eyes and shook his head minutely. "Heard 'em all, Ace. So you just go ahead and get all the penis jokes and double entendres out of your system while we're still in the office. As to who I ticked off, let's just say that you'll be doing any necessary interfacing with the computer jockeys here at HQ. My last partner was one of them—not a field agent. But we still might need their support on this op."

"Op?" Ace snorted again. "This is barely a book report. A bunch of anarchist groups—there's an oxymoron—hack into the computer chips in various car models and insert a virus that turns off the brakes. Then the same suspects chat about 'great crack' and a 'south side rift' preceding some big 'east coast action.' That's got the Subsidiary's oversight board all frowny-faced and concerned? Bullocks! I could work that entire vocabulary into a Facebook invitation to a rave. Yet prissy pants, the Subsidiary's Worldwide Director of Operations, assigns two agents to it? Based on that standard of actionable intelligence, I'm surprised we're not looking for secret underground bases established by ancient aliens. I mean, it's on The History Channel, for God's sake. It must be reliable information."

She noticed the Dickster closed his eyes for a few seconds before responding. Anger management technique?

"Look, Ace. I don't know if this is a meaningful assignment or not and, if it is, how it might fit into the bigger picture. That's need to know, too." He set down the folder and glared at her. "Maybe I got drudge work to do with you because I'm being punished for something I did on my last mission. Maybe I got the task because I'm between partners and somebody has to make sure you don't shit yourself the first time an op goes sideways. Maybe somebody knew you make great 'dick' jokes. Or maybe somebody thinks I have some experience relevant to this task and you could learn a few things. I don't care. I don't need to know and neither do you. I just do the job I'm given."

Now it was Ace's turn to close her eyes and shake her head. *Sakra!* Why were middle-aged guys always so cranky? Maybe because they feared their declining years more than they feared death? She shook off the philosophizing and focused on her own situation. She supposed she should try to make a good impression, even on a partner who was well past his "best used by" date. This case might only be a minor stepping stone, but she was determined to have a real impact on world events. After all, isn't that what spies do?

She opened her eyes. "Relax, big guy. I'm just trying to fit in with you crazy Americans."

Her alleged mentor shrugged. "You got the accent down, at least. I can't make out half of what the office cleaning lady says, even when she's speaking English and not Polish."

She reverted to a low class Czech accent. "De Czech peoples, dey are no Pollacks, *kokot*. Dey, cultured, edjicated peoples." She switched back to Americanized English—a flat, Midwestern R-drawl according to her instructors at the Defense Language Institute. Let him think she was a natural. "Lots of Hollywood movies and TV. Why do you Yanks always think foreigners can't do at least as good an American accent as you can do a Scottish, French, or Pakistani accent?"

She paused for a beat. Better to shift the subject away from her for now. "You got any ideas from looking at the chatter as to where to start this mission?"

"One thought—maybe the real reason I got assigned to this particular piece of intel."

"What's that?" Ace asked.

"This phrase 'south side rift,' it could be referring to the south side of Chicago. I was a cop there once upon a time. And Joliet, the epicenter of brake failures, is just thirty or forty miles southwest of the city."

"Really? South side necessarily means Chicago? Why not the south side of Boston or New York or L.A.?"

39

Dick smiled. "Idiomatic English ... well, American. Every big metro area has its own nickname. In L.A., the south side is called South Central. You know that if you're from the area. Just like you would know where 'The Inland Empire' is. In Boston, you're a Southie, not a south-sider. In New York, it goes by borough, and so on. The south side of Chicago is the poor, tough side of town, where gangs are strongest. This could be about cocaine trafficking, maybe referencing some influx from a new East Coast supplier or rival. It's a place to start."

"So it's off to the Chicago metro area?"

Dick laughed. "Chicagoland. They call the area Chicagoland."

Ace furrowed her brow. "Chicagoland? Sounds like a theme park."

Dick shrugged as he stood. "Have the quartermaster's office make the travel arrangements and meet me at the airport." He started to go. "Oh, and bring a jacket."

"It's June," she replied. "Isn't it warm in Chicago during the summer?"

"Sure," replied Dick. "But ChiTown is right next to the world's biggest air conditioner."

"Huh?"

Dick smiled. "That's what they call Lake Michigan: The World's Biggest Air Conditioner."

Great. Now the cranky guy was making sport of her.

Kurva to hovno. Fuck that shit.

At least she knew the important American idioms.

Chapter 6

She'd flown through O'Hare International Airport before, of course. You could barely fly around the U.S. these days without hitting Chicago, Denver, Atlanta, or Dallas-Ft. Worth. America probably had as much acreage dedicated to international airports as the Czech Republic had acreage. Just the United terminal—one of four main terminals at the airport according to the in-flight magazine, despite the International Terminal being designated Terminal 5—was so big they had enough room to tuck a dinosaur skeleton between a bank of TSA inspection stations and a juice bar. Working here was a whole new world.

Her big ox of a companion trudged down the busy airport corridor without looking at the gates, overpriced vendors, or other passersby— his eyes focused forward, with an odd occasional glance at the polished floor. She decided it was best to remain quiet and take his lead.

That was the smart approach, but of course it couldn't last. Once they were out of the secure zone, he ignored the baggage claim area, turning sharply toward the rental car kiosks.

"Hold up," she said. "I need to grab my bag."

She saw him roll his eyes at her. "Jeez" he sighed. "You checked a bag?" He shook his head. "The first rule of all business trips, whether you're a lawyer, a sales rep, or wastewater treatment consultant, is you never check a bag. It slows you down when your flight arrives, makes you late getting to wherever you're going."

She forced a tight smile. "Point taken. But I still need to pick up my bag."

She found Carousel Nine and waited twelve agonizing minutes before it belched a warning alarm and coughed up her bag. At least Dick didn't tap his foot the entire time they were waiting, although he did check his phone more than once. Finally, she was ready and they headed off toward the rental counters at a brisk pace.

She was confused when he led her past the kiosks for the brand name companies to the dingy desk of a rent-a-wreck vendor, but she said nothing. Not at the counter; not even during the ridiculously long, slow shuttle ride. Eventually, they arrived at an off-airport rental lot which sported fewer cars than her favorite teenage make-out spot overlooking the Vitava River back home.

"Great selection," she groused.

Dick-boy threw an irritated glance her way. "I don't care if they've got fewer cars than Jay Leno's third auxiliary garage, as long as they have the one I need."

She bit back a reply as long as she could, but that wasn't long. When Dick used the key fob to pop the trunk of an aging Lincoln Continental that looked like it had been bought second-hand from a liquidating limo company, she spoke her mind.

"Need for what? A demolition derby?" She gritted her teeth, attempting to calm herself, but gave up. Screw anger management. "Why the bullocks are we driving this piece of crap? Does the Quartermaster's office hate you? Or were you hoping to get lucky in the big back seat?"

Dick sniffed. "Quartermaster probably does hate me. But, more important, he knows me. Large, decent power, and none of the bullshit modern accoutrements."

She wrinkled her brow at him. "We talking about you now or your preferences for a car?"

"Neither," growled Dick. "I regard small talk a modern accoutrement."

Sakra! Her partner got it right when he insisted on being called Dick. "Fine," she exhaled with a huff. "Let's stick to business. Where to?

Medical Examiner's office in Joliet? Impound lot to look at the vehicle that went into the canal?"

Dick snorted, wrinkling his forehead and looking at her as if she'd suggested an impromptu game of tag. "No," he snapped, then paused. She could almost see him counting to ten, which had to be difficult since he wasn't using his fingers. Finally, he continued. "You tell me, Ace. What's that going to accomplish? We know the guy drowned. That was in the briefing. We also know the onboard computer in his car was tampered with by hackers. Hell, thanks to the nerds back at the office, we know the hack originated in the Philippines and who did the work, even if we can only identify him by his online handle. Unlike cops, we don't have to gather evidence and bullshit confirmations for a future prosecution. We just need to find out what's going to happen and stop it. That means interviewing a few sources about those 'south side' and 'crack' references. I still have a few contacts down that way from back in the day."

"So, what am I supposed to do?" she bristled back at him. "Take copious notes during the interviews?" She flicked a few buttons of her blouse open. "Play a drugged out crack whore?"

Dick shook his head and clambered into the car. "My contacts, they know me as a cop. They're CIs, confidential informants. They'll just assume you're my partner or a trainee on a ride along. And they'd be right."

She glared at him for a moment, got a few essentials out of her luggage, then slammed the trunk shut and got in the car, biting back a retort.

He looked over at her. "Buckle your seatbelt."

"Bad driver?" she spat out, without turning to look at him.

"Nah," Dick chuckled. "It's the law. First rule of being a spy. Always obey the law when you can. It simplifies your life."

#

Fourteen hours later, Ace couldn't make up her mind if Dick was just a lousy mentor or an epically ineffective investigator. They'd cruised Dick's rent-a-tank all over the streets and alleyways of the south side and chatted up half a dozen CIs, all to no avail. Dick didn't even let her join in the questioning, so she had nothing to do but stare out at what pulp detective novels would refer to as the "mean streets" of the inner city and try to assuage her growling stomach with a roll of Mentos she'd gotten at the airport in Philly.

The streets of the inner city, she realized, weren't so much "mean" as they were "depressing." Lower middle class row houses, identical except for the color of their aluminum awnings and the style of their after-added detached garages facing the back alley, gave way to run down, three-story walk-ups, identical except for the color of their graffiti tags and the style of their after-added protective window bars. At least in the bad neighborhoods in Europe the buildings were old enough to have some architectural details to class up the poverty.

She had to give the big guy credit for one thing; he was an equal-opportunity employer when it came to CIs: black; Hispanic; Vietnamese; and a strung-out Aryan with a shaved head and copious prison tats who reminded her of an asshole from a mission back home. But it didn't matter who Dick talked to, the conversation was the same.

"Long time, no see."

"Yeah, I was working counter-terrorism for a few years, but now I'm back on Narcotics."

"Who'd you piss off to get shoved back to Vice?"

"None of your fucking business."

"Hey, at least they partnered you up with some bad kitty trim for the prostitution stings."

"Shut the hell up before I shut you up. Look, I heard there's some big south side rift about crack. What's that all about?"

"Ain't no south side rift 'bout nothing. Where'd you hear that shit? This some kind of test? Cause I know better than to make shit up for you, man."

"Yeah, it was a test. You passed. Now what about some big east coast action coming up?"

"East coast action? What you been smoking? Everything sold on the streets these days is south-of-the-border shit, exceptin' the meth from Arkansas. No one be messin' with no cartels and live to talk to the likes of you."

Kecâŝ kraviny! Bullshit. A complete waste of time. Their only break was to stuff down dinner. Dick insisted they go to a local place for Italian beef, calling it "Chicago's best, but least known, food delicacy." The sandwiches were soggy and messy, but the ultra-thin-sliced, spicy beef was excellent. Dick ordered his in a combo with Italian sausage. Of course, she'd never encountered this combo during her trips to Italy when she was working out of the Prague office, but the fact the food wasn't any more Italian than pizza didn't mean it wasn't delicious.

After chowing down in the car and tossing the trash into the back seat, they returned to cruising the streets for more dealers, hustlers, and informants. Fun times.

About two a.m., she made a point of no longer covering her mouth during her increasingly frequent yawns. Nothing. So she started looking at her watch every three minutes. Nothing. Finally, she took off her watch and tapped it, as if to see if it was still running.

Dick curled a lip at her and growled, "Just one more stop."

He parked the car in the loading zone for a bodega tucked underneath the elevated train tracks and clambered out, heading toward a tall punk wearing flashy high-top sneakers, dark pants, and a

Bulls pullover hoodie. The punk loitered about thirty feet away, where an alley intersected Cottage Grove Avenue. Ace took her time getting out of the car. She already knew what Dick was going to say; she could guess what the punk was going to say. She wasn't in any hurry to listen to the latest encore performance.

Just as Ace was about to hip-check her door shut, she heard an angry voice.

"Don't touch me, you motherfucking pig. I know what Chicago cops do when you get hold of a brother. Lemuel, he still walks with a limp."

"C'mon, Kenan, you know I had nothing to do with that ..."

As Ace looked up, she saw the punk reach into the pocket of his hoodie and pull out what looked like a weapon.

"GUN!" she shouted, diving back into the car through the still open door and snatching up her purse. She looked back up to see her partner grappling with the punk. A Glock 17, nine millimeter, was in the kid's left hand. Dick grabbed the kid's gun hand, forcing it straight up. The two guys pawed and punched at one another with their off-hands. Ace pulled her own weapon out of her purse. She also preferred the fourth generation Austrian-made Glocks, but found the Glock 26 a better fit for her hand and an easier concealed carry.

She crouched by the right front fender and aimed over the huge expanse of the hood, but had no clear shot as the two men struggled. Dick appeared to have the strength advantage, but the punk had reach and height. Dick could keep the gun pointed away, but he couldn't wrest it from his attacker's hand.

Suddenly, Kenan kneed Dick in the privates. Dick involuntarily doubled-over, losing his grip on Kenan's gun hand. The kid pushed off and back, then swung the automatic pistol toward Dick.

Bullocks!

46

Ace had no choice. Her aim tracked the bad guy as he pushed off her partner. She fired four times at his center of mass, standing and moving toward him as he stumbled back from the impact. When he didn't immediately go down, she fired another four shots in an identical grouping. He collapsed to the sidewalk. She rushed forward, her gun still held out, her left hand bracing her right, ready to fire again. She still had seven rounds left in the standard fifteen-round magazine.

She didn't need them. The dead kid's gun clattered out of his hand as he fell backward, the hood of his sweatshirt shielding his dead eyes from her view. Dick kicked the gun away and looked at her with a blank, dumbfounded expression.

"What?" she snapped, still holding her gun on the perp. "I had to do it. He was about to shoot you."

Dick held his hands out and to the side, palms toward her. "I got no problem with that, honey," he proclaimed. "I just wanna know where you got the gun."

She smiled. "I never leave home without it." She lowered her weapon and looked Dick in the eyes. "Rule number one, partner. Always check a piece of hard-sided luggage when you travel, so when you get attacked in a strange city you've got something to pull out besides your dick. What do you generally carry? Italian sausage?"

Dick laughed. "You read my file. You know I have a penchant for explosives." The wail of a siren in the distance interrupted their survivors' revelry. "Police your brass. We need to get out of here. The cops have surveillance equipment that tracks the sound of gunfire. Even in this neighborhood, there'll be a CPD response soon."

She knew he was right. Even as a former Chicago cop, Dick was a spy just like her. They both understood getting the local constabulary involved in a mission for the Subsidiary was not going to do either of them any good.

In less than a minute, they were back in the car, leaving the scene of the crime.

Dick steered through a few alleys and side streets before entering onto a main thoroughfare. It wasn't long before he popped their behemoth onto the Skyway and headed for Indiana. The orange sodium vapor streetlights ended abruptly at the border, leaving Ace with a sweeping panoramic vista of the stark white lights emanating from power plants, oil refineries, and dark factories dotting the blackness south and east.

Sakra! Where was he going now? "Fleeing the jurisdiction?" she asked.

Dick's eyes flicked toward her for the briefest moment. "It never hurts," he muttered. "Plus, there's a riverboat casino just across the border."

Ace looked at the industrial wasteland fading into the blackness, now that the orange glow of Chicago was in the rear view. "What river?"

Dick laughed. "None. There's no river. They just float the casino in a man-made pond of water so they can call it a riverboat. Early on, the Coast Guard made 'em carry lifejackets and everything, even though the boat can only probably sink about eight inches before it hits the bottom of the cement pond, but I heard they finally nixed that piece of foolishness."

"Why do casinos have to be on riverboats here? The ones in Atlantic City and Vegas aren't."

"Midwestern politics. Part Puritan morality play, part machine-style patronage, and an even bigger part big money corruption, all papered

48

over with a historical reference to riverboat gambling back at the turn
of the century."

"You mean when I was in primary school?"

Dick's brow furrowed and his upper lip quivered as if he was about
to snarl. "The century before that."

A brown sign indicated a casino at the next exit. Dick nudged the
right blinker on and faded toward the deceleration ramp.

"And why," Ace continued, "are we looking for a casino? Surviving
a shootout making you feel lucky?"

Dick smiled. "Now you're asking a good tradecraft question." He
looked over at her, but she remained silent. "The casino hotels are
decent, clean, and safe compared to the neighborhood rent-by-the-hour
flophouses. Reasonably anonymous, too."

She nodded. It made sense. "One more question. Do you snore?"

Dick snorted. "You'll never know. Two rooms, connecting, but
separate." He took his left hand off the steering wheel and held it up,
fingers splayed. "A good spy would have noticed the wedding band in
the first ten seconds after meeting me and known I was a married
man."

Ace shrugged. "Maybe you're sentimental; maybe you wear it for
cover. A good spy knows enough to read a personnel dossier from
cover-to-cover before she takes an assignment. Married, yes. Happily?
Recent events don't seem to bear that out."

Dick pulled into the lot for the hotel-casino complex and parked in
the midst of a sea of empty spaces. He turned off the engine, then
looked at her. "Thanks for saving my ass. And, thanks for the offer, but
a really good spy knows when to shut the hell up."

"What offer? I was imagining the same room, Dickie, not some
dickie from a stout, hairy co-worker old enough to be my ..."

Dick glared at her.

"... uncle."

#

Ace listened at the door for a moment before she knocked, but heard nothing. Hotels might have thin walls, but they spent money for solid metal-core doors. They saved on lawsuits by preventing sexual assaults and didn't show dents and damage from room service and housekeeping carts banging into them on a constant basis.

Dick was stuffing a piece of bacon in his maw as he opened the door. A room service cart was parked by the bed. Local morning news blared from the TV. His lip curled when he saw her.

"What the hell?" he growled by way of greeting. "What's your hurry? Drug dealers aren't exactly morning people, you know. They stay up kinda late."

She smiled. Obviously, her mentor had not checked in with the office yet. Too busy chowing down on smoked slices of hog fat. "The computer geeks at the Subsidiary apparently stay up late, too. They intercepted another transmission from one of the people connected with the hackers behind the sabotaged brakes, once again mentioning 'great crack' on the 'south side.'"

Dick wandered back to the room service tray and snatched another piece of bacon, dipping one end in an open packet of honey sitting next to the crusts from his toast. "So?" he mumbled with his mouth full. "Nothing new there."

She nodded. "Yeah, but the person on the other end of the transmission answered with 'Man, those tourists at Waikiki are going to shit when they see that wave.'"

Dick stopped cold, his right hand three-quarters of the way to his open mouth. As he paused, the honey slid down the greasy bacon, oozing onto his fingers. "So, 'south side' means the south side of Oahu, where Waikiki is located?' He chomped down on the slice of bacon and chewed it slowly. "That could make sense, I guess."

"Could? It blows away your south side of Chicago theory. After all, islands have beaches and beaches have waves ... and tourists. Tourists who apparently are going to shit 'when they see that wave,' whatever that means."

"Wave? They're sure the guy talking didn't say 'rave?' It's not the designer drug of choice for partiers, but I can see a coke-fueled bash as a way to announce a new syndicate is taking over the drug trade in the tourist hotspots."

Ace shook her head. "Crystal clear, digital sound. Uploaded it and listened to it myself."

Dick made a face as if the honey he had just eaten had gone bad, except, of course, honey never goes bad. "Wave." He interrupted his sour scowl to lick off his fingers. "What the hell does that mean?"

"It means," Ace replied. "We're going to Hawaii." She nodded toward his carry-on suitcase. "Grab your gear. The Quartermaster's booked us on a flight to the islands. It leaves in just over two hours and my cell says we're more than an hour from O'Hare. Given the speed of that damn shuttle, I'm not sure we'll make the flight."

Dick finished sucking honey off the fingers of his right hand while he grabbed his toiletries and stuffed them in the case.

An hour and twenty-three minutes later, Dick steered the big car into the "Departures" lane at O'Hare.

"You missed the turn-off for the rental place," Ace noted as she looked up from her phone.

"Screw that," growled Dick. "We'll just leave the car in front of the terminal with the keys in the ignition. I'll call from the gate and tell the rental place that if they want it, they should come pick it up."

"Ježíši!" exclaimed Ace, "won't that spark an incident? I mean, a parked vacant car could be viewed as a bomb threat. They might close the airport while they check it out."

Dick shook his head. "Nah. Happens all the time. You don't think movie stars and billionaires actually return their rental cars to the off-site lots, do you? Rich, famous people do this kind of crap all the time. Security will deal." He shrugged. "If it makes you feel better, I'll pop the trunk when we get out. That way they can see it's not loaded with explosives."

They rushed through the terminal, using counterfeit Mileage Plus cards to access the short line for TSA inspection. As promised, Dick used the brief wait to call the car rental agency with his Subsidiary-provided cell. So Ace was surprised when she saw him whispering on a cell phone on the other side of Security. It wasn't that she was spying on him. She was just killing time while she made her way through security behind a bearded man who slowed up the line with a bulky laptop and what he called a CPAP machine, whatever the hell that was.

She marched up to him as he huddled over his phone at a recharging station, his back to the hallway. "C'mon, lover," she called out as she reached out to tug on his arm. "Don't want to miss our flight to paradise."

Dick whirled on her with so much speed she was astonished.

"Don't do that," he seethed.

"Touch your arm?"

"Interrupt my phone calls."

Sakra! "Reporting in to Glenn with a transfer request already?"

"Maintaining my cover," he hissed. "Some of us aren't single and carefree. Some of us have family ... responsibilities. Some of us have to lie to our families to maintain cover."

She gave him a hard stare. "You're right. Some of us don't have families." She turned and headed for the gate without looking back.

#

Less than an hour later, Dick was winging his way to paradise with a woman other than his wife. Life as a spy was complicated ... and risky.

He hoped Ace hadn't noticed he'd been using a non-secure cell phone—the burner he'd picked up in Singapore—at the airport. That was his mistake and he wasn't forgiving of sloppiness on the job. He'd disabled and dumped the burner the first chance he got afterword, just to make sure that particular fuckup couldn't happen again.

Jesus. He prayed Melanie hadn't overheard Ace or, if she did, she understood it was all part of his cover. His marital relationship was complicated enough without unwarranted suspicions of infidelity. Calling in to Melanie when on assignment, which he promised her he'd do, might be reassuring for her, but it led to a lot of awkward conversations—conversations he had avoided when he'd pretended to be overworked fixing wastewater treatment systems in some third-world country with non-existent cell phone coverage. He loved his job with the Subsidiary, but he loved his wife even more. Sure, Ace was smart, athletic, and sexy—all useful things in the world of espionage. Still, he wished Melanie was flying to Hawaii with him, a lazy, relaxed, one-dimple smile on her beautiful face. Their marriage needed a little aloha.

Not that his relationships at work were any better. Glenn and Dee were on the edge of firing his ass, the entire computer department was so hostile he'd terminated his online banking access just to make sure his meager savings didn't disappear into the fog of the World Wide Interwebs, and his new partner pointedly ignored him as she passed his row, heading to her own seat farther back in the plane, though their physical separation was probably just a result of having booked the flight at the last minute.

Making a difference in the world had certainly made a difference in his world ... and not for the better.

Chapter 7

Thank God and United Airlines for in-flight WiFi. Instead of wasting time on sleep, snack boxes, and second-run second-rate film entertainment, Dick had hours to surf the web, investigating. The Subsidiary had all sorts of high tech surveillance, NSA-level intercepts, satellite imagery, and on-the-ground assets in all sorts of obscure and dangerous places. But from the discomfort of his coach seat in an over-packed flying tin can, Dick had the power of the internet. And even though he was no tech wizard like his former partner, Luke, he had two fingers and Google.

That was all it took.

The flight landed in Honolulu just after sunset, but the airport was still bustling. Dick waited at the top of the jet way for his partner, who seemed surprisingly keyed up for having just come off a twelve-hour flight, counting the forty-one minute layover dash at LAX.

She didn't even bother to stop when she got to him. Instead, she brushed past, calling out over her shoulder. "C'mon. If we hurry, we can pick up my luggage and still make the last flight to the Big Island."

He quickstepped to catch up. "We're not going to the Big Island." He caught her by the arm. She turned and looked at his hand on her elbow, her eyebrows rising, but said nothing. "At least not yet," he continued, letting go. "We need to do some investigating here."

She huffed at him. "You waste your flight time by sleeping?" Before he could deny it, she continued. "I didn't. I spent my time researching. This "great crack" thing, I think it has to do with the Big Island ..."

He held up his right hand, motioning her to stop. "That's all well and good, but Waikiki is on Oahu. We're here at the moment and we might as well make good use of our time and get some information on what this 'big wave' at *Waikiki* might be. Maybe it's a tidal wave—a tsunami. That's as big as a wave can get. The Pacific Tsunami Warning

Center's in Ewa Beach, just on the other side of Pearl Harbor from the airport. I think we might get better information about big waves there than hooking up with some surfer dudes on the Big Island."

"The Big Island isn't known for surfing. That would be the North Shore ..."

"So, you don't think getting some detailed *scientific* information about big waves is relevant to our investigation?"

"I wasn't suggesting ..."

"Good," he interrupted. "Then, it's settled. We'll pick up your bag, pick up the rental car, and drive to the hotel the Quartermaster booked for us, then go to the Tsunami Center first thing in the morning."

"What are we going to do all evening? Hold hands and stare at the ocean from the terrace of our room, then douse the lights and pound on the headboard for ... a few minutes ... to maintain our cover?"

He shook his head. "Two-bedroom suite. Given the age difference, we'll be posing as a divorced dad taking a vacation with his daughter."

Ace shrugged. "More credible, I guess. That way we can argue incessantly without anyone being suspicious."

"And," added Dick, "you can spend all of your time staring at your cell phone, while I do all the talking."

She pursed her lips, as if pouting. "Yes, Daddy."

He spun around and marched off toward baggage claim.

#

Ace woke to the smell of salt air and the delightful caress of light tropical breezes. A dawn chorus of birdcalls sang to her from outside her open balcony door. This was what she had fantasized about as a teenager in Prague. Warmth, beauty, freedom—an escape from a cold, gray life and a cold, gray future. Sure, there was danger and work, too, even here in paradise, but she preferred to think of those things as exciting and fulfilling—a job description few in her circumstances could ever hope to achieve.

She savored the luxury of the morning for a few moments, then grabbed her cell to find a text from the Dickster: "Meeet me at brkfastt buffey."

Either dear old Dad was a crappy speller or he had fat thumbs and little experience texting. She'd bet on the latter.

The message was only a few minutes old; the buzzing of her cell had probably been what woke her. She didn't rush her shower or morning routine, putting on a pair of tan linen slacks and a loose, flowered top. She knew her "dad" would appreciate the extra time at the all-you-can-eat bacon buffet.

She tucked her weapon into her purse, perched her special Subsidiary-issue sunglasses on the top of her head, and sauntered downstairs to the open-air courtyard restaurant. Sure enough, Dick was sitting with his back to her along the black, lava rock wall at one side of the dining veranda, with a mound of bacon, eggs, and toasted English muffins on his plate and a half-dozen opened plastic honey containers littering the table. A pair of Leica binoculars and a floppy white hat sat on the right side of the table within arm's reach.

She approached from behind, giving him a friendly shoulder squeeze as she veered off and seated herself in the empty chair to his left. "Good morning, D ..."

A booming voice in a thick Brooklyn accent interrupted her from the center of the veranda. "Hey, Dick. Dick Thornby. Great to see ya." She turned to see a wiry, mustachioed, Hispanic wearing shorts and a Polo shirt striding toward the table. *Ježíší*, had Dick already been setting up meetings before breakfast?

By the startled look in Dick's wide eyes as he looked up, she guessed not.

"Edwaldo," Dick called out in a soft voice in response. "Didn't expect to see you here."

Edwaldo reached the table, simultaneously grasping Dick's outstretched hand as he leered down Ace's loose top. "Obviously not," he replied, innuendo oozing from every syllable.

"Uh, yeah. Edwaldo, this is my ... uh ..."

"Daughter," Ace interjected. "Acacia."

"Oh," replied Edwaldo, his eyes jolting up to her face from her cleavage. He turned his face toward Dick. "I ... uh ... didn't know you had a daughter. Only a son ... Seth. Right?" He glanced around the restaurant. "Are Seth and Melanie over at the buffet?"

"Uh ... no," replied Dick, his face flushing. "It's just me and ... uh ... Acacia. Right, honey?"

Her partner's discomfiture delighted her, but Ace knew this was a dangerous situation, not just an awkward moment. Running into someone you knew from real life was a horror story for anyone in their line of work, whether working undercover narcotics in a biker gang or black ops in a third world nation. Unfortunately, Disney World was probably the only place that rivaled Hawaii in terms of high risk of running into someone you knew far from home. And she could tell that New York Eddie, here, wasn't buying that Dickie-Boy had an adult daughter who didn't bother to wear a bra to breakfast with her dad. So she did the only thing she could.

"Yes, Daddy," she cooed with a wink at Dick. "It's just the two of us, all alone in that great big hotel room." She leaned forward, giving them both a good look down her loose blouse. "Should I go back up to the room, Daddy, and wait for you while you talk with your friend?" She got up from her chair.

"Uh ... sure, Acacia. Why don't you finish getting ready for our ... sightseeing tour ... while Edwaldo and I catch up."

She cast her eyes down. "Yes, Daddy. Whatever you say, Daddy."

She walked a few steps away from the table, then turned back to the two men. "You can bring your friend up to the room if you want, Daddy. I'll be a good girl. Promise." She winked and sashayed away, swaying her hips so suggestively a hula dancer would have blushed.

#

Dick exchanged pleasantries with Edwaldo for only five or ten minutes before he made his excuses and headed up to Ace's room ... without inviting his friend. He didn't really pay any attention to the conversation. Instead, his mind was awhirl running alternative scenarios on how he could explain all of this to Melanie without her demanding a divorce, interrupted only by running alternative scenarios on how he could get Glenn Swynton to replace his newest partner in the middle of an operation. He counted to ten ... then twenty ... before he pounded on her door.

Ace opened the door mid-pound. "You didn't bring your friend," she said, making a pouty face and speaking in the little girl voice she'd used with Edwaldo. "Was I a bad girl, Daddy?"

"What the hell was that?" he growled as he pushed into the room, kicking the door shut with a resounding slam behind him. "Maybe this is all fun and games to you. But I've not only got a career to worry about, I have a life and a family. I thought you understood that."

Ace's pout dropped away in an instant and transformed into a stern expression. "I do understand that. Bullocks! That's why I just saved your bacon, as you Americans put it. Something you, of all people, should appreciate both literally and figuratively."

"What?" Dick bellowed. "You think you did me some kind of favor there? If my wife finds out ..."

She cut him off. "*Sakra!* That's just it, Dickie. Your wife isn't going to find out anything. My little scene made sure of that."

WTF? "Explain that. How does your play-acting the set-up for a soft core porn flick mean Edwaldo won't go blabbing to my wife?"

"Because you're not the only one."

Dick closed his eyes and shook his head hard, trying to rattle some semblance of sense loose. "The only what?"

Ace looked heavenward for a beat before staring him straight in the eye. "The only dick in the world. Most guys are dicks ... or at least they think with their dicks."

Dick grimaced. "Is that your 'go-to' advice for dealing with people who recognize you when you are on the job?"

Ace laughed. "Never happened. Never going to happen. My chances of running into anyone from the state-run orphanage in Prague is essentially zero ... and I don't have a life before the Subsidiary other than that."

Dick arched an eyebrow. "Wouldn't know. You got to see my dossier; they didn't show me yours."

"Too thin to bother, probably."

"More likely Glenn Swynton's passive-aggressive way of telling me where I rank in the grand scheme of things. After all this is over, he's more likely to ask you about my job performance on this mission than quiz me about yours."

He stared out the window a few seconds before Ace broke the silence. "Still, not much to see in the file. I was recruited straight out of school. Not that many missions since training finished."

"Enough to get you promoted to HQ, so somebody was impressed. And, trust me, I can see why the Subsidiary might prefer operatives without, you know, family entanglements. Hiring orphans before they marry ... or shack up ... fits that profile. But, how's that kind recruitment work? I mean, I got approached privately when I was a cop, but I can't imagine guys in trench coats approaching high school girls in the park would work out so well."

She offered up a wan smile. "The orphanage has an employment festival in the spring for the kids who are aging out. It's held a few weeks before school finishes."

"I doubt the Subsidiary has a booth with pamphlets about the exciting life of being an international spy."

Ace looked out the window, focusing on the palm trees near the beach as she answered. "The recruiting officers, they sit in various classrooms to do interviews, one after the other. There are sign up sheets which describe the different companies hiring."

"Are there a lot of those?"

"No, of course not. A few factories and maybe a half-dozen companies supposedly looking for secretarial staff or retail clerks."

"Supposedly?"

"Many of them are fronts for pimps or porn producers. Even the real companies that recruit at the orphanage are the kinds of places that have handsy bosses who expect you to sit on their lap while they give dictation. Like I said, most guys are dicks."

"Oh."

"Yeah. Of course, the Subsidiary wasn't exactly what it purported to be either. They pretended to be recruiting entry-level security personnel for a big, international hotel chain opening a new location downtown. I liked the idea of having a gun and getting an outside chance for a little travel, so I signed up." She turned back to look at him. "That's how I ended up here with you, saving your cover and your marriage."

Dick frowned. "Yeah. I'm still not convinced about that last part."

"Think about it. So Edwaldo thinks you've got piece of ass half your age on the side. So what? You think that's gonna make him run to your wife? Not on your life. Especially if he thinks there's any hope ... the slimmest, slightest, flimsiest chance in the world that he's gonna someday, somewhere, somehow get in on the action and tap that hot little Lolita fetish himself? Not a chance. If you don't see him lounging at the pool leering at the teeny-boppers when we head out to our appointment, it's because he's wanking off in his hotel room and dialing up pay-per-view threesomes."

Dick pressed his lips together. She had a point. He'd never been that close with Edwaldo, but the guy had never seemed to be the sanctimonious type. And, Edwaldo had only ever met Melanie a few times quite a few years back. Would he even recognize her if he saw her out shopping?

Ace continued. "Where do you know this guy from?"

Dick let out a long exhale. "Chicago. He transferred in from the NYPD. We were cops in the same precinct."

"Worst case, he intimates to your old pals in Chicago you're a stud. It's not like he's gonna run into your wife at Walmart or something. The chances are astronomical."

Dick closed his eyes a moment as his blood pressure settled down. "Odds were against me running into him here."

"One unlikely, unpleasant event is a coincidence," Ace replied, her voice becoming softer, more chipper. "Two unlikely, unpleasant events ... is a global conspiracy of evil we're sworn to stop."

He threw her a half-hearted smile. "Yeah. Best be getting back to that."

She bit her lip. "Too bad," she murmured.

"Too bad we've got to get back to work?"

"Too bad you didn't bring him back to the room," she replied, her eyebrows crooking up. "That would have absolutely guaranteed he'd never tell your wife."

He gave her a sidelong glance. "You mean ..."

She smiled. "I'm like you, Dick. Younger, smarter, better looking, and more physically adept, but like you, I do what needs doing."

"But ... but ..."

She fixed her eyes on him. "It's just sex. *Žádné velké věc*. No big deal. Did you think hotel security guard was the only 'interview' I signed up for? Did you think infiltrating gangs in the Czech Republic for the Subsidiary was all piercings and pickpocketing tourists? You Yanks make such a huge deal about sex, especially the older generation, but that's on you. Tab A into Slot B and lots of screwing—it's really not any more complicated than assembling furniture from Ikea."

Dick's mind suddenly flashed on the Beatles song *Norwegian Wood*, and the lyrics the way he'd always interpreted them. *Isn't it good, knowing she would.* Knowing Ace would was not only need-to-know information he didn't *need* to know, it was something he preferred *not* to know. He didn't need another layer of complexity in his life, thank you. It was already falling apart and he couldn't make any more sense of it than the poorly translated instructions that came with the computer desk he'd assembled for Seth a bunch of Christmas Eves ago. Everything he was trying to put back together in his life should come with the standard Ikea advisory: *Some assembly required.*

When he tuned back in, Ace was still jabbering about the wonders of on-the-job sex. "After all, it's safer and smarter than hooking up with locals. Besides, who wants to go for days, maybe weeks, at a time without fucking?"

"You don't need me for that," Dick replied. He pointed at his cell phone. "Phone sex. It works." He started to turn away, but then twisted back. "Use the speakerphone setting if you need both hands free."

She glared at him for a few seconds, then suddenly Ace was all business, gathering up her things and heading for the door. "Yes, Daddy. Now, are you ready to go talk with some scientists about killer waves? Or do you need to go wank off first?"

Damn. He hated working with a fucking partner.

No. Amend that.

Fuck. He hated working with a damn partner.

Chapter 8

The drive to the Pacific Tsunami Warning Center was blissfully short and quiet. Even though the temperature was in the mid-80s, Dick didn't bother with the air conditioner. The open windows brought fond memories of driving to Patterson Lake in his old beater, with Melanie slid over next to him on the bench seat. Besides, the trade winds off the water provided a touch of coolness even when stopped at an intersection.

The car was a five-year-old white Cadillac, the best the Quartermaster could do on Oahu to match Dick's somewhat antiquated and eclectic taste in rentals. Beefy and powerful, though not much trunk space compared to the old Caddies. It would do; they probably wouldn't be on the island long and he didn't anticipate any car chases. Of course, he hadn't anticipated the fiasco at breakfast. Being a spy was unpredictable.

The PTWC was located in in a generally residential neighborhood just a couple of blocks off of Ewa Beach. The low-slung, tropical style building sat behind a chain link fence on a mossy-looking grassy expanse.

"Not very impressive," noted Ace as they approached a few miles per hour below the posted speed limit. "Not very secure, either. I'd hate to have to defend this place."

Dick shrugged. "It's a bunch of geeks and a much bigger bunch of computers. I don't think they need to worry about being a target in the event of the zombie apocalypse."

She threw a half-smile his way. "That's why I'll survive the zombie apocalypse and you won't, boss."

"Let's stick to the cover. Call me 'Dad.'"

She opened her mouth to reply, but he cut her off.

"'Dad.' Got it? Not 'Daddy.' No more screwing around."

"Yes, sir ... er ... Dad."

Dick drove past their target to get the full lay of the land before turning around and approaching from the east. "I called ahead this morning and told them I was a freelance reporter for *The Des Moines Register* on vacation with my daughter, but looking to get some background information for a feature on tsunamis. Let's us ask a lot of questions without raising too much suspicion."

Ace's nose wrinkled. "Seems pretty suspicious to me. Why the hell would anyone in Iowa give a damn about tsunamis? And what if they check the newspaper's website and don't find your name?"

"Iowa's smack dab in the middle of flyover country, where the people aren't completely jaded and cynical like they are on both coasts. Iowans care about everybody and everything. As for them checking the website, that's why I said I was freelance. Of course I wouldn't show up on the site."

"So, what am I supposed to do? Wait in the car?"

Dick eased the big car into a parking spot shaded by a tall coconut palm. "Not at all. You're hanging with Dad while he works during vacation because ... you're a dutiful daughter and, I don't know, you feel obligated 'cause I paid for the trip, 'cause you're buried in student loans. You tagging along makes my visit and my questions seem that much more mundane. Toss in some questions of your own, if you want."

"Fine, but I still think this is a waste of time. We should be on the Big Island investigating the Great ..."

Dick held up his right hand, motioning her to stop. "Yeah, yeah. We're here now, so listen and learn. Okay?"

Ace gave him a slit-eyed look.

Jesus. Daughters were even more of a pain in the ass than sons.

#

Ace played her part as Dick checked in with the receptionist, smiling and nodding when introduced, and letting her dad take point. The interior of the facility was the same dingy white as the exterior of the building, but with the people providing a colorful accent. Not only was there a surprisingly varied assortment of colors and races among the staff, but almost everyone was wearing casual, comfortable clothing. Younger members of the staff tended toward board shorts topped with a brightly festive T-shirt; older employees gravitated toward khaki slacks offset by wildly patterned, button-down aloha shirts. If this was normal day-to-day attire, casual Friday must mean swimsuits and beach cover-ups.

The facility manager, Dr. Akiro Hansebi, had just enough graying at the temples to look distinguished despite wearing sockless penny loafers to complete his island ensemble. He spoke in the clipped, precise tones typical of Japanese businessmen, but with no trace of an accent. Although he denied Dick's request to use a cell phone to record the visit—citing government policy—Hansebi seemed happy to show them around, maintaining an energetic description of the various computers, seismographs, and relay gear, finishing up in the main control room.

Hansebi gestured toward the wall opposite the door, dominated by a lighted map of the Pacific basin, with rows of computer screens with assorted feeds—pictures, graphs, scrolling data—beneath and on either side. "Here's where everything comes together: seismic reports about tremors and quakes, tidal and weather inputs, data re volcanic eruptions and magma swelling on volcanic slopes, and tsunami buoy data from throughout the basin."

Dick looked up from the pad on which he was half-heartedly scratching notes; Ace assumed that, like her, he had set his sunglasses to record both audio and video. "Seems like kind of a boring gig. Just waiting around for something to happen, so you can analyze it and maybe, just maybe, send out an evacuation order."

Their guide wrinkled his brow. Ace thought he might be offended by Dick's remark, but his quick reply showed no hint of irritation. "Not at all. Plenty is going on all the time. We are a constant source of information for both civil defense authorities and scientists in dozens of countries. Much of the information gathered here is disseminated in real-time even while it is being analyzed and run through our computer simulations to determine whether it warrants a tsunami alert."

"What do you mean," Ace asked, "by 'disseminated in real-time?' You mean you just give out all of this data to anyone anywhere?"

Hansebi tilted his head toward her. "Exactly. The entire reason for the Center is to facilitate communication of information that may save lives. You can, for instance, follow a Twitter feed which will alert you about earthquakes anywhere in the world. Of course, if you don't filter it by area of geographic interest or delimit it by magnitude, your phone just buzzes at you constantly. Earth's crust is much more dynamic than most people realize. And even smaller events which are of insufficient energy or displacement to cause noticeable tsunami effects in any significant portion of the Pacific basin can have local effects important to shipping, fishing fleets, or to local populations. Earthquakes and seaquakes which do not cause destructive waves or building degradation can still impact power grids, whether by downed lines or, perhaps, triggering the scrambling and shut down of power generation facilities under safety protocols."

Dick spoke back up. "Isn't some of that kind of ... I don't know ... peripheral to your main task? I'm not sure the average taxpayer wants to be spending money so some guy in a village in Vanuatu knows whether a tiny tremor has upset the morning fishing routines."

Hansebi threw an eyebrow shrug and a tight smile toward Dick. "The information has to be gathered for our purposes in any event; not sharing useful bits of that information with others would seem to be the bigger waste. Besides, such reports not only generate a significant amount of goodwill with our neighbors while training our staff and inculcating them into a regular routine of rapid, accurate analysis and quick dissemination, but, more importantly, they ensure that everyone who should be paying attention to our reports in the event of a time-sensitive alert is accustomed to monitoring them on a priority basis."

"Why's that so important?" asked Dick. "I seem to recall that after some big earthquake a few years back in Chile or Peru ... someplace down in South America ... the tsunami wave didn't get to Hawaii for six or eight hours. CNN ran the same six clips from stock footage for hours before anything happened and, even then, it was pretty much a non-event."

Another tight smile. "Well, Mr. Thornby, think about what you said for a few moments. When you flew here on your connecting flight from L.A. or San Francisco or whatever, you were flying at almost five hundred miles per hour, and it took you about five hours to get here. Hawaii is a very remote place—the most remote place in the Pacific basin. Yet a seismic event thousands of miles away, even farther from here than L.A., caused a modest wave to arrive here six or so hours later. That means the shock wave was transmitted through the ocean at the speed of a jetliner and was strong enough to push water along an extremely broad front with impressive force. When Krakatoa erupted in Indonesia in 1883, there was an admittedly small, but measurable, impact on the sea level in London, in an entirely different ocean, a day later. But things were much quicker and much more devastating for those nearby. Tsunamis in Java and Sumatra were well over a hundred feet high, killing thousands within minutes after the explosion which destroyed the island—almost all from the impact of water, not lava or gases."

Dick mouthed an "Ohhhh ..." as he nodded at the doc. Ace wasn't sure if he was acting or was truly as clueless as he appeared. "So that's why you have the warning center out here in Hawaii, because you'll get hours and hours of warning before a tsunami can take you offline."

Hansebi's brow furrowed. "Well, that certainly is an advantage for tsunamis generated by volcanic activity or landslides along the tectonic plates which circle the Pacific Ocean—the Ring of Fire. Of course, due to a thin spot on the crust of the Pacific Plate, the Hawaiian Islands are right on top of—and, in fact, were created by, a volcanic hotspot, which spews out magma which builds up and collapses to form these volcanic islands. So, while we would generally have hours of warning for a tsunami generated by activity along the Ring of Fire, a sizeable earthquake or explosive volcanic eruption here in the islands—most likely on the Big Island of Hawaii—could generate a sizeable tsunami which could come to shore here on Oahu in a half an hour, give or take."

"Jesus," muttered Dick.

Ace couldn't restrain herself. "So ... if something cracked off of the Big Island, all the tourists on Waikiki might see a huge wave rushing toward them only minutes later?"

The doc swallowed hard. "Well, yes, in theory. The actual dynamics of a tsunami are complex. Where and how a wave hits is not only affected by the size and precise location of the generating event, but by the topography of the sea floor, coral breaks, and the outline of the shore. The highest waves are often generated by narrowing bays with open access to deep water."

Ace tipped her head down and glared at him. "Like a deep harbor for ocean-going vessels, like battleships and aircraft carriers."

Hansebi looked at the floor. "Yes."

"Then why the hell is the warning center practically next door to Pearl Harbor, a block and a half from the beach, and only a couple feet higher?"

"Well, uh, that's really not a very likely scenario ..."

A burly native-Hawaiian tech looked up from a nearby screen. "The short answer is that we're just an offshoot of the weather service facilities which were here first." Hansebi shot the tech a stern look, but he either didn't notice or didn't care. "Keaweaheulu Maleko," he said, proffering a meaty hand. You can call me 'Ulu.'"

Ace took it and tried to give it a single shake, but it barely moved. "You can call me 'Ace.'" She let go of his hand. "What's the long answer?"

"The long answer?"

"What's the real reason the Center is sitting on a beach instead of sitting up ..." She gestured toward the back of the building.

"*Mauka*?" Ulu asked. "That means 'towards the mountains.'"

"Yeah," said Ace. "Why isn't the center *mauka*?"

Hansebi's stern look deepened. "This topic is not really within Ulu's area of special expertise," he interjected. "I'm sure he needs to get back to his monitoring."

Ulu's lip quivered, but he stifled the snarl that was forming. He angled his head deferentially toward Hansebi and turned back to his station, muttering under his breath. "*Haoles* are stupid."

Ace glanced at Hansebi. Their guide had turned and headed out the door with Dick. He apparently hadn't heard Ulu's remark. She started to go with them, then interrupted Hansebi's latest tour patter. "Restroom?"

Hansebi nodded down the hall in the opposite direction they were headed. "Second door on the left."

"Go ahead," Ace said with a smile. "I'll catch up."

"Sure," said Dick. She mentally gave the big guy credit for the assist. He obviously knew she didn't need to hit the loo. Large bladder capacity was practically the only genetic trait required to be a spy.

The two men continued down the hall. Ace headed to the restroom, opening the door and watching as the guys turned the corner at the end of the hall, then scooted quickly back to the control room, rapping once on the door to get Ulu's attention.

He scowled. "I'm not supposed to open the door for non-employees."

"I forgot something."

He got up and opened the door, scanning the floor on the way. "What? You lose an earring or something?"

Ace stepped inside and shut the door behind her. "No, I forgot to ask why *haoles* are stupid."

"That's a lengthy conversation," grunted Ulu, dropping back into his chair and throwing a quick glance at his terminal.

"Let's start with the basics. Who are *haoles*?"

Ulu barked out a laugh. "Non-natives."

"Foreigners?"

"Non-Hawaiians. White people mostly. Loud, obnoxious, hyperactive, rich people, especially."

"So, what particular aspect of *haole* stupidity triggered your comment as we were leaving?"

Ulu snorted. "Their propensity for building houses, businesses, and governmental buildings on the shore, so they can be near the ocean ... so they can see the ocean." He shook his head. "You're on a friggin' island, brah. You go outta your house, you're going to see the friggin' ocean. It's right there, man."

Ace shrugged. The information was less useful than she'd hoped. "Tastes differ, I guess. You pay your money, you make your choice."

"But, it's a stupid choice. *Mauka*, the climate is cooler, so you don't need no air conditioning. And there's more rain, so you can grow your own food. And the breezes are cleaner and cooler and the heat and the salt spray doesn't destroy all your electronics. You know how often we have to replace cable connections and circuits on all this stuff?" He shook his head. "And, your question was on point. Uphill is way safer in the event of an ... event. A decent-sized tsunami would take out this place in an instant."

"I dunno," replied Ace. She knocked on the interior wall next to the door. "Cement's pretty tough stuff."

"Sure, it'll stand up to a hurricane, though the wide eaves mean the roof would lift right off in a big blow, but wind's nothing ... *nothing* ... compared to the power of surging water. Even something the size of the Ritter Island tsunami or the Sri Lankan surge would take out this place. If ... when ... Alika Three happens, there'll be nothing left of *haole* civilization here. Just bruddahs hanging out *mauka*."

Kurva! She had to watch her time. She held out her hand. "Give me your number. I'd like to call you later."

Instead of handing her a card, he grabbed a felt-tip pen and wrote seven digits on her palm, like they were in fucking school. "What's the area code?"

"Eight-oh-eight," he replied. "Everything in the islands is area code eight-oh-eight." He chuckled. "You're a *haole*, but I could look past that ..."

73

Wet Work

She looked at his massive bulk and had a fleeting image of being crushed having sex with the local. She smiled at him. Let him think what he wanted. "Only if I get to ride out the waves on top ..."

Chapter 9

Dick raised his eyebrows as Ace rounded the corner to the lobby, where he stood conversing with Hansebi, who he'd managed to position so the doctor wouldn't see Ace as she approached.

Hansebi was talking: "While the decades-long eruption of Kilauea on the Big Island, principally through the Pu'u 'Ō'ō vent and in the Halema'uma'u Crater, generates a regular stream of small to modest tremors, the flow of lava is not likely to cause a tsunami of any sort. Tsunamis are generated by sizeable shifts of rock within or into waters, causing a massive displacement of water volume. A constant lava flow releases pressure from the magma chamber on a regular basis. It's only when pressure of both magma and sulfuric or steam gases builds rapidly ... or at least more rapidly than it can be released through flows and steam vents ... that explosive events can occur, like Mount St. Helens or Krakatoa. Such explosions can dislodge considerable volumes of earth and rock, which can be very dangerous in a marine environment."

Ace strolled up. "So, is that what happened in Alika one and two? Big explosion because of pressure build up?"

"Alika ... what?" stammered Dick. He looked back and forth between her and Hansebi, shrugging his shoulders. "Seems my daughter prepared better for this interview than I did." He readied his pen and pad for more notetaking. "What's an Alika?"

"And," Ace interjected, "how overdue is Alika three?"

Hansebi frowned, as if the subject was somehow distasteful. "Alika one and two are distant historical events. Alika one occurred approximately two hundred forty thousand years ago and Alika two about one hundred twenty thousand years ago."

Ace let out a low whistle. "Which suggests Alika three is due anytime ..."

75

Hansebi waved away her concern. "These things are not that precise. There are innumerable variables. This isn't Old Faithful we're talking about. It's a complex system of magma chambers, rift zones, steam vents, lava tubes, and tectonic movement."

Dick tried his best to run some interference. "Yeah, sure, doc. We're talking about geologic time here. We understand that. But a whiff of danger can get people to read an article they might otherwise just skim past. Maybe, just maybe, that means they might learn something in the process ... or not gripe about governmental expenditures on science." He motioned with his pad, showing the doc he was ready to take notes. "So, were these Alika things big blow-offs after a period of building pressure?"

Hansebi seemed to settle down, though his expression remained hard. "Not at all. The Alika occurrences were subsidence events."

Dick scrunched up his face.

The doc apparently noticed his confusion. "Landslides. Massive landslides."

"Uh-huh ..." murmured Dick.

"You understand," continued Hansebi, "that the Hawaiian Island chain is formed by volcanic magma coming out of a hot spot on the ocean floor?"

"Sure," interjected Ace. "Everybody knows that. The Earth's crust is moving over the hotspot at a slow speed and each island was formed when it was over the hot spot. The older ones, like Kauai and Oahu are ancient and more worn down."

Hansebi nodded. "Exactly. The oldest, Niihau, is practically a flat, desolate plateau at this point." His face softened as he continued his lecture. "What people forget is that the volcanoes are immensely tall—not just tall enough above sea level that there is snow on top of Mauna Kea at times, but *hugely* tall from their base on the sea floor. Measured

76

from top to base, they are taller than Mount Everest is above its base and, accordingly, much, much greater in total volume. Only a small percentage of the actual volume pokes out from the surface of the sea."

That made sense when Dick thought it through.

"The other thing," the doc continued, "is that the volcanoes are actually quite steep, so there is a significant amount of natural subsidence which occurs on a regular basis. Some of that occurs in a constant, regular stream, but it is often punctuated by larger events on an irregular and unpredictable basis."

He noticed Ace nodding as the doc spoke. "Oh, I get it. So, it's like when the kids at the beach try to make a sand tower and the sand keeps sliding down hill and collapsing when it reaches a certain height."

"Yes," replied the doctor. "But more like a mud castle, where the dirt may initially adhere, but clumps off as it dries and heavier, wetter mud is placed above it."

"So," asked Dick, "these Alika earthquakes shook some of the volcanic deposits loose?"

Hansebi tipped his head. "More like gravity finally overcame the adherence of the initial deposit and a landslide started which was so massive it mimicked an earthquake."

Ace's face was grim. "How massive are we talking about?"

"More than a hundred times the volume of earth displaced by the Mount St. Helens collapse."

"Fuck ..." whispered Ace. Dick threw her a stern look. "Pardon my language, D-d-dad, but ... holy shit."

The doctor held out his hands, palms down, in a calming gesture. "Don't get too excited. It's very, very unlikely to occur within any of our lifetimes."

"Sure," said Dick. "But, just to be thorough. What kind of tsunamis did these Alika events cause?"

Hansebi returned to a professorial tone. "Scientists have gone about looking at that in two ways. Some have analyzed the debris fields in the ocean containing the detritus from these landslides, calculating how much power it would take to move boulders of various sizes the distances involved and calculating the volume of water displaced. Others have looked at evidence of coral debris on Lanai and Oahu, trying to calculate the height of the waves by measuring how high such debris occurs and how many miles inland. This latter method has some detractors, as some believe the older islands are, in fact, rising as the crust beneath them rises in counterbalance to the sinking of the mantle below the Big Island as it grows and gets heavier over time."

"Sounds complicated," replied Dick. "Do the two theories differ much in their conclusions?"

"Not really," answered Hansebi. "And recent studies on the Kohala uplands on the northwest side of the Big Island, which everyone agrees is slowly sinking, indicates the tsunami was somewhere between twelve hundred and sixteen hundred feet high when it hit Kohala a few minutes later, and at least seven hundred feet high when it swept over Lanai shortly thereafter."

"Wow," muttered Dick.

"*Sakra!*" echoed Ace. Dick saw her wince a half-second later when she obviously realized she'd broken character. She quickly tried to recover. "How big of an explosion or earthquake would you need to trigger something like that before, you know, it would naturally occur." She shrugged. "Say, along the Great Crack."

Dick watched as Hansebi stared for a few moments at Ace, as if calculating the chances she wanted a do-it-yourself primer. His face became stern as he squinted at her. 'Please tell me you're not one of those?"

"One of what?" Ace asked, her voice saccharin sweet.

"Disaster porn junkies. Conspiracy nuts. End-of-the-world whackos."

"I don't know what you mean," replied Ace. "Why would worrying about stuff that might happen make you a whacko?"

"Yeah," gruffed Dick. "Don't call my daughter a whacko."

Hansebi sighed, then closed his eyes a moment before dialing up a tight smile and continuing. "I'm sure you ... both of you ... are well intentioned and that ..." He nodded toward Dick. "... your article is not intended to be sensational or gratuitously alarming. However, there are certain fringe elements, especially within the end-of-the-world prepper movement, who like to panic others with predictions of imminent disaster of, well, Biblical proportions. I'm not sure if it's because it makes them feel important or they're just trying to sell more freeze-dried, long shelf-life foodstuffs."

"MREs," mused Dick. "Yeah. Only the prospect of starvation could prompt a civilian to stockpile meals-ready-to-eat."

Ace interjected, practically twitchy with impatience. "What's all this got to do with the Great Crack? I mean, as I understand it, there's ... well ... a big crack running across the south end of the Big Island. Doesn't that suggest that hunk of land is going to ... well ... crack off and slide into the ocean creating a splash that will engulf Maui and Lanai and wash this cinderblock beachside warning center over the Pali Lookout?"

Hansebi fluttered a hand in Ace's direction. "The Great Crack, as it is called, is a mere thirteen kilometers long. Eight miles as the crow flies in, er, Iowa. While it is an impressive sight, given it is up to fifty feet wide and almost sixty-five deep in some places, I'd hardly call it evidence the entire south side of the Big Island is sliding into the ocean."

Ace pressed. "But if it did, that would be bad."

The scientist failed to take the bait. "The Great Crack is not an omen. It's probably not even a subsidence crack. It's more likely a result of crustal dilation as the result of lava flows and incursions."

"But what if it widened suddenly?" Ace asked. Dick almost found himself shaking his head. She was like a teenager with a smartphone. She just couldn't let go.

Hansebi wrinkled his nose. "Certainly I've seen no credible scientific evidence it is widening or about to burst at the seams. Although there was lava flow from the crack in the early 1800s, neither the 1868 nor the 1975 quakes—magnitude 7.9 and 7.2—caused any lateral slippage."

"What about a bomb?"

The doctor looked heavenward, but apparently was too polite to count to ten out loud. "I think, Miss, you should let your father do the fact-gathering for his own story. ISIS is not sending over swarthy men with backpacks to detonate as they leap into the Great Crack. Besides, if they had explosives of sufficient size to *chance* causing a tsunami here, why would they set them off where there are so few people? Why wouldn't they just set them off in a major metropolitan area?" He tapped his foot. "Don't believe everything you see on the SyFy Channel. Or the Discovery Channel either. And don't get me started on A&E and History. It's shameful what educational television has devolved into."

The trio stepped to one side as a bevy of scientists passed by discussing lunch plans. Dick was just about to wind things up by thanking the doc when Ace dragged them back into conversation.

80

"And a big earthquake is the only thing that could dislodge a huge landslide on the Big Island?"

Jesus. It's like she couldn't shut up. Time for Dad to intervene. "I think we've taken up enough of ..."

"Well, there was the silent earthquake on the Big Island back in 2000," mused Hansebi.

"What the hell is a silent earthquake?" Dick blurted. Jeez, he hoped it wasn't as deadly as a silent heart attack.

"Well, silent is probably a misnomer, since noise is not a reliable indicator of earthquake intensity. Aseismic is probably a better term. The November 2000 event was exceptionally slow-moving, lasting almost thirty-six hours, but causing almost no noticeable shaking and registering a mere 5.7, but moved a prodigious slab of material."

"How'd it do that?" interjected Ace.

Hansebi shrugged. "The most high-profile theory is that it *slid* due to an extremely high-volume of water which percolated down almost three miles into the fault systems below Kiluea on the heels of a torrential deluge of almost three *feet* of rain slightly more than a week earlier. The influx of the water into the quite porous lava rock not only added significantly to the weight of the angled layers of old flow, but lubricated them like oil ... or the flow of an air hockey game." The doctor nodded. "Quite impressive."

Now they were getting somewhere. "How far?" asked Dick.

"Hmm?"

"How far did the lava slide?" Dick clarified.

"Almost nine centimeters," declared their host.

"Is that all?" Ace replied with a dejected whine.

Dick threw her a quizzical look.

"Less than four inches."

"Oh," said Dick. "Is that all?"

Hansebi snorted. "Is that all? Moving a half-mile thick slab the size of ... a national park ... or a small state ... four inches without anyone noticing is a most impressive feat." The doctor glanced at his watch. "I really need to check on several projects. I hope this suffices for your article, Mr. Thornby." He bobbed his head. "Nice meeting you ... both of you. Enjoy your stay in the islands." He turned and left, leaving them in the hallway near the lobby.

They were well out of range of being heard, almost to the car, before Dick spoke up. "Well, that was interesting. Educational even. I'd never heard of the whole silent earthquake business."

Ace sneered at him as she reached for the passenger side door handle. "Four inches? Sorry, Dad, but no matter what they say, girls are never impressed with anything under six inches."

"Shut up and get in the car."

Chapter 10

Kurva! The car seat was burning hot. Dick, in his khakis, didn't seem to notice. She leaned back on the vertical portion of the seat, which had been more shaded, and propped her sandaled feet up on the dashboard to save her thighs from third-degree burns.

"What next?" asked the Dickster, oblivious to her discomfort.

She gave him a hard look. "What do you mean, 'What next?' We go to the Big Island and check out the Great Crack, like I wanted us to do yesterday."

He backed out of the parking spot, then shifted the car into drive and headed for the exit. He wasn't subtle about giving the behemoth gas, but she didn't mind the breeze coming in the window as he turned out on to the street without bothering to stop at the familiar red sign.

"You heard the doc," he said. "The Great Crack is a bust ... a myth ... a dead-end. What's the point?"

She twisted in her seat, shifting to position her legs out the passenger window. "Just because the first alleged expert we talked to thinks it's a myth, doesn't mean it is. Besides, it certainly doesn't mean the bad guys think it's a myth. Maybe they think it'll work. Or maybe they're not thinking of a tsunami apocalypse, just a smaller event. Something that won't propagate across the ocean—just a smaller slide that will inundate the coastal regions of the islands, themselves. Either way, we still have to take a look. Besides, we've got no other leads, unless you want to start shaking down local hoods, *Hawaii Five-O* style."

"I guess," groused her assigned mentor. "But who would want to drown a bunch of clueless tourists ..."

"*Haoles* ..." she interjected.

"What?"

"*Haoles* are non-natives. Most of the native Hawaiians apparently like higher ground, where it's cooler."

Dick suddenly hit the brake, causing her ass to slide uncomfortably forward as the edge of the window held her feet in place. "What the hell?"

"Exactly," said Dick as they sat in the middle of the damn residential street. "What the hell. It could be the damn PPIPF."

"Pfffft," she groused as she clumsily repositioned herself to a more standard sitting position. "What the hell is that?"

"P-P-I-P-F." Dick looked at her as if she was an idiot. "The Pan-Pacific Indigenous People's Front. I thought you said you read my file, including the details about my New Zealand assignment."

"Oh, sure," she replied, drawing out the last word. "The one where you blew up a port to recover a laptop. Subtle work that."

"Shove it up your ass," growled Dick.

"Dad! Such language!"

"Cute. But if you spent more time reading and less time being cute, you'd know the PPIPF is a violent fringe group that wants to reclaim the whole Pacific basin for the natives and take out as many tourists and colonial interlopers as they can along the way. They'd love a caper which did maximum damage to the tourist economy and took out the houses of rich retirees and vacationing one-percenters."

"Caper? Seriously? You *are* old."

"Shut up and switch seats with me." He grabbed his special Subsidiary-issued aviator sunglasses from out of the pocket of his aloha shirt. "I need to check in with the office and get some leads on local PPIPF members while you drive us back to the hotel."

#

Almost five hours later, Ace dialed up the magnification on her own shades, a European wrap-around style that, like Dick's, had all the communications equipment, low-light vision, and other features the Subsidiary techs could fit into the sleek frame. She gazed up at Diamond Head from the lanai of Dick's hotel room. She'd wanted to lounge by the sparkling clear waters of the spacious hotel pool while he finished quizzing the research division about PPIPF members in the islands, but the big guy was concerned she'd run into his friend from breakfast. No doubt he also thought she was goofing off during the mission by catching some rays; she preferred to think of her touristy activity as reinforcing their cover.

"Looks like a tough climb," she said as she amped up the power and swept the crest of the extinct volcano. "Not real mountain tough, like the Alps, Himalayas, or Rockies, but more arduous than the hefty-sized PPIPF doughboys you've been showing me pictures of would want to tackle for what basically sounds like a natives-R-cool pep rally." She squinted. "On the other hand, I do see a few people up there, along with some kind of squat building, so there must be a route."

"There is," replied Dick, "but not from the outside."

She lowered her sunglasses and gave him a stare. "How else do you climb a mountain? No snow, so I doubt there's a ski lift." She scrunched up her face in thought. "Scenic tramway out of view?"

Dick chuckled. "You've got to remember that the mountains here are all volcanic. Diamond Head is just the tallest point on a circular ridge that surrounds an ancient caldera."

"So you climb up at a lower point on the circular ridge and walk around the circumference?"

This time the old guy snorted. "Better yet. You take a city bus halfway around the outside and follow the road that goes through a tunnel to the flat plateau in the center of the ring, then follow the path at the park that takes you up to the top along the less steep inner slope. There's a somewhat awkward, steep stairway at one point, but most of the way is easy going. Only a mile or so if I recall correctly."

"Stairs?" she blurted. "Americans install stairs on their hiking paths?"

"No. Well, at least not in this case. The United States Army did." He pointed at the mountain—a useless gesture given the distance and the fact both of them were using magnification when they looked at the summit, but she understood his meaning and slid her shades back down to her eyes. "See those squat, boxy features near the top? The Army installed lookouts and pill-boxes—machine gun emplacements—on the crest during World War II, when they were worried about a Japanese invasion of the island. There's two sets of concrete steps on the steeper parts of the slope connected by a short tunnel, plus a spiral staircase near the top to aid the climb up with packs full of ammo and equipment. There's even an old cable line partway up to assist hauling larger loads up and down."

"You mean a zip line?"

Dick shrugged. "Kind of, I guess. Though I doubt they ever used it that way. Didn't pay much attention to it when I climbed up several years ago during a layover on a return flight from ... well, you know ... an assignment."

"And that's where the guys at the Subsidiary who monitor PPIPF communications say the local contingent is congregating tonight?"

"Yeah," said Dick. "Not normally something that would be on the Subsidiary's radar. Routine gatherings just don't rate any concern. After all, lots of separatist and secessionist groups around the world are nothing but talk. But, given what the Maori faction of the PPIPF was up to in New Zealand a while back and my request for info, the reshuffled the deck of monitoring priorities to shake out a lead."

Ace maxed out the magnification on her sunglasses and studied the pill-boxes. "Still seems like an arduous trek to get to a desolate spot for a clandestine meeting just so they can swap stories about how stupid tourists are." She dialed back to normal view and looked at her partner as he took off his sunglasses and sat in one of the lanai's deck chairs.

"I dunno. It's desolate, but nearby. You can get within a mile or so by public transportation. Summits and headlands are always prominent features to a native population, but this one's got obvious colonial scars, plus a killer vantage point to look not only at the stars and the ocean, but also the ..." He gestured at the tightly packed beachfront hotels and the throngs along the expanse of Waikiki. "... commercialization of island life by the evil colonialists."

"Whatever," Ace replied. "If they want to see what being taken over again and again by imperialist powers is like, they should spend some time in Eastern Europe." She inclined her head toward her own room. "Guess I'd better go change into long pants and better hiking shoes. I don't think flip-flops and a beach cover-up are going to cut it, even for a stroll tourists take."

"Yeah. I figure it's easiest to head up late this afternoon, when the park at the bottom is still open, then find a spot along the way to take cover until after dark, when the PPIPF members will be gathering." He glanced at his watch. "Let's plan to leave here a quarter to four. In the meantime, I'll make a quick run to pick up some gear I arranged for the Quartermaster to put together for us locally."

"Don't want to have nothing but your dick in your hands when you're the only *haole* at a native gathering? I thought we were just going to listen in, not try to arrest the entire gang."

"I was a Boy Scout ..."

"No shit," Ace drawled. She pursed her lips and gave him a seductive wink. "I'd never have guessed."

Her mentor ignored her faux advances. "... which means I like to be prepared."

"Really?" she said. "I rifled through your wallet when you were in the restroom an hour ago. Didn't find a condom." She winked at him again as she sashayed into the room and headed for the open door connecting their rooms. "So how prepared are you, really?"

#

The hike up the inside of Diamond Head was an easy trek, practically a stroll. When he was in the Rangers, he did five times as much before breakfast on most days. Ace didn't even seem to break a sweat keeping up with him. Finding cover part way up presented no obstacles, either. Waiting, however, was a whole different story. While Dick could handle even the most tedious parts of his missions, he was having a hard time tolerating his new partner's fidgeting.

"Jesus. Sit still," Dick growled as Ace shifted for the third time in five minutes. "Or take a nap. You're worse than a toddler at church." He glanced over at his teammate. "You'd make a crappy assassin."

She stopped moving and seemed to settle in place. "Nah," she whispered. "I'd make a crappy sniper. I've done my share of snuff jobs. I'm just more the seduce-and-stab type." She gave him a once-over. "I could gut stab you twelve times in four seconds and there wouldn't be any visible blood until after I walked away. By the time you hit the ground, I'd be in the next room, asking the valet to retrieve my car." She leaned closer to him. "And it would be a damn fine car ... a fast car ... a sports car. Something appropriate for a spy."

Dick said nothing. One of them, at least, should practice maintaining appropriate protocol for hiding in place.

"Of course, I never wear white, just in case there is an errant spot of blood. Besides, white isn't appropriate for my usual cover. Something red and flowing; something that doesn't inhibit my movement ... or my mark."

Jesus. It was going to be a long, long wait. The park officially closed hours before the bad guys were slated to meet, and most of the natives seemed to operate on island time—a flexible construct that corresponded with good surfing conditions and a relaxed approach to life.

Dick couldn't remember the last time he'd had a relaxed approach ... to anything.

Chapter 11

Waiting for gang members to assemble was like standing in the kitchen waiting for microwave popcorn to pop. First there was a lone pop, then a long wait for the second, less for the third. Then the pace picked up until a cacophony of pops defied counting before dwindling off into groups or two and three. Eventually, you found yourself counting off seconds between occurrences. Finally, things died down enough, you figured you were done and you'd better get down to business before you waited too long and got burned, missing what you were trying to accomplish. He had mentally ticked off the PPIPF members he'd recognized from the photos supplied earlier by the Subsidiary. All the head honchos had arrived.

Dick double-checked there were no more locals headed up the switchbacks leading to the summit access, then nodded at Ace. The two of them moved out from their cover between the first lookout and the first stairway to finish their climb to the top of Diamond Head. Seventy-four steep concrete steps later, they entered a dim tunnel. The lights installed to assist tourist access were turned off for the night, as the park closed at six, but enough ambient light leaked in to reveal no guard blocked the way. They exited at the bottom right of another concrete staircase with a rest area on the opposite side. Dick eschewed taking the additional hundred or so steps to the bottom level of the gun emplacement and its easily-guarded internal spiral staircase to the lowest level of the Fire Control Station. Instead, he opted to take the gentle slope of the shorter of the two new exit loop trails and creep up a modern metal staircase installed where the trails intersected on the inner slope of the crater. From there, he could assess where their target congregated.

Ace stalked closely behind without saying a word. A nice change of pace, that.

The bunker to the left was empty, as was the walkway to the right and the additional metal stairs to the summit and its flat-roofed, heavily-graffitied, concrete station. He nodded toward the right, and they sprinted along the summit trail and up the steps to the station. Still no one in sight.

Dick took the lead, motioning for his less stealthy compatriot to follow as he crept along the inside perimeter of the concrete cube, avoiding the well-trod tourist pathway on the other side. He hesitated at the far edge and dropped to his belly to scope out the scene. While the trail railing and a rocky outcropping blocked part of his view, he could make out a circle of gang members sitting along the crest pathway between the summit pillbox and the more camouflaged Fire Control Station lower on the ridge to the west. The setting sun off the coast past Waikiki backlit the conclave, making it nigh impossible to make out individual features on the participants. All he could see were nodding heads, bulging muscles, and extra-husky waistlines. Too much *loco moco*—gravy drowned burger, rice, and eggs—on their island diet; you didn't get a gut like that on poi and pineapple.

Although he'd heard voices as he neared, the conversation had lulled as the sunset approached—all eyes no doubt on the fiery sky streaked by wine dark clouds as the sun still peeked out above the azure waves on the horizon. Tourists on the beach were probably holding their breath, leaning forward in an attempt to catch the vaunted green flash of the perfect tropical sunset. He stayed focused on the mission, elbowing his way forward. It's not that he could see more, but he had some hope of hearing something nearer to the group. He turned his head so he could hear better when conversation flowed once more as the gloaming gave way to twilight.

91

His dedication to duty paid off. As soon as the sun was down, the conversation resumed. It was like music to his ears. Unfortunately, he didn't know the lyrics to the song.

Damn.

They were speaking Hawaiian. Of course they were speaking Hawaiian. Isn't that what an organization dedicated to wiping out colonial interlopers and imperial taskmasters would do? Sure, the natives had Niihau all to themselves and Hawaiian was the only language spoken there. But the Forbidden Island was a windswept plateau wasteland for the most part; the PPIPF wanted all of the islands for the natives. They funded secessionist efforts, a growing sentiment on the islands. They also backed the push to allow native access to Kahoolawe, despite the fact the uninhabited island was a fucked up jungle of unexploded ordinance, having been used as target practice by the U.S. Navy for the better part of half a century.

Sure, some of the PPIPF's desires might sound honorable, but even if he couldn't understand what they were saying right now, he knew they were willing to murder and maim thousands of innocent people to accomplish their goals. Violence was their true language, even if the soothing tones of the Hawaiian tongue made it sound pleasant, even melodic.

Still he listened, just in case they switched over to English or even Pidgin, the local patois combining Hawaiian and English dialects into a mishmash of laid-back drawls and clipped phraseology in a sing-song accent. At least, then, he might be able to make out a few words—a date, a name, a place. Not that it would be easy. With only thirteen letters, the local geographic names were a confluence of similar sounding syllables to Dick's ears. Besides, different islands had towns with exactly the same names. Things were not going Dick's way.

If this was a movie, this is where someone would suddenly growl "Speak English! Our beautiful language does not deserve to be sullied by the violence and destruction we are about to rain down on the vile pestilence that has befouled our way of life." Then everyone would speak in English, repeating the earlier conversation for good measure. Or maybe the bad guys would sneak up and capture them, then reveal their entire nefarious plot before devising some tediously slow and arcane method of killing them that allowed them to escape after the bad guys left. But this was real life. Nobody in the real world would let themselves be captured on the off chance they could gather information, then escape unharmed.

He listened to the unintelligible conversation for a while, but nothing changed. Then he felt a tap on the back of his leg. He kept his combat instincts in check and craned his neck to look behind him. Now that the island was fully dark in the way only a hunk of rock dropped in the middle of the world's biggest ocean can be on a moonless night, he barely could make out the outline of Ace behind him. He reached into his pocket and pulled out his special, Subsidiary tech shades, pressing the temple to activate low-light mode as he donned them. He could see now that Ace had her wraparounds on, too. He didn't know why. He could hear fine; he didn't need to read lips. Especially not when they were speaking Hawaiian. It's not like they were acting out their sinister plot by using their hands and bodies to speak in hula motions like at all the touristy luaus.

As he stared at her, Ace mouthed the words: "Did you hear that?" I guess he could read lips after all. He furrowed his brow, not that she could probably tell, since he had on shades. He shook his head minutely. "They're leaving," she mouthed. She motioned with her thumb. "We need to go, now!"

93

Wet Work

He had no idea how she could know that, but there's no point to having a partner if you don't trust them in a tight spot. It did sound like the unintelligible conversation might be winding down. He also heard the sound of shuffling feet and the sumo-like grunts of overweight thugs getting up from the ground.

He nodded and got up with slow, stealthy movements. They could back off up the hill and scramble down the path on the other side of the concrete block at the summit, maybe even get back to their earlier hiding spot while the gang members navigated the choke point at the spiral staircase in the station right below their conclave perch. All they had to do then was wait while the conclave trickled down the path in the dark. Ace was scrambling up, too, but he suddenly realized neither of them was moving fast enough. The group wasn't going down through the darkened spiral staircase. They were taking the other side of the tourist path loop, the exit path he and Ace had come up earlier. Maybe the spiral staircase couldn't bear the heavy load of so many Spam-fed natives at once or maybe the big, bad secessionists were afraid of the dark. It didn't matter; he'd made a mistake assuming which way they would go when they left.

A big mistake.

He felt the footfalls of thundering heavyweights approaching much too close. He and Ace certainly weren't going to make it back to their earlier cover in time. And here, up on the crest, there wasn't any real vegetation to hide them, just the silent silhouettes of concrete machine gun nests from a bygone time. The summit station was just a few yards away. If they could get behind it, the gang might still pass them by unnoticed.

Ace clearly had the same idea, but instead of trying to dash around the side of the concrete fortification, she jumped lightly atop it. What the …? Dick had no choice but to follow suit. Ace began rolling along the flat top of the bunker; Dick was doing the same when a dim flashlight suddenly shone on both of them, starting at their feet, but rapidly moving up their torsos.

Dick was about to jump up, ready for fight or flight. Instead, Ace grabbed him, pulling him closer and wrapping her legs around him. "Kiss me!" she hissed, pushing up both their sunglasses, flicking open her blouse, and pressing her face to his as she rolled him over so she was on top.

"What? Huh?" replied Dick as the moving light centered on them.

"Like you mean it," Ace whispered, shoving her tongue in his mouth, preventing any reply, as she grabbed his right hand and shoved it on her breast.

The lead thug kept his light steady as he approached them. "Yo. What you doin' here, brah?"

Dick let Ace's tongue exit his mouth as she sat up, but he kept his paw on her tit. Instinct? Pleasure? Maintaining his cover? Protecting her modesty? He hadn't been so confused about second base since high school ... and his confusion had nothing to do with the infield fly rule. Worse yet, while his mind was confused, his body was responding with gusto. Fortunately, Ace covered Dick's confused silence.

She looked over at the thug *du jour*. "What's it look like, brah? Fucking in fucking paradise."

A low, animalistic growl rose up from the darkness as a throng of fellow locals began to bunch up behind their interrogator like looky-loos at an accident scene. "Looks more like you're disrespecting our sacred ground."

Ace barked out a laugh. "Yeah, like you wouldn't do me on the spot if you had the chance ... tall, dark, and hunky." She pointed a finger at her accuser. "Not that you ever will."

Wet Work

Dick desperately wanted to give her a non-verbal signal to back off, not to escalate the confrontation, but what was he supposed to do? Squeeze her tit? Somehow, he didn't think that would convey the intended message.

She somehow seemed to read his mind, though. "Besides, that's why we're doing it up here on the top of the bunker ... or whatever the hell you call these things. Seems like your sacred land already got disrespected by war-mongers the better part of a century ago. We're just counteracting the violent mojo with the power of love." She made a classic peace sign with the fingers of the hand she'd pointed at him a few moments before. "Make love, not war. Right, brah?"

There was a moment of silence ... of indecision. Dick dropped his hand to get ready to push up for a fight, but just then one of the stragglers near the back of the approaching group hooted "Nice tits, babe!" and the mob disintegrated into catcalls and whistles. In the midst of the ribald revelry, Dick heard a low voice say "Let it go, brah. I know her. She's cool." Dick recognized the voice of Ulu, the tech from the Tsunami Center. "Besides, we got bigger fish ... you know?"

The throng began to move past them on the tourist path below. A few flashed lights or muttered encouragements as they ogled the dimly-lit make-out scene. Dick relaxed. They were going to make it, after all.

Then another of the flashlight beams flitted over his face. Suddenly, he heard Ulu's voice again, but this time it was much louder.

"What the fuck, *wahine*? Isn't that dude feeling you up your *dad?*"

The foul accusation hung in the air for a moment between heaven and paradise. Then Dick encircled Ace's waist with his arms and rolled toward the opposite edge of the concrete slab.

"Run!" he hissed. "Now."

Chapter 12

Ace didn't hesitate. She leaped from the pillbox toward the fifty-plus metal stairs descending from the summit on the east side. She avoided the bulky bodies of the gang members already blocking the staircase by aiming for the railing on the outside edge of the crater. She hit the rail with the hardened plastic plate in the crook of her hiking boots. Absorbing the shock with her knees, she slid down the railing with practiced ease. If she'd had a skateboard, the trick would have been flashier and her speed greater, but it was impressive enough to be effective, given the shocked looks on the faces of the thugs she slid by. She doubted Dick could match her feat. In fact, she had no clue how her mentor intended to escape the PPIPF members she was rapidly leaving in her wake, but she didn't have time to look—not that she'd be able to see much in the dark.

At least she could fix that last part. She reached up while she was still running along the path to the metal staircase which led to the rest stop along the inner rim of the crater, pulling down her wrap-around shades, still in low-light mode.

Much better. A quick glance showed a herd of beefy guys thundering down the steps behind her, but they had no hope of matching the speed her lithe form and extensive training afforded her. She hit the corner to the metal steps and grabbed the railing to pivot without slowing. As her body jerked up with the sudden change of momentum, she twisted in mid-air and sat on the pipe railing this time, kicking the opposite rail to push off and sliding down the length. The intermittent joints where the railing was affixed to posts would leave a few bruises on her derriere, but gravity was definitely her friend. She continued to outpace her pursuers—enough so she risked a look up and to the west for Dick.

She hoped he was okay. She didn't mind giving the big guy a hard time about ... well, almost everything, but she didn't want to see him beat senseless by a gang of thugs who, at best, thought he was molesting his own daughter and, at worst, knew he'd been spying on their clandestine terrorist planning session.

She might have to go back up and save the asshole. Worse yet, she might have to carry his dead body down the mountain. Dead weight and steep slopes were a bad mix, usually followed by a long fall.

At least she didn't hear any gun fire. At least, not yet.

#

Dick spent half-a-second watching Ace parkour down the railing past a bevy of angry Hawaiians and sprint away. He could never top that move. Hell, he couldn't equal that move. Sure, once upon a time he'd been young and reckless, but he'd never been that nimble, that light on his feet. No, he was a brute force kind of guy and right now a throng of brutes was approaching in force. He jammed his low-light shades back down and scanned both sides of the crest. The tough guys were on the path on three sides of the concrete structure, beginning to scramble up to accost him. He didn't have the speed to outrun them if he leaped over and tried to use the crest path to escape. He could probably clear the group on the path skirting the outside edge of the fortification, but that left him on the towering outer slope of Diamond Head. He knew that to be steep and treacherous. The good news was no one would follow him if he jumped off a cliff. The bad news was that he knew the outer edge of the iconic landmark was the kind of place the authorities occasionally had to use helicopters to rescue people from. He wasn't going to jump off that cliff even if besieged by a lot more than peer pressure.

He turned, focusing his attention on the downslope of the inner crater. Still steep, but not near as scary as the other side. The first of the toughs reached the flat top of the concrete slab and surged toward him, reinforcements clambering up behind. No more time to think. He reacted by instinct, leaping off the pillbox in the direction of the inner slope of the dormant volcano, bending his knees again slightly as he became airborne to absorb the shock of his landing. The hiking boots he'd gotten earlier in the day kept his right ankle from breaking as he hit rough, slanted lava off-kilter, then leaned left and tucked for a roll.

Given the steep slope and rugged terrain, his best hope was that he could maintain a controlled tumble with no sudden stops as he attempted to slow his pace. With at least two alternate routes down the mountain, the beefy locals probably wouldn't mimic his suicidal leap. At least, he hoped not; if any did, they would likely dislodge debris which would pummel him throughout his descent.

He got lucky. The scrubby brush on the inside of the crater slowed and cushioned his drop. The not-so-controlled tumble was jarring, painful, and awkward, but no bones were broken. He scrambled back to a standing position and assessed his situation. He'd ended up not far from the rest stop at the bottom of the upper set of outside stairs where the halves of the tourist loop met.

He could certainly use a rest stop while he waited for his partner. Sure, she moved fast, but he had covered a much shorter distance as the crow flies.

Screw that; they didn't have crows here. As the magpie flies? More like "as the body plummets."

His luck held. There was Ace, sprinting down the tourist path at a helluva speed. She looked even better running than Pierce Brosnan did in his Bond movies. Of course, he didn't generally run with his shirt half-open.

"*Sakra!*" huffed Ace as she jogged to a stop, her chest heaving from exertion. "How the hell did you beat me here?"

"The bruises will show in the morning," Dick snapped. He jerked his head to the opposite side of the rest area and stairwell. "Through the tunnel and down the path. If we can beat them to the bottom, we can hide and wait for them to leave."

"I vote to just leave. Or did you forget we drove through a tunnel to get inside this crater? I don't like to hide in a place with only one good exit."

"Copy that."

Dick grabbed his partner's arm and scrambled toward the short tunnel leading to the lower set of stairs. As they did, pursuers streamed down the path Ace had come. A separate throng of enemies emerged at the top of the upper stairway, lumbering inexorably toward them from above.

He dropped Ace's arm and rushed into the darkness of the tunnel, relying on instinct and gyroscopic memory to curve just the right amount not to smack into a concrete wall. Ace's steps echoed behind him, following his lead. Suddenly, he slammed into something softer than concrete, but somehow rock hard all the same.

"Ooof!" exclaimed the pile of muscle blocking his path ... their exit. "What the fuck?"

Dick didn't hesitate. The park had been closed for hours. This wasn't a lost tourist; this was an enemy. As he pushed off his adversary with his left arm, he delivered two quick upper cuts to the guy's gut. Too much muscle and flab for Dick to damage the hulk's ribs, but he did hear two satisfying grunts as he connected. As his opponent reached out with both hands to grab him, Dick fell back, kicking out and up with his right leg to crush the guy's balls.

The only people who play fair in a real fight are losers, sometimes known as corpses.

But, just before the anticipated satisfaction of his hiking boot connecting with the soft squishiness of its intended target, Ace collided with Dick's back, spinning him clockwise. His extended right leg continued upward, unimpeded by muscle or rock. At the same time, Ace's falling body hit him in the back of his left knee. He buckled, tumbling them both to the floor of the curved tunnel in a jumble of flailing body parts and coursing curse words.

The anonymous jumbo they'd literally run into compounded the confusion and pain of their collision. He collapsed on top of them, his fists tight, and his arms flailing and punching as he came down.

Dick tried to give as good as he got and assumed Ace was doing the same ... if she hadn't already been reduced to a greasy spot on the tunnel floor by the combined weight of the MMF threesome. For a few moments the pile of mixed martial arts meat writhed and shuddered in a confused collection of jabs, gropes, pinches, bites, scratches, slaps, and hair-pulling—which accomplished nothing except to prove why a light should always be left on during an orgy.

Then Dick felt a series of quick, staccato vibrations and heard six wet shucks. Almost immediately, a hot, coppery gush of wetness flowed over his body as the bulk of the meat pinning him down lost its muscle tone and melted into motionless flab. He felt like the rice at the bottom of a bowl of *loco moco*, though the acrid, salty tang of the gravy in this dish reeked more of Spam—an island favorite—than grass-fed beef.

"Move!" urged Ace, as he felt her attempting to extricate herself, mostly from below and behind him. "The herd of natives is going to stampede through here any second."

Wet Work

Dick shouldered the dead weight of their opponent to the right side of the tunnel and pushed off the bloody torso to get his own feet back under him. Dick wasn't squeamish, but he had to admit he was happy he couldn't really see what their victim looked like ... or what he and Ace looked like. He twisted counter-clockwise and reached backward, flailing with his left arm until it collided with his partner's forearm. He circled it with his bloody paw and pulled her forward. "C'mon. There's no hiding now. We'd be too easy to track."

He took off at a lope, exiting through the asshole of the twisty tunnel. He dropped her hand as they emerged from utter blackness into merely enveloping darkness and rushed down the lower set of steps, quickly reaching the tourist path. The low-light setting on his amazingly still intact sunglasses helped some, but not as much as they had before they'd become spattered and smeared with what he hoped was merely blood. He put on a burst of speed once on more gently sloping ground, glancing back to make sure she was still close behind.

"Hurry. We need to outdistance the bastards and hope they didn't leave any more guards along the way."

"Yeah," grunted Ace as she ran. "No duh. Great fucking plan. Awesome leadership skills."

English had to be her third language because sarcasm was definitely in the top two.

Even at full speed, he thought he had enough breath left to shoot her a muttered "Screw you" over his shoulder, but then shots jabbed out of the darkness behind them. He instinctively crouched lower to provide a reduced surface area to the gunmen and hugged the right side of the path, the side with more overhanging vegetation. More shots followed, followed by a lot more shots, the last few tearing through the large leaves of a vine hanging down from one of the upslope trees.

Crap. Someone brought a Mac 10. That put a lot of lead in the air at a time, though at full auto the shooter would need to reload every three or four seconds. The next time he spied a hanging vine, he grabbed it without slowing, twisting it in his grip and hanging on, snapping off a length and letting it trail behind him as he continued down the path. He stopped abruptly at the next post for the metal-pipe railing.

Ace's eyebrows turned inward as she approached. "What the ..."

Dick waved at her to go past him. "Lookout is just ahead," he panted, "the one with the old winch and cable they used for hauling crap partway up the hill."

Despite Dick's motioning, Ace slowed. "That vine won't stand up to a rusty metal cable for zip-lining."

"You're right." Dick reached down and unbuckled his belt. "But this will." He slipped off his belt and tossed it to her. "Loop it around the cable and buckle it. That way it's easier to hold onto than the loose ends."

Ace nodded as she snagged the belt out of the air. "Then what ..."

"Just to slow them down. Have the belt ready when I get there. I'm grabbing it. You're grabbing onto me."

Ace sped up as Dick tied one end of the vine to a post a few inches off the ground, then strung it to a post a bit ahead on the opposite side, then back to the next post on the inside. It was a crude trap; he wished fervently he had some explosives he could hook up to the vine as a tripwire, but they only needed a few extra seconds if all went as planned. And groups moving in a pack didn't do well at spotting traps.

Once he tied off the end of the vine, he sprinted to the lookout, picking up as much speed as he dared. When he saw the looped belt hanging on the slack cable, he knew they would need all the momentum possible to get their makeshift zip-line moving. Ace looked startled to see him barreling toward the edge of the lookout, but didn't hesitate when he yelled: "Grab on as I pass."

He dove for the loop, thrusting his left arm and shoulder through the makeshift harness and hooked his left hand with his right, the curled fingers of each hand interlocking in a G.I. Joe Kung Fu grip. Given the size of his waistline, Ace couldn't do the same around him when she grabbed on in mid-dash. But she managed to latch on to his right side-pocket with one hand and, after pawing at his crotch for a few moments, thankfully snagged one of his belt loops with her other hand. She tucked her chin into his hip bone and squeezed his left leg and butt for dear life as Dick flung himself off the lookout.

At first, the loop held where it was on the cable and the ungainly package of human cargo swung forward and up as the belt accepted their weight. Then momentum overcame friction and the belt began to slide along the rusty cable. Gravity helped fuel their speed as they fell away from the lookout into the darkness.

Dick didn't really know exactly where they were going and what the hell they were going to do when they got there, but he had the exhilarating feeling they were going to make it.

#

Sakra! Kurva! Do prdele! Damn fucking fuck! *Zmrd! Debil!*

Her partner wasn't just a dick; he was an idiotic bastard.

Ace pressed her face into her mentor's burgeoning middle-aged, ex-athlete's paunch and held tight as he swung out over the black void of the cliff like a pendulum, then suddenly lurched forward and alarmingly fast downward in their flight to escape the PPIPF thugs who were trying to catch them. As she did, a wave of nausea passed through her as speeding air whistled by.

Tonight's escapade proved three things: First, there was even more crime and violence in the islands than the jacked up episodes of the *Hawaii Five-O* television show portrayed. Second, her headmaster had been right in school when he said if her friends all jumped off a cliff, so would she. And, third, as ridiculous as it might sound, there really was a goddamn plan to create a giant, killer tsunami that would scour paradise clean of tourists, soldiers, bureaucrats, and *haoles* of all types.

Sakra!

The bumpy, jerky slide down the mountainside also proved one other thing as Dick's belt skidded and caught and slid roughly down the ancient cable. If you are going to risk your life by grabbing on to someone's pants as they rocketed down an ersatz zip line, you'd be a lot better off if they still had their damn belt on. She could feel Dick's pants sliding down his torso in fits and starts with each bump and jerk. No doubt, a new moon would surely rise before they hit the end of the line and she would plummet to her death holding a pair of dirty, bloody cargo pants, while Dick escaped pantsless into the night. What would the crime scene investigators make out of that?

Ježíši, she hoped he wasn't going commando.

#

As they plummeted down the cable, Dick felt his pants sliding down his torso. Ace clung to his body, her chin jutting into his kidney, her forearm crushing his nuts, and her dangling legs flailing in an attempt to gain purchase and vice-grip his hiking boots. But he never looked down or let go of his death grip. He knew if he unlocked his hands, he'd only be able to keep his shoulder and arm wedged into the belt for a few seconds. If Ace actually started to drop, he'd make a desperate grab, but he couldn't do that yet.

Besides, his focus was above.

Not on their pursuers. They'd gotten enough of a jump the goon squad probably didn't even know they'd escaped via zip line. No, his full attention was on the belt being ripped apart by the frayed, ancient cable as they tore through the darkness. He could see the belt tearing as bits of leather and stitching flew off it. He could smell the friction burning through the soft leather. He could hear the material ripping in short bursts beneath the high-pitched whine of the descent.

He was about to die a stupid death in paradise with a girl half his age entangled in his pants.

Sorry, Melanie.

Suddenly, he felt the button atop his fly burst open and his pants jerk downward. He let go with his right hand and thrust it down to catch Ace, crooking his left arm tight to his chest as it took all the weight of their purchase on the belt. He instinctively leaned to extend his reach to the maximum, his fingers spread, his arm flailing, fishing for something to grab or something to grab on to him.

Nothing.

Fuck. Fuck. Fuck.

#

Bullocks!

Dick's pants burst open and stripped down his body. Ace plummeted, her hands too caught up in the pants to reach up to snag a hand or a foot or a fucking dick.

Sakra!

There was nothing she could do, but bend her knees to absorb the coming impact of sharp, rock hard lava ... if she wasn't impaled by a tree on her way to the ground.

Fuck!

#

A heartbeat later Dick felt a hard tug on his feet as his falling pants got caught up on his hiking boots and Ace's weight jerked down with momentum. He flung his right hand back up in an effort to regain his locking hold on the belt just as a curious thing happened.

They bounced. The release of weight followed by the sudden yank on the line as that weight returned with the added momentum of falling a few feet whipsawed the cable. For an instant, the belt hovered weightless above the cable, not only allowing Dick to regain his Kung Fu grip, but to rotate the belt a quarter turn before it slammed hard back onto the cable. The leather took the shock and the cable started chewing through a fresh spot on the belt as they finished their descent into darkness.

Landing would be a bitch, since Ace hung below him and his feet were hogtied by his trousers and her arms.

On the other hand, he was alive, a tropical breeze was whistling through his boxers beneath the bright stars in paradise, and he was pretty sure they'd figured out who the bad guys were.

All in all, he'd call that a win.

Chapter 13

Ace didn't mind the long, long walk back to their hotel. She was happy to be alive and the hike let her burn off the adrenaline which had coursed through her system during their fight and flight. The edge faded along the way as the threat of imminent danger decreased.

At her suggestion, they avoided the possibly guarded or even blocked tunnel though the crater ridge. Instead, they circled around the volcanic crater to a much shorter portion of the ridge, hiking up and over in a spot with passable vegetative cover, landing in a residential neighborhood. Even if the PPIPF thugs tracked their escape, they'd be unlikely to stage a full-scale assault in a place with security cameras, neighborhood watch signs, a smattering of foot and vehicle traffic, and good police response times. Given their nefarious terrorist plans, keeping a low profile was essential for the bad guys. Getting arrested was not recommended when you were conspiring to commit mass murder.

And, even though Ace and Dick were the good guys in this scenario, they couldn't afford to attract attention either. The local constabulary had no clue the Subsidiary existed; its agents were sworn to keep it secret. And there was the very real chance the Subsidiary wouldn't do anything to save their asses if they got picked up for jaywalking, much less aggravated assault, manslaughter, or even murder.

Maintaining a low profile was essential to their cover, their mission, and their freedom.

Fortunately, the nice thing about running a covert op on a tropical island was that being covered in blood wasn't nearly the problem it would be in other locations. Given the intermittent showers of a mid-Ocean tropical clime, finding a puddled erosion gully while they were still back in the crater let them wash off the most obvious evidence of their knife fight. After that, all they had to do was find a public beach access (there were convenient signs!) and walk into the dark ocean to scrub themselves and their clothes relatively clean. Ace asked Dick whether the blood would attract sharks, but he just laughed, saying he bet she could take one in a close-quarters fight with nothing but her pocket blade. Walking around in wet clothes didn't seem to be an issue, either. Frankly, their footwear got more stares than their dripping attire. Sandals were the norm here, even at night. That and the fact Dick had to hold his pants up, having left his belt behind at the bottom of the zip line.

"We can grab a pedicab when we get near the zoo in the park," suggested Dick as they left the rocky shore and began their trek back toward the bright lights of Waikiki. "Even if Ulu remembers our names from the Tsunami Center, I doubt they have the connections to sift through all the hotels on Oahu and find out where we are staying before at least midday tomorrow."

"No problem, then," replied Ace. "And now that we have confirmation of the basics of the plot and know who's behind it, there's no reason not to take a flight out first thing in the morning."

Dick stopped walking. "Wait. What? We do?"

Ace stopped a half-step in front of him and turned to talk. "Sure. Weren't you listening up there? They weren't telling ghost stories; they were confirming everything was set up for the big event. Some details would have helped, but it sure sounded like actionable intelligence to me."

Dick's brow furrowed and she noticed his fists clench. "Did it? Sounded like they were speaking Hawaiian to me."

"Yeah. So what?"

"Oh, I beg your pardon. You see, while you may have read my entire file in enough detail to allow you to make snide remarks about

109

the state of my marriage, I didn't get to see your dossier. I didn't know Hawaiian was taught in the public school system in the Czech Republic ... or even the Eastern European field office for the Subsidiary."

"It's not. I don't speak Hawaiian."

Dick glowered at her.

"You had your sunglasses with you. I assumed you did what I did."

"Yeah. Low-light setting. So what?"

"Sure," she replied before she continued on slowly, doing her best to find the right words to explain the situation simply without sounding condescending. "Well, we use the sunglasses for audio communications back to the Subsidiary's offices all the time to check in or request supplies, so I just opened the feed to the translations division in Philadelphia, turned up the gain, and asked them to relay back the conversation in English in as close to real time as they could muster."

Dick's face softened and his posture slumped. "Oh."

"There was a bit of time delay, of course, which is why I didn't realize they were wrapping things up until it was almost too late."

Dick looked away from her. He seemed to be staring into the darkness over the ocean. Finally, he turned back. "That was good work. Smart, even." He nodded. "Nice job, Ace."

She smiled. Dick could be gruff, but he was one of the good guys. Most of the macho squad back in the Czech Republic wouldn't think of telling her she'd done a good job.

She threw him a half-smile. "Well, you did a good job saving our lives by using that zip line."

He wheeled around in an abrupt motion and grunted. "Fuck you."

Apparently Dick wasn't into mutual admiration societies. "What? I can't say thanks for saving my life?"

He spun back, his contorted face looming above her own. "No, you can't."

"Bullocks! I can if I want."

"Not this time." His face softened a bit. "Look, if we remain partners, I hope we save each other so many times we lose track, but you can't thank me for this one."

She no longer filtered her sarcasm. "And why the hell not?"

He shook his head, as if he couldn't understand how she could be so clueless. Then, in a low, soft voice, he replied. "Because I let you fall. I felt my pants sliding down and I still let you fall."

This was a whole different level of macho bullshit than she'd had to deal with back home. This was some kind of tough guy code of honor. Chivalry gone ape shit. She tried her best to give him an out. "Bull. You knew ... subconsciously at the very least ... that your pants would get stuck on your hiking boots."

He rolled his eyes at her and turned away again, resuming their trek away from the shore.

"You knew," she repeated, then tried to ease him out of his apparent self-loathing by making a joke. "Thank God bell-bottoms went out of style half a century ago."

"Hmmpf," he snorted without looking back. He kept walking. "At last a statement everyone can get behind."

She let the matter drop and scurried to catch up. They walked in silence for a few minutes before Dick spoke again.

"So, what exactly did these terrorists have to say?"

"I'll have HQ email you a complete transcript, but basically they were congratulating each other about how everything was in place at the rift for the big quake that would wipe out the coast of the whole island chain. Maybe do some damage on the west coast and Japan, too."

"Rift?"

"Rift, crack. The translator said it might mean either."

"And did they say how they were going to accomplish that, given Hansebi, back at the Tsunami Center, says the whole Great Crack thing is crap? After all, they've got one of their guys working with him; they must know his expert opinion on the subject."

She shook her head even though Dick was focused on the path ahead instead of her. "No details. Maybe they simply think he's wrong; scientists disagree all the time. Besides, Hansebi did say inundating fracture lines with water could cause a sliding displacement rather than a traditional earthquake."

"I guess. The thing is, it's not even rainy season right now. Does that mean we're months away from this operation being put in motion?"

"I don't think so," replied Ace. "A partial side conversation at the beginning of the translation had something to do with finishing up laying in supplies for the coming flood. Then someone else said they'd bought all the toilet paper in stock at the local grocer."

"Everybody talks big about the good ol' days, but nobody gives up their toilet paper," muttered Dick.

"Would you?"

"Not my point." He paused before continuing. "Make sure the Quartermaster has us booked on the first flight to the Big Island in the morning. Now that you've gotten your feet wet as my partner, we've got to make sure these assholes don't get everyone's feet wet."

Chapter 14

"This is a waste of time," griped Dick as he drove westward on Highway 11 past the entrance to Hawai'i Volcanoes National Park on the Big Island. He didn't turn in. "What do you expect to find here? An eight-mile-long line of plastic explosives? Or the world's longest watering hose?"

"Just keep driving. The instructions on the internet say the turnoff is somewhere between mile markers forty-six and forty-seven, on the *mauka* side of the road. That's ..."

"I know *mauka* means inland towards the mountains," Dick responded, an edge to his voice. "Ever watch a weather report here? It's all leeward, windward, *mauka,* and *makai.* It's like they don't even know the compass points."

Ace sighed. Dick had been grouchy all day. She doubted it was the bruises and bumps of last night's run in with the PPIPF thugs—those kinds of encounters were a routine part of the job. No, more likely it grated on the big guy's ego for her to have thought of a simple way to translate the gang's discussions when he hadn't. According to what she'd read in his file, Dick was actually a pretty tech savvy guy for someone his age, especially when it came to explosives. His last big mission had a virtual reality company run out of a mammoth tech center. As she understood it, he'd had to navigate in the virtual world of Reality 2 Be, which meant he had to be a bit more cyber-proficient than the AOL and MySpace crowd. She let his latest remark slide. Espionage partnerships were like marriages; you had to let a lot of the little stuff slide if you were going to make them work.

"There it is," she said as she spied the paved turnout. Big enough for at least four vehicles, it wasn't hard to spot.

Dick parked and they both grabbed items from the trunk. Ace loaded a small knapsack with two liters of water, some granola bars, a plastic bag with lip balm and sun tan lotion, binoculars, her pistol, and two spare clips of ammo. Dick brought water, rope, binoculars, a 9 mm automatic pistol, six spare clips of ammo, three grenades, a large hunting knife, matches, a foil survival blanket, six Tootsie Rolls, and, oddly, a book about Hawaiian birds. Both of them donned hats and their Subsidiary-issued shades.

Ace motioned to the other side of Highway 11. "The trail starts over there, behind the gate on the left."

Dick sauntered across the lightly traveled asphalt road without, she noticed, bothering to look for traffic. She followed. A few moments later, they'd climbed over the gate and were strolling down the road behind it, basically a parallel series of indentations through the tall grass and interspersed rocky terrain of a huge lava field. Dick led the way, his steady gait and longer stride forcing Ace to occasionally quick-time to keep up. Their only stop on the way was as they approached a large stand of red-flowered bushes. Dick stopped, bringing his binoculars up to scan the line of bushes after hauling his bird book out of his backpack. Ace simply hung back, bending to rest with her hands on her knees while Dick looked, first at the bushes, then at the book, then at the bushes, then at the book. Finally, he put the bird book back in his pack, shouldered the pack and started walking again. She jogged to catch up with him.

"Rare native bird nesting in the bushes? I couldn't see any movement from back where I was."

"Nope," replied Dick without slowing or even looking at her. "Saw a flash of red. Thought it might be something interesting for a second, but it was just a Brazilian Cardinal. Rats have wiped out most of the unique native species. They're all ground nesters and the rats like the eggs. Feral cats don't help the situation, either." He glanced up, where a smoky plume of vog—volcanic fog—streamed from the Kiluea Crater not far behind and to the left of them, muting the glare of the sun in the otherwise clear, blue sky. "Wrong time of day, too. Doubt you'd even see many birds at Kipukapuaulu this close to midday."

"What the hell is Kipuka ... pulu?"

"Kipukapuaulu," he corrected her with a gruff chuckle. "It's a kinda redoubt nearby—a patch of scrub and trees that's gotten missed by all of the lava flows in the last century or three, so it's got more extensive and developed vegetation. Local birds and critters have taken sanctuary there in the bad times." He glanced over at her. "There's a loop walk for birders. Read about it when I was mapping out our course for the day."

"I see." She matched his brisk pace with three steps for every two of his. "So, you got into the spy biz to expand your opportunities to engage in your birdwatching fetish."

Dick shook his head. "Nah. Other way around. Got into birding to cover my spying activities. Handy excuse for traipsing about, stopping at odd intervals to look through high-powered binoculars."

Ace shrugged. "Whatever. If I wanna stop and stare at a fixed point for a bit, I just hold my cell phone at arm's length and pretend I'm taking a selfie."

"Yeah. That would blend in with your demographic better than mine."

"And," Ace continued, "If you click the shutter every once in a while, you get a supply of selfies on your phone which look perfectly innocent should anyone ever investigate. Plus, if you occasionally press the button to change which side of the phone is in the frame, you can intersperse a few candids of your surveillance target with none the wiser."

Dick's nose twitched. "I can see how that could work."

They fell into companionable silence as they continued onward, the shrubs diminishing in number and size until finally the road turned along the edge of a newer flow of relatively smooth, black rock. Eventually a man-made cairn of rocks marked a trail which turned out onto the expanse of black lava. Before too long, the lava fell away, plunging into a giant crevasse.

Ace gave a low whistle. "Gotta say, that is one great crack there." The meandering slash in the lava extended away from them as far as they could see in either direction. "Looks pretty empty, though. No signs of activity by PPIPF bad guys or anybody else."

Dick began to clamber down the near side. "We have to look, all the same. They'd have to be pretty stupid to do anything here, where tourists and everyone comes to snap vacation shots. We need to reconnoiter a larger sample."

Once Dick was down and to the side, Ace followed him. "Should we split up? You go *makai* while I go *mauka*?"

Her mentor looked upslope for a few moments, then shook his head. "Seems more likely if this thing is rigged, it's between here and where it peters out short of the ocean downhill."

She screwed up her nose and looked at him.

He squinted. "If the plan is to get this crack to break away, so a big chunk of real estate slides into the ocean, you wouldn't put your explosives too far uphill." He pursed his lips. "More accurately, you wouldn't put your explosives *only* uphill from here. Otherwise, you might just cause a jumble of rocks to rumble and tumble downhill, but stop well short of the ocean. You'd want to make sure the chunk nearest the water, but still situated on a steep part of the slope, gives way. That way it has some hope of reaching the shore. After all, tsunamis are all about water displacement."

116

"Makes sense." She stared down the length of the crack extending toward the ocean. "Makes for an uneven, unpleasant hike, though."

"The very definition of work. So unpleasant, you wouldn't do it if they didn't pay you. Fortunately for the Subsidiary, I'm a hard worker."

"Well, then ..." She tipped her head to the left. "Let's get to work. I'll take this side and you take the right."

"Righto," said Dick. "Looks like it is going to be a long day."

#

Hiking the Great Crack was slow going. Searching the Great Crack as you hiked it was downright tedious. They'd been at it for hours, probing holes and voids left by the vagaries of cooling lava, as well as open intersections with lava tubes—tunnels left by fast-moving lava created when the rock on the outer edge of the flow cooled, but the hotter lava inside kept flowing, vacating the straw-like hollow.

Dick gave his partner credit. She kept up with her share of the work and didn't complain, even though the sharp edges of the lava were wreaking havoc with them both, slicing the soles of their hiking books and cutting into legs and hands when they misstepped and took even the slightest tumble. If fact, Ace was almost twenty feet farther along on her side than he was when things finally got very interesting.

"Yo! Ace! Mark where you quit looking and come over here. Watch your step ... and not just for sharp rocks. This area might be booby-trapped."

He thought about making some crack about Boobies—the blue-footed variety could be found on the islands, though generally in lusher coastal enclaves than here—but only a birder would get the joke.

Dick remained still while Ace made her way to him without incident. He pointed at an oblong void in the floor of the four-foot diameter lava tube descending away from the right side of the Great Crack.

"See the small, square lump right on the edge of that hole? Anything about it strike you as odd?"

Instead of sliding her glasses down her nose and peering at the spot as he expected her to, Ace reached up to the right stem of her Subsidiary-issued shades, fingering the minute controls.

Dick went on: "It's duller than the rest of the tunnel wall, which is glassy from the heat of the passing lava. It's also too regular in shape."

"Fuck that," replied Ace. "The surveillance detection setting on my sunglasses says it's got an electronic signature. Cell phone?"

Dick nodded. "Too clunky to be a newer model, though."

"2G," Ace agreed. "If it's new, it's a cheap burner."

"Perfect for a cell phone detonator." He fished out his flashlight and played it over the area, probing into the void with the beam. "Couple of wires snaking down and out of sight."

"Yeah, I see them. *Bullocks!* Looks like we found a genuine improvised explosive device, boss."

"Roger that. That phone's not tucked down there so somebody can call up the Menehune and chat."

Ace just gave him an odd stare.

"Mythical little people ..."

"You mean, Leprechauns?"

Dick growled before continuing. "Native Hawaiian spirits who come out at night and build things." When she just kept staring at him, he shook his head. "Don't you read the guidebooks and magazines in your hotel room when you've got time to kill?"

118

"How would I keep up with my TV shows if I did that?" She paused for a second. "Just kidding. American TV sucks. I spend my spare time reading your file. Given its size, maybe I should call you Moby Dick."

Dick flipped her off. "Whatever. I can't think of any plausible reason for that kind of phone to be where it is that doesn't end with a big boom."

Ace's voice flattened to an all-business tone. "I agree. But it doesn't make any sense to me. Given the remote, barely accessible location, whatever is in the void can't be that big. Even if it's a pretty big bang per cubic centimeter explosive—military grade C-4 or some shit—I can't see how there could be enough in that spot to do much damage. I mean, not earth-shattering, tsunami-inducing damage."

She had a point.

Dick studied the spot for a few moments, then looked carefully at the jumble of lava surrounding the opening. The sun assaulted his back as waves of heat rolled up from the black rocks, baking the still air and softening the thick soles of his combat boots. The silence was as oppressive as the heat; Ace was apparently smart enough not to interrupt his thinking.

"I suppose that oblong void could be an intersection with another lava tube which goes down, deeper, and fed into this lava tube. If so, that hole could lead to a sizeable space. Put enough C-4 down deep, as deep as a spelunker might be able to go down such a tributary, and there could be a big-ass explosion deep enough to bounce this portion of the crust just enough to create a momentary loss of friction and start it sliding, especially if it goes off in coordination with a series of similar explosions elsewhere along the crack." He rubbed his hand along his stubble. "That's a lot of 'ifs,' though."

"Best not to take chances," replied his partner. She bent down and studied the lava tube. "No way you're getting down into the intersecting hole." Ace exhaled noisily. "I can probably get down there, but you're going to have to walk me through what to do when I get to the explosives."

Dick harrumphed. "Screw that. This ain't the movies."

"You mean you don't want me to risk my life?"

He barked out a laugh. "If the job required you to risk your life, I wouldn't hesitate to risk it. That's why we do what we do. That's why we're here, to risk our lives for the greater good if that's what the mission requires. But that doesn't apply here. What I meant ... what I mean in this situation ... is that no one needs to crawl down a hole filled with C-4 to solve this problem. All I have to do is clip the wires connecting the cell phone to whatever is down below. Whoever put this here wasn't expecting it to be found. And now that I've looked closer, it's clear there's no booby-traps on the approach and no evidence of disarming countermeasures on the device at all—no mercury switches, no tremor sensors, nothing. Which makes sense when you're mounting something in an area which gets hundreds of tiny tremors every week. I'll cut the wires and we'll take the phone with us. Maybe the numbnut PPIPF bozos left prints or bought the burners in bulk and we can trace how many and who bought 'em."

"Oh," said Ace as a bead of sweat trickled down and caught at the end of her nose. "That's kinda anti-climactic."

Dick shrugged. "Not every encounter has to end with a bang."

Ace smiled. "What? Now you're giving dating advice? Thanks, Dad."

Chapter 15

Ace took a photo of the location of the device, allowing her phone to tag the spot with its GPS. Then Dick shouldered past and squatted down near the intersecting lava tube. He leaned on the opposite wall for support and lowered himself until he was stretched out on the floor of the main tube. Then he shimmied forward until he could reach the cell phone. He stretched out and picked up the two wires connected to the phone and gathered up the slack to form a six-inch oval loop above his grip. Taking the hunting knife from his right hip, he held it with the blade up and inserted it into the loop. Ace saw his grip on both the wires and the knife tighten as he pulled up, the keen edge to the blade slicing cleanly through the insulation and wires.

"Oops," he muttered.

"What?" gasped Ace in response as she straightened from looking over his shoulder and took an instinctual step back toward the mouth of the lava tube.

Dick guffawed. "You are just too easy ..."

Ace scowled. She didn't need her mentor making her flinch for sport. She did her best not to let her irritation show. "Haven't had any complaints on that score so far."

Dick shifted to all fours, then a kneeling position, before standing and turning toward her holding the cell phone by the cut wires. "Here. Drop that in that plastic bag you have without touching the phone. Don't want to damage any possible prints on the case."

Ace walked the few short steps to take her out of the lava tube and back to the jumbled "V" of the Great Crack. She dumped out her lip balm and suntan lotion with her free hand and bagged the phone.

Dick followed Ace to the middle of the rift, brushing coarse black sand off the front of his clothing. "I guess we've done our dirty work for the day."

"Yeah, well, all the really dirty work gets done at night." She looked at the position of the sun, then upslope toward where they'd left their vehicle hours and hours ago. "How many more of those you think are planted in the crack? If we spend too much more time looking, it's going to be dark by the time we get back to the car."

Dick stretched while he apparently made the same assessment. "Assuming we didn't miss any along the way, my guess is two or three, but it's just a guess."

"So, how do we go forward from here? I mean, it's great we ... you ... found a needle in the haystack, but the odds of finding three more needles in time don't strike me as so favorable." When Dick responded with nothing but a grim look, she continued. "Look, Dick, don't misunderstand what I just said about it getting dark before we're back if we keep at this. I think you know me well enough by now to know I'll do whatever needs to be done to finish the mission. And I know from your file the same is true for you. That's the most consistent through-line in your entire history with the Subsidiary. So if you want to spend all night looking for black phones with black wires in black holes in black rocks, I'm game. After all, I hear once you go black you never go back. It's just ... I don't know if we'll find them all in time ..." She trailed off. *Sakra!* When was her partner going to say something?

Dick rubbed his chin, then stared into the distance for a few moments. "You're right. This is a situation that just needs a shitload of manpower at this point. We've got proof somebody's setting bombs in lava tubes along the Great Crack. If we call this in to HQ, they can use their connections to get Homeland Security or the U.S. Army or even *Hawaii Five-O*, for all I care, to look for more bombs. They don't even need to know why they were planted—Hansebi certainly doesn't think this whole blowing up the Great Crack to create a tsunami plan has any hope of success anyhow. Let the local authorities think it's some

122

psycho loner targeting tourist hikers or a bunch of militia types practicing their bomb-making skills. Let the grunts ferret out the C-4, while we get back on the investigative track. There's still plenty of questions to answer on that front."

"Including what the hell any of this has to do with hacking cars. How's that fit in with the PPIPF's agenda?"

Dick shrugged. "The hack was done in the Philippines. Maybe they're connected with a local PPIPF group there." He pondered for a moment, then shook his head. "Of course, most hacks originate in the Philippines or Russia, so I'm not sure that really proves much."

#

Glenn Swynton handed Dee Tamany the latest status report from Thornby and Zyreb, then stood by silently as she skimmed its contents. A minute later, she set the folder down and glowered at him. "Your assessment?"

Glenn didn't need to think out his response. As Operational Liaison, he not only knew the Director would ask for his assessment, it was his job to guide her on such matters. The fact it was the middle of the night didn't slow him for a second. "Using local contacts to flood the Great Crack with manpower to find the additional explosive devices is easy. Truckloads of men can be deployed at first light. And our people concur with this Dr. Hansebi that the Great Crack is not a likely focal point for a subsidence event. The explosives, even should they go off, are unlikely to trigger a tsunami. This entire plot has an odd character to it—more flash than substance."

Dee Tammany got up and paced behind her desk, pausing to stare out at the lights of the city below. "It's like sugar in the gas tank of a car."

Glenn was bewildered by her comparison, but he refused to let her know he was flummoxed. "A modest amount of sugar has no effect on the efficacy of an internal combustion engine," he replied in a matter-of-fact tone.

"Exactly," agreed the Director. "But people think it does. They think that bit of sugar in the gas tank will caramelize when it gets burned in the pistons, causing the engine to seize. But that's simply not true."

Where was she going with this? "The common man believes a great many things which have no basis in reality," he replied, hoping she would continue to play out the metaphor.

"In fact," the Director mused, "I've heard it said the most destructive thing you can do with sugar and a gas tank is to leave a half-empty bag of sugar on the ground next to a car with the gas cap removed. The owner, thinking someone has tried to ruin his vehicle by sugaring the gas, goes to great lengths to drain and flush the tank, with all the inconvenience and expense attendant with such process. Yet all they had to do was put on the gas cap and drive away."

"So," Glenn responded, "you believe the goal of the PPIPF is to induce panic rather than to rack up a large body-count." He folded his arms and pondered. "There's a certain similarity with the hacking of the brakes in the inciting incident for Thornby's mission. While harrowing, the hacking had limited casualties. Most of the ensuing accidents were minor fender benders. Air bag deployments were effective in preventing loss of life in most of the more serious incidents."

"Except where the car happened to plunge into a canal."

Glenn nodded. "True. But the parallel construction breaks down when you analyze the situation more deeply. Taking over control of a moving vehicle causes minimal loss of life, but induces broader public panic, impacting such items as automotive sales figures, insurance premiums, and driving patterns. On the other hand, the detonation of explosives along the Great Crack might induce temporary panic as people worry about an impending tsunami. But if the underlying causality is faulty, that panic rapidly dissipates when no tsunami results from the explosions." He sighed. "And, of course, none of this explains why the Pan-Pacific Indigenous People's Front wants to cause apprehension over purchasing and driving modern automobiles, even though communication intercepts suggest the same people are behind both schemes."

Dee Tammany headed back to her chair and sat. "Agreed. There's got to be something more to these explosives. At least with Thornby, we've got an explosives expert on the case."

"Indeed." Glenn unfolded his arms as he shifted from contemplative mode to reporting mode. "On that score, I am pleased to report Thornby and Zyreb seem to be working together without any outward evidence of difficulty. More importantly, Thornby hasn't blown up any major transportation hubs ... so far."

Chapter 16

Ace scowled as the sun slowly sank. Dick was at the wheel. After turning around and heading east when they'd gotten back to the car, he had inexplicably turned southeast when Highway 11 intersected with Route 130 in Keaau. She scrolled through screens on her cellphone.

"You know, there's not anyplace much to eat at besides a Subway and a couple of local diners and bars in Pahoa. There's some good reviews on here for Turtle and Moon and Hilo Bay Café back in, you know, Hilo."

Silence.

"Don't know about you, but I don't relish the thought of coming all the way to the middle of the Pacific Ocean for pizza or Mexican food, especially when I just spent the better part of eleven hours hiking over sharp black rocks in the hot sun."

"We're not stopping in Pahoa," grumbled the Dickster.

Ace toggled to the map she'd called up earlier, when her boss had turned off from the main drag. "Nothing south of Pahoa 'til you get to Kalapana. You do know most of that town was wiped out by lava not so many years back, right?"

"I'm sure there's something to eat at Uncle Roberts." He looked over at her. "Job first. Food's a secondary consideration."

"I don't recall having this discussion when you were jonesing for Italian beef back in ... Chicagoland." She looked away from him, out the window at the scrubby juggle struggling to flourish in the endless lava fields. "And who the hell is Uncle Robert? You got contacts here, too?"

"Uncle Robert's dead, but the clerk at the rental place said there's a conclave or gathering of some sort at his bar and grill at the end of the road in Kalapana on Wednesday evenings. Music, arts and crafts vendors, tropical drinks, and crap. Guess what? It's Wednesday evening."

"If I wanna soak up Hawaiian culture, I can book a luau at one of the big hotels." She exhaled with a huff. "What are we going to do at a craft fair? Look for postcards with topless hula dancers?"

"You don't get it ..." Dick groused.

"No," snapped Ace. "I don't get it. You're the boss. You're supposed to be my mentor. Wanna let me in on why we are driving to the edge of a town covered by lava to party on with a bunch of tourists and local artists? I'm not really into poetry slams."

Dick drove on a while before responding. "You're right. I'm supposed to be teaching you the craft, so I need to keep you informed as to who, what, when, where, and, most importantly, why."

She turned to look at him.

He sucked on a tooth before continuing. "When you were hitting the ladies' room at the car rental center, I quizzed the clerk about places where the locals hung out and actually mixed with the tourists. You know, in the guise of not wanting to stumble into an area where militant secessionists held sway. He said he'd avoid areas around South Point after dark, but this Kalapana shindig was a good mix of locals—mostly of the friendly persuasion—and artsy fartsy tourists."

"Yeeaahh ..."

Dick shrugged. "So, I figured it was the only place where we might be able to gather some info on the local PPIPF crowd, but wouldn't stick out like a sore thumb."

Ace looked at her thumbs. "Huh?"

Dick shook his head. "Another idiom. Where our presence wouldn't be obvious and aggravating."

"Fine," she replied. "As long as there's food there, I can work the crowd for info at the same time."

Wet Work

Dick turned right at the intersection of 130 with 137. Almost immediately, they were in the midst of a conglomeration of parked cars, bamboo booths, and cavorting throngs of people. Dick pointed to a bevy of aloha-shirt clad tourists exiting from a shack that advertised Thai food. "Apparently, they have meat on a stick."

"That'll do," said Ace. "I love me some meat on a stick."

They got lucky and Dick was able to ditch the car in a spot vacated by a mini-bus that had apparently ferried attendees from a nearby yoga center. The crowd was a mixed bag—along with the yoga practitioners attired in way-too-revealing Lycra, there was a motley assortment of aging hippies, younger neo-hippies in bright, free-flowing fabrics, bearded hipsters in board shorts and too-tight tees, and downscale tourists wearing baggy shorts and, all too often, white socks with their sandals. The locals, whether native Hawaiian or of Japanese or Filipino ancestry, wore mostly work clothes: worn jeans, faded, loose shirts, and sweat-soaked bandanas. Signs advertised a variety of food and wares, including dirty soap, art prints, kites, kombucha, smoothies, poké, shave ice, mangoes, and beer on tap.

Dick grabbed a couple bottles of Longboard from Uncle's Awa Club while Ace snagged an array of various meats-on-a-stick, scarfing down one even before she returned to the middle of the open area to connect up with Dick after his beer run. Between the crowd noise, the music blaring from various stalls, and the televisions in the open-area tropical sports bar *mauka*, it was difficult to be heard without shouting.

Dick pointed makai, where the edge of the parking area abutted the open lava fields extending south to the coast. A few signs peppered the edge of the expanse, one declaring in white block letters "Hawaii Star Visitor Sanctuary." Another sign explained in much smaller letters how the land beyond was formed by lava flows occurring since 1980 and was part of the "Kingdom of Hawaii." A larger sign to the right

128

advertised eco-trail hikes to the black sand beach where the lava met the ocean.

Dick motioned toward the sign. "Want to hike across the lava before full-on dark?" He glanced around the revelry surrounding them. "My bet is this place probably won't really be hopping for another hour or so."

"Oh, boy," grumbled Ace. "A stroll across sharp, black lava rocks in dimming light. Just what I've been dreaming about all damn day."

Dick's nose twitched. "There's a path."

Ace relented. "Okay, but I'm not looking for bombs as we go."

Dick smiled. "Fair enough."

The lava here was fresher and, thus, more barren. The din of Uncle Robert's party quickly faded as they walked along the desolate flow as twilight gave way to full night. Surprisingly, the lava field was dotted with a smattering of shacks, tents, and even a full-blown house or two, though Ace couldn't imagine how the squatting residents managed to haul water, food, supplies, or lumber, much less biological waste, across the broken gullies and sharp cracks of the lava field or why they would even want to do such a thing.

Before long the noise of the crowd fell away completely and the darkness deepened until there was nothing but black lava below and black sky above bedazzled with more stars than Ace had ever imagined, featuring a broad, bulging band of glittering light extending at an angle almost from horizon to horizon. She couldn't help but stop to gaze at the spectacle.

"*Sakra!*" she whispered in awe.

"Damn impressive, isn't it?" said Dick. "Most people who grow up anywhere near a big city have never even seen the Milky Way, much less the bright, expansive version you can see from the middle of the Pacific Ocean. Puts things in perspective, I guess."

Ace responded without looking at Dick. She couldn't draw her eyes away from the heavens. "You mean it makes you feel small and insignificant, like nothing you do here has any real impact on the universe?"

She heard her companion give out a short huff. "Some people see it that way. Me, I think that if ... just possibly, mind you ... if we're the only intelligent life in the big, wide universe of which the Milky Way is only an infinitesimal fraction, then keeping the world safe and its inhabitants as happy and healthy as possible is the most important, most monumental, and most sacred task in the universe." He paused. "And, I think I'd damn well better not screw it up."

"*Ty jseš debil!*" She turned to look at him in the dim light. "You are such a fucking idiot! The happiness of the entire universe doesn't rest on your shoulders." She shook her head violently and looked back to the heavens with a muttered: "Men! Everything's always about you."

Her accusation hung in the air for a few moments before Dick replied, his voice soft. "Maybe. But I'd rather believe my life matters and try to live up to the calling that implies, than decide nothing I can ever do will make a difference and prove the point by only fulfilling that potential."

Ace wanted to believe him, to believe her life mattered, that she could make a difference, but so far her life ... and this mission ... seemed trivial in the grand scheme of things. And with the weight of the darkness enveloping her while the stars above twinkled at her from billions of light years away, feeling important was nigh impossible. Unexpectedly, she noted a light moving steadily across the sky—too high for a plane, too steady for a shooting star.

She pointed, then turned her head toward her companion. "What's that?"

She saw Dick look over to her, his glance flowing from her shoulder to her fingertip, then beyond to the heavens. Her focus followed his and as she glimpsed the light once more it had already passed where she had pointed, continuing to arc its way steadily across the sky.

Dick harrumphed. "Satellite. International Space Station, maybe. Something artificial in low Earth orbit."

"Spy satellite?" She glanced back to her companion. "Communications?"

"Maybe a spy satellite. Military or NSA." He paused. "Not a communications or television satellite. Those are in fixed, geosynchronous orbit ... above the equator, but situated to mostly service the mainland." He pointed makai, farther along the path they'd been following, but with an eastward shift and at an angle up into the sky. "Thereabouts, somewhere. That's why all the dishes for satellite TV in the islands point that direction."

He dropped his arm and shifted his gaze back, obviously tracking the moving light with her. "Haven't seen a satellite, not with the naked eye, in years, back when I was camping with my dad in the Boundary Waters ... up on the Canadian/Minnesota border."

Soon, the satellite dropped out of sight below the horizon. Ace stayed silent.

Finally, Dick spoke again. "Let's head back. Things should be in full swing by now and we need to start asking some subtle questions. I don't want to make this too late of a night. I need to call my kid in the morning and see if he knows when they're going to release him from the hospital."

"You're a good dad," Ace said. "I'm sure you were a good son, too. Your dad would be proud of you, taking on the weight of the whole universe and all."

"Right back at you," Dick murmured.

"Not so much," Ace said. She sighed. "Orphaned. Remember? Besides, you're a much better father figure than he ever was, *Dad*."

Sakra! Why'd she say that? Sure, it was true, but showing vulnerability wasn't in character. It wasn't her, at least not the her she had decided to be, to show to the world. She wanted to take it back, to make a joke, but that would only make it worse.

Fortunately, the pop of a rifle shot and the crack of the bullet ricocheting off the lava near their feet broke them both out of their respective reveries.

As another shot rang out, Ace hunched down by instinct, squatting as she turned her head from side to side to see if she could locate the source of the attack. She noted Dick had done the same. He pointed toward a jumble of broken lava perpendicular to the pathway, but slightly *mauka* of their position.

"Up there, I think."

She trusted his analysis. "What's the plan? Fight or flight?" She nodded makai. "We can move faster than him on the path, make for tougher targets moving fast in the dark."

Dick shook his head. "Don't want to get trapped with the ocean to our backs if he follows." He tilted his head *mauka*, up the path from where they'd come. "If we move back toward Kalapana with speed, we can get past his position and head toward the safety of the crowd at Uncle Robert's. Given the sound and the pause between shots, I'd bet my life ... and yours, I guess ... that our opponent has a bolt-action rifle shooting full metal jackets, not a semi-automatic with frangible bullets. If we move immediately after his next shot, we have a good chance of making it past his perpendicular position before he can get the next shot off. And we could probably survive a shot, even two, if worse came to ..."

132

Another shot came from the darkness, but this time Ace caught the flash of the barrel. Dick had been right about the position of their attacker.

"MOVE, NOW!" Dick growled.

Ace ran as fast as she could, knowing Dick would have no trouble keeping up with her. She crouched as she ran, leaning from side to side, weaving as much as the path and her speed allowed to make their attacker's targeting as difficult as possible.

One more shot was fired during their sprint for safety, but the crack of the ricochet was well wide of their position. When they came into sight of the lights of the Kalapana gathering, Ace slowed to a gentle jog and Dick followed suit. She scanned the partiers for any sign of hostility or weapons, but it was a happy throng. Nobody seemed to be paying them any special attention.

As they passed the signs on the edge of the lava field and stepped onto the level ground of the bustling crowd, she let out an audible sigh of relief. "What the fuck was that?"

She could see Dick scanning the crowd, too. He didn't turn to look at her as he spoke. "Damn if I know. The PPIPF would have better firepower and more guys. Maybe it was just some crazy who lives out on the lava and doesn't like company."

"Yeah," she replied, "but the sign says the lava field is a sanctuary. Some sanctuary."

Dick shrugged. "It's a sanctuary for aliens, not *haoles*. Maybe. Let's head for the car. I don't need the extra trouble tonight. You know?"

"Roger that."

They made their way through the crowd to their rental car. They found the tires slashed and a message scratched into the windshield. "*Haole* go home!"

133

"Bullocks!" spat Ace, then turned back toward the crowd and yelled: "If you want us to leave, don't slash the fucking tires!"

Dick merely shook his head and pulled out his cell phone, whether to call a taxi, the rental company, or a tow truck, she didn't care.

"Relax," he said. "It could be worse."

"How's that?" Ace growled.

"They could have disabled the brakes ..." He turned to his cell phone for a minute, then clicked it off. "We got about thirty minutes before we have a ride." He nodded his head back toward the crowd. "At this point, I think we've pretty much lost any chance of subtly questioning the locals. So let's get some more meat on a stick while we wait ... and some shave ice or maybe more beer. I don't have to drive anymore tonight and we deserve a treat."

Chapter 17

Dick sat out on the lanai to his room, overlooking the early morning light on Hilo Bay as he used the hotel's clunky wireless handset and dialed into Seth's room at the hospital. All the cushy, fancy resorts on the Big Island were on the Kona side, from the crowded beach bungalows packed along the main thoroughfare in Kailua to the high-end places on the Kohala Peninsula where the *hoi poloi* frolicked with tamed dolphins, but he had no complaints about the Hilo high rise. The room was spacious, the view fine, and the tropical breezes a pleasant alternative to the miasma of industrial smog in New Jersey when the prevailing winds blew from the direction of the chemical plants.

Seth picked up on the third ring. "Hello?"

"Hey, champ. It's Dad. How's it going? Any word on when the docs will be letting you head home?"

"Doing PT four hours every day now. Two before lunch; two before dinner. Works up an appetite."

"Chow down all you want. All that hospital food is nutritionally balanced, you know. Probably much better for you than normal fare, not that your mom isn't a great cook."

"Tastes like it's nutritionally balanced." He paused. "Speaking of crap, how's work? You gonna be home soon?"

Dick sighed. "Might be longer than I thought. Had a bit of a complication."

"Bummer. Mom's not gonna be happy to hear that."

"Well, nothing's for certain. Let's just keep it between the two of us for now ..."

"Uh ... er ... too late, Dad." Dick heard a voice in the background. "Hang on, Dad. Mom's here and she wants to talk to you."

135

Uh-oh. Dick thought he'd called early enough Melanie wouldn't be at the hospital yet. Maybe he'd miscalculated the time differential. Daylight Savings Time always confused him.

"Dick?"

"Hey, sweetie. I was hoping I'd catch two birds with one call."

"I'm worried about you." She lowered her voice to a whisper. Dick could imagine her cupping the mouthpiece of the phone and turning away from Seth's bed, maybe taking a couple steps to the hallway door. "Are you still in the same place?"

"Sure. Hawaii ... just like I said before. Just like we agreed." Dick knew Melanie thought of his job as gallivanting away to exciting destinations, rather than dodging bullets while he dealt with criminals and scum. He tried to make the best of the situation. "Look, maybe we should take a trip out here once this job is done and Seth can travel. You know you can hike up to the top of Diamond Head? Great view and all."

Melanie didn't sound enthusiastic. "I don't know. I don't think Seth will be up to any mountainous hikes for quite a while. Besides, I saw on the news there was a stabbing on the Diamond Head trail just the other day. A local man died. Must be a pretty violent place for it to show up on the national news. That didn't have anything to do with you, did it?" Now she sounded simultaneously frightened and accusatory.

"Um ... ahh ... you know I can't talk about what I do. I'm breaching protocol just letting you know where I really am."

"That's not an answer. That's dodging the question."

Dick took a deep breath. Ahh, maybe this would work. "Look, I'm not even on Oahu. I'm on the Big Island. So no worries, right?"

Melanie's voice was cold. "You said you were in Honolulu."

"I called from Honolulu. I said I was in Hawaii."

Melanie's flat tone continued. "So you went someplace new and didn't tell me, like we agreed."

"It's not someplace new. It's Hawaii. The Big Island is literally called Hawaii."

"It's a different island."

"Yeah, but it's the same state. It's like I'm in Trenton instead of Newark."

"No it's not. You took a plane to get there, didn't you? You don't fly to go from Newark to Trenton."

"Look. I don't want to fight. When we visit, we'll go to both Oahu *and* the Big Island. Okay?"

He heard Melanie sigh. "Someplace warm and beautiful would be nice."

"You bet, sweetie. We'll come here—the whole family. You'll like it." He heard the door to his hotel room open as he finished the call. "Hawaii's a great place. You'll love it."

He turned to see Ace standing in his room, giving him a stern stare. "Who the hell are you talking to?"

Dick clicked off the hotel phone and stepped in from the lanai, but said nothing. When he didn't immediately reply, Ace continued. "It can't be your family, because from what I recall from our briefing ... and I recall everything from our briefing ... you're supposedly in South Korea consulting on a malfunctioning wastewater facility just outside of Seoul."

Dick ignored her accusations. "How'd you get in my room?"

Ace rolled her eyes. "Please. If I can't pick a hotel lock with the electronics in my sunglasses in less than thirty seconds, even with my laptop in my off hand, I'm not much of a spy now, am I?"

"Fine," Dick snapped. "Forget how. Why? What about my privacy?"

"In case you hadn't noticed, the Subsidiary's not really big on the whole privacy thing. That's what comes from having wiretaps, keyhole spy satellites, and codebreakers at your beck and call twenty-four seven." Her stern stare softened. "Besides, I knocked. You didn't answer. I was worried our sniper pal from last night followed up on his effort. Thought maybe I might be saving your life."

"Yeah. Well, thanks, but you weren't." Hopefully, Melanie hadn't heard Ace's interruption. Hopefully, Ace hadn't done further damage to his marriage. Hopefully, she wouldn't tell his superiors about his clandestine call.

He was about to make up some lie about who he was talking to when the ring of a phone cut through the silence between him and his partner. He looked stupidly at the handset still in his hand. It wasn't ringing. Neither was his Subsidiary cell, still tucked in his pocket. That's when both he and Ace turned toward the source of the noise. The cell phone in a Ziploc bag on top of the dresser, the phone they had recovered from the Great Crack the day before. The one that was supposed to trigger the explosion in the lava tube ... most likely at the same time as other phones hidden in other spots along the Great Crack were triggering their own blasts.

Shit! It was happening. The PPIPF was trying to trigger a tsunami. Now. Right fucking now.

They both dashed for the door, Dick grabbing the ringing cell on the way. "Take the stairs!" Dick yelled. Together, they plummeted down the emergency exit toward ground level—the exact opposite of what they should be doing if a tsunami was headed their way.

The Secret Service has nothing on the agents of the Subsidiary.

#

Ace led the way down the staircase, her partner lumbering behind her at full speed. She hip-checked the panic bar on the emergency exit, setting off an ear-splitting alarm as they crashed through into a garden area on the side of the main parking lot.

Sakra!

They didn't have a car. They'd left theirs behind in Kapalana for the rental agency to take in and repair or replace. She skidded to a stop, pondering what to do next. Dick slowed, but never stopped, thrusting the PPIPF's cell phone into her hand as he jaunted toward the currently unmanned valet station near the main entrance to the hotel.

"Call in a tsunami warning to Hansebi, now. I'm jacking us a car."

She froze for a second in bewilderment. "I have a cell phone," she called to Dick's back as he headed away from her.

"Use theirs," he called back over his shoulder. "Harder to trace. Better for our cover."

Made sense to her.

It took more than a minute to get patched through to Hansebi. Two agonizing minutes to explain to him that some bad guys just set off a series of explosions along the Great Crack, attempting to trigger a giant tsunami on the south side of the Big Island. She had the feeling he was humoring her, but thought she was, quite literally, a crack-pot, when all of a sudden she heard a sharp intake of breath, then the words "Shit, shit, shit!" before a clattering as if the receiver had been dropped.

Fifteen seconds later, the tsunami sirens along the bayfront in Hilo blared out their warning—a long, continual blast which could have passed for an air raid siren in Europe circa World War II.

Dick pulled up in a white Range Rover, reaching across to throw open the passenger door for her. "Get in!" he barked.

She was barely in the door before he gunned the pricey vehicle forward, without bothering to wait for her to close her door or buckle her seatbelt. *Sakra!* Fortunately, she had good balance and reactions or she would have spilled out onto the asphalt.

"Where are we going in such a hurry? There's no way we'll get anywhere near the Great Crack in time to do anything."

Dick turned his head to look at her, his face a mask of scowling brows and wrinkled puzzlement. "Jesus Christ. Are you kidding? A tsunami may be rolling to shore any second. *Where are we going?* Uphill. We're going uphill as fast as possible. That's what you do when the tsunami sirens go off. You get as high as possible as soon as possible, then you assess the situation when you have the luxury of potentially surviving for more than a few minutes."

"We could have stayed safe high in the hotel and accomplished that."

"If the wave was small enough. Even then, we might have been trapped there for ... who knows how long?"

She held onto the flip-down hand hold on the ceiling above the passenger side window as Dick made a sharp right out of the parking lot, then gunned the engine to a throaty roar.

"Nice car for a change," she said between gritted teeth.

Dick grinned like the maniac he surely was. "Thought we might want something a bit more rugged, with decent ground clearance, if we're going to have to get around in the middle of a disaster area."

She hung on as Dick made a sharp left and they roared along a wide, flat road. "I don't know. Hansebi said the Great Crack wouldn't ... couldn't ... cause a major tsunami."

"And, yet, the sirens are blaring. What convinced him? What did he say?"

"I think his exact words were 'Shit. Shit. Shit.'"

Dick pounded the dash of the car with his fist. "You need a lot of ground clearance to go through that much shit." He slammed the car *mauka* and they started climbing past a motley assemblage of nice and not-so-nice houses in a residential subdivision on the south side of Hilo.

Ace folded down the visor on the passenger side and flipped open the vanity mirror imbedded in it. The ocean view in the distance behind her was unremarkable, serene and blue beneath the morning sky. But when she tilted the mirror up, shifting her view down, closer to shore, she saw a giant swell of water rising up, not such much crashing into the shore, but inexorably flooding the beach and the rocks.

Next, it overwhelmed the changing facility near the parking lot and the shave ice stand nearby without slowing. It continued forward swallowing the road behind them, engulfing parked cars, snatching up trash bins and vegetation, somehow not diminishing, but still growing higher as it sped toward them. She turned her eyes toward the side view mirror and the devastation looked even worse, crashing in windows, picking up household debris, rolling forward without respite as it gained on them, despite, she read, already being closer than it appeared. *Do prdele!*

"Faster! Faster! Faster!"

Dick floored the car and it charged forward, bottoming out as the road suddenly inclined sharply. But her partner never let up, weaving to miss parked cars as he shot through the schizophrenic subdivision of middle class homes next to cars-on-blocks and chicken coops in the front yard shacks on the east slope of Mauna Loa.

His eyes flashed over to hers; he nodded at the rear view. "Let me know when the coast is clear."

She nodded back. Given their rate of climb, she suspected they would be safe in seconds, but with all the detritus the thirty-plus foot surge had picked up as it rolled over the shore, she knew the coast wouldn't be clear for months.

"I think we made it," she sighed.

Dick didn't let up on the gas. "The first wave usually isn't the biggest," he explained. "It could be the third or the fifth or even later, depending on the series of shocks."

Ace laughed nervously. "Oh, boy. I don't know about you, but I could sure use a fifth right now."

#

Jake Sutter finished his morning exercise routine and sauntered out to the hot tub for a soak, settling in his favorite corner to let the jets knead his back and calves while he enjoyed the view of the Pacific Ocean far below. Morning was the best time to enjoy the panorama from almost twelve hundred feet up on the southwest side of the Big Island thirty miles south of Captain Cook. Suddenly, he felt an unfamiliar tremor and a faint, steady whine. Damn. He should have insisted the seller replace the spa pump when he bought his dream house last year. Getting parts to the middle of the Pacific Ocean was a bitch. And, of course, everything imported to the island—which was pretty much everything besides ti leaves and poi—was damn expensive.

He twisted his body to the controls and turned off the jets.

There. There it was again. But the pumps were off.

Of course. Probably an earthquake. Bigger than usual, but no big deal. The island got them all the time. He was just settling in to continue his soak when movement caught his eye. A faint, curved line seemed to be streaking across the calm sea. Barely discernible in the deep water, but more pronounced in the shallows. He skipped his gaze ahead to one of the few outcroppings of coastal white water he could see from his privileged vantage and was shocked by the size of the wave which pounded across it, fountaining spray higher than he had ever seen before—even when he'd ventured out to anchor the spa cover during the big hurricane last fall.

Holy crap! He was witnessing a tsunami from the comfort of his Jacuzzi.

Life in paradise was a constant wonder.

Chapter 18

Traffic was light as Dick continued uphill, eventually connecting to the wide highway over the saddleback between Mauna Loa and Mauna Kea. Still, he flashed his lights at all traffic headed downhill, just in case they didn't have on their radio and hadn't yet noticed the distant wail of the sirens. As soon as he reached a clear spot above the scrub trees, he jerked the Range Rover into a scenic lookout and stared out across Hilo and the ocean beyond.

"Where's the next wave?" Ace shielded her eyes from the morning sun, scanning the horizon. "I don't see it."

"Tsunamis are hard to see in open ocean. In deep water, they may be only a few inches or feet high." Dick's eyes tracked nearer, at the city of Hilo below. "Besides, looks like the biggest one already hit," he said, pointing toward the center city, the streets awash with debris and churning water, but the most of the buildings were still standing, though the windows in the first several stories were almost all blown out. "The seawall out in the bay apparently took some of the *oomph* out of the surge, but it was still high enough to push out of the official tsunami evacuation area—that puts it at thirty, maybe forty, feet high or so."

Ace snatched up the PPIPF's cell phone from the dash. "I'll check in with Hansebi and get an update."

Dick glanced at his watch. Jesus, more than forty minutes had passed since the bombs had been detonated. He shook his head. "Not a mega-tsunami or anything. Not by a long shot. But, given Hansebi's location, the Tsunami Warning Center is either already underwater or much too busy evacuating to take non-essential calls."

#

Suki stared at the yellow pictographic sign, then pointed at it, elbowing her boyfriend, Takahiro, to pay attention. "I don't think we should go that way. I think the sign means it's dangerous."

The metal sign on the northeastern edge of the sand beach at Hanauma Bay, the most popular amateur snorkeling spot on Oahu, showed a series of scenes depicting a stick figure on a rocky cliff getting engulfed by a wave easily six times as high, then washed out to sea.

Takahiro glanced at the sign and chortled. "I think the sign is hilarious. Even more hilarious because there isn't any text to explain the danger. I mean, sure, not everyone reads English, but you'd think they'd give those who are proficient a clue as to what their comic book pictures are supposed to mean."

Suki frowned. "I think it's obvious. It means 'don't walk along these cliffs or a giant wave could wash you out to sea.'"

Her boyfriend waved his arm toward the expanse of the ocean beyond the entrance of the bay. "Really? It's super-calm this morning. There's not even any whitecaps out past the break. Bet you big time nobody ever got washed out to sea from a giant, killer wave hitting this cliff."

Suki pursed her lips into a pout. "Then why did they put up the sign?"

"That's easy," laughed Takahiro. "They don't want people hiking around the point to the Toilet Bowl."

She furrowed her brow. "The comfort station is just down the beach the other way."

"Not the restrooms. The Toilet Bowl. It's this hole in the rocks about five meters across and not quite as deep. It's connected to the ocean through a tunnel at the end of a narrowing inlet, so every set of waves tons of water gets pushed through filling it up, then emptying out again only a few seconds later. Awesome! I saw on YouTube how you can stand on the bottom near the tunnel when it's empty and the water rushes through and knocks you on your feet and throws you towards the sharp rocks on the other side ..."

"Oh my god!"

"... but the water always beats you there and bounces off the opposite face and pushes you back and suddenly you're, like, floating, then the water all starts to flush out until it's less than knee deep and it all starts over again."

"That sounds dangerous."

Takahiro motioned toward the sign. "So's walking along the beach, according to this." He tilted his head down and stared at her. "C'mon. It'll be fun."

She couldn't deny him, not when he was so intense about having fun. "Okay, but I'm not getting in. I'll just watch you."

He started out along the path and she quickly followed. "We'll see. I'm betting once you get there, you'll want to get wet, too." He winked at her.

Suki shushed him. "Stop that." She looked around. "Someone might hear."

"Who?" he replied, spinning around as they walked. "There's nobody here. It's still early for the sun worshippers." He smiled and skipped along ahead of her a few steps before turning his back to the ocean to smile a her. "A giant wave could wash us to sea and nobody would even notice."

That's when she noticed the water had receded from the bay, exposing an intricate series of boulders and coral, trapping fish which flopped about in shallows interspersed with small, deep pools amidst the jumble of jagged rocks and coral. "I think the tide's gone ..." she said, then faltered as a gigantic bulge of water appeared beyond the

146

bay entrance, careening toward shore faster than anything she could ever have imagined.

"Wave!" she yelled, pointing behind Takahiro toward the sea.

He smiled and waved at her.

"No," she screamed. "Tsunami!"

The wave crashed through the bay and thundered toward the cliffs, towering above her, above Takahiro, and well above the yellow pictographic sign. A moment later it crashed against the lava rock, throwing Takahiro at her as it rushed to scour the cliffs clean.

#

Carlisle didn't panic when the Waikiki tsunami sirens blared as he trotted off to recover a guest's car from the valet parking area. He'd been through the drill before when the big Japanese quake and tsunami had taken out the nuclear power plant, and, before that, when there was a big quake in Chile. Six, eight hours of sirens, bunches of anxious, pissed-off tourists bitching about being told to stay in their upper floor rooms while the beach access was closed—and, for what? A minor push of water that didn't even come up to the high-tide mark on Waikiki? Big deal. A few boats damaged at a badly configured marina somewhere on the Big Island, but nothing major.

He fetched the guest's vehicle, cranked on the air conditioning, maneuvered the car quickly up the circular drive to the main entrance to the open air lobby, and accepted his tip with a hearty "Aloha!" Then, he quickly sought out the Head Porter to volunteer for beach closure duty. There wouldn't be much in the way of tips at the valet station for the rest of the day and God forbid he be assigned to the third floor lounge, where anxious guests would mill about eating fresh fruit and complaining about their ruined vacations all day.

Wet Work

He shooed away the few early beachcombers and set about his task of folding and storing the dozens and dozens of lounge chairs the hotel had arrayed on the white sand for clientele. Just him and Julio, one of the other bellmen, and an endless series of heavy wooden chairs. Routine, boring, hard work in the hot early sun. He would have soaked a bandana in the cool ocean water and tucked it under his hotel-mandated, logoed ball cap, but the tide was too low for easy access to a clear pool. Instead, he found a shady spot cast by one of the hotel's trademark palms and squatted to catch his breath, looking out over the broader than usual expanse of beach at the calm ocean.

He saw a flicker of white on the ocean, then another. Was that a whale breaching this late in the season? Maybe a pod of dolphins frolicking in the surf? If so, he hoped the guests were watching from the outdoor terrace on the third floor lounge—it would break up their miserable day.

He heard a collective gasp from above and behind and concluded the crowd had seen the frolicking sea life, too. He stood, trying to get a better view, but saw nothing but a line of foaming, surging water rushing toward him. Then he heard the shouts from the third floor veranda.

"Oh, my god!"

"Grab the kids!"

"Holy crap!"

"Run! Run for your life!"

Carlisle ran for the safety of the hotel, but the wave caught him, picked him up and carried him through the open air lobby, and out the main entrance past the valet stand, across the parking area and into the street. The surge slammed him against the front window of the boutique shop across the street, flattening him against it for a moment before the pressure cracked and shattered the glass, impaling him on a large, heavy shard as the water swept past, battering his bleeding body with detritus picked up along its trek: furniture, broken tree limbs, bicycles, newspaper boxes, and people. Then the shard impaling him broke off and he joined the relentless push of water crashing into displays, mannequins, and counters. Heavy, wet racks of designer clothing clutched at him, holding him down under the surface, until his head hit something hard and his shift ended.

#

"Nice work," growled Glenn Swynton. Dick knew it wasn't a compliment even before his boss continued on with: "Less flashy than your cockup in Dunedin, but greater devastation."

Dick gripped his cell tighter, but didn't rise to the bait. "What's the damage report?"

Dee Tammany chimed in. "Casualties in the hundreds so far, but they will go higher. The volcanologists say something called the Hilina Slump—basically a big pile of debris in the ocean off the southeast coast of the Big Island—acted as a kind of doorstop, preventing the slide from reaching the size of the Alika events off the southwest side of the island hundreds of thousands of years ago."

Glenn took over. "Preliminary assessment indicate the tsunami ranged from twelve to forty-five feet high on the coastal areas of the islands—depending on what direction the coast faced, the configuration of the shore and the underwater geology, etcetera, etcetera. How these things propagate is not just a matter of size, but the precise location of the underwater displacement."

"Yeah," said Ace. "Hansebi's people explained all of that to us a few days ago." She let out a deep breath. "But all of that's said and done. And, odds are, so are they. I guess that's not important anymore."

"More important than you can imagine," Glenn responded. "Hansebi and his people survived—I guess they take their evacuation drills more seriously than the average resident. They've set up a temporary command post someplace high and dry. They've done their calculations, sent out warnings to other islands and coasts which might be affected, and reported in to FEMA."

Dee interrupted. "We ... uh ... listened in."

"Quite," continued Glenn. "The interesting part is that they determined the epicenter of the quake giving rise to the displacement and the tsunami. Other locations have confirmed and refined their numbers. The earthquake centered on ..."

Ace finished the sentence for him. "Let me guess. The Great Crack."

"No," replied Glenn, with a chill Dick could feel even in the warmth of Hawaii. "West of Hilo, along the main rift line separating Mauna Kea and Mauna Loa."

Dick's mind boggled. "That's where we're at right now, more or less." Another thought crossed his mind. "I didn't do this. I swear. You know I don't even have any heavy duty explosives on this mission. Besides, the burner cell we recovered from the Great Crack rang. Somebody tried to set off the explosives there."

"Calm down, Thornby," interjected Dee. "Nobody's accusing you of anything. And eye witness accounts and seismic reports do indicate some minor shocks or explosions along the crack at about the same time—maybe a minor contributing factor or, perhaps, just a distraction from the main event."

Glenn spoke up again. "The rift west of Hilo is reasonably active. A lava flow threatened the outskirts of the city proper as recently as 1985. Perhaps a larger explosive device was detonated there. But, if so, it was a much more sophisticated placement than the lava tube bombs like

150

the one found along the Crack. The math indicates the epicenter was more than fourteen thousand feet underground."

"Below sea level?" blurted Ace. "They planted the bomb underwater?"

"Islands don't float," responded Glenn, his voice as dry as his martinis, no doubt. "Deep in the mountain. Remember, from the seabed to the peak of Mauna Kea, you're on the largest mountain on the face of the Earth. It dwarfs Everest in total volume."

"Give me the exact coordinates of the epicenter," said Dick. "We'll check it out."

"Precisely our thought," said Dee. "Do be quick about it. We don't know if another shock is about to go off."

Dick copied the coordinates from Glenn and hung up to search Google Earth for how to get to the spot. Unfortunately, his cell began to buzz almost immediately with another call. He glanced at the Caller ID. Shit. It was Melanie. No doubt worried, possibly frantic, but he couldn't take the call. Sure, he could make and take calls from family on his Subsidiary-issued phone—family being able to reach you through what they thought was your work number at Catalyst Crisis Consulting helped maintain the cover story you sold to them. But Melanie wasn't supposed to know he was in Hawaii and he couldn't control what she might say or explain how he was okay despite the tsunami with Ace sitting right next to him. Worse, he was pretty sure Pyotr Nerevsky's goons in Internal Audit listened in—or, at least, recorded—all conversations on the Subsidiary's equipment, which was why he had avoided using it for family calls since Denver. He thumbed the button to decline the call. There'd be hell to pay at home later for doing so, but there'd be hell to pay at work even sooner if he didn't.

I love you, honey, but I just can't talk.

151

Wet Work

He thumbed the screen, scrolling through the satellite maps of Google Earth until he found the coordinates. The picture showed a scattering of trucks and something that looked like a crane or maybe a drilling rig close by. It was hard to tell; there was no "street view" available. It probably didn't matter anyway. Google Earth images could be years old. It's not like they had up-to-the minute views of any place on the planet when you wanted it. For that you needed to be able to access top secret military spy satellites.

For that you needed the Subsidiary.

They depended on him; he depended on them when need arose.

But right now, he just had to take a drive through paradise in a stolen car with a woman who wasn't his wife.

Work was complicated sometimes.

Chapter 19

Taren Sykes sipped Glenfiddich as he leaned back in his swivel desk chair and watched the repetitive and largely inane news reports of damage roll in from the Hawaiian Island chain. The maximum wave height recorded—forty-nine feet—was a disappointment, but within acceptable parameters. And the congratulatory message from his stooges in the PPIPF left him with a wide smile on his face.

Stage One of his latest project was complete. Chaos sown. Damage done. Paranoia piqued.

On to Stage Two. Mass destruction and chaos, whether it worked or whether it didn't. That was what filled him with joy. Death was a bonus, but chaos was the key.

He mused for a few moments on how long to let the current round of confusion reign. Fear and paranoia took time to travel around the globe. Too soon and the fear would not have a chance to spread and fester. Too late and the fear would begin to fade; logic and order would threaten to take hold.

There was no secret formula; no algorithm for how to time things to achieve maximum pandemonium, just his gut and his years of experience fomenting hysteria around the globe.

He decided and made the call. Satellite phone, of course. No cell phones out there and he'd never trust a radio. Not secure. And he was always very secure when propagating insecurity.

#

Kurva! Ace hung on for her life. Dick drove like a crazed maniac at the best of times, but when Dee Tammany, his boss' boss and the head of the whole damn Subsidiary, said to be quick about something, he didn't hesitate. Hell, he didn't even slow for curves, stop signs, or small animals. According to Dick, that mongoose deserved to be splattered into road kill; they ate the eggs of Hawaii's dwindling native bird population, after all.

Fortunately, they didn't need to go back to the coast and all of the attendant flooding, destruction, debris, and chaos of the inundation zone to get to their intended location. Of course, according to the map on the cell phone Dick had thrust into her hands before spinning the wheel and jinking the Range Rover into gear to rocket off from their overlook above Hilo, the epicenter looked to be in the middle of the jungle ... or tropical rainforest ... whatever they called it here. She was about to tell the big guy he'd need to pull over in a half-mile and hike in when he hit the power brakes hard with both feet.

Her combat senses took hold; in his current mood, she didn't think Dick would brake to avoid hitting a baby carriage, and there was nothing but feral pigs and mongeese ... mongooses ... out here. When she rocked back from her own near collision with the dashboard, she saw her partner pointing at a small sign on the left side of the road, next to an overgrown dirt road into the trees: "Hawaiian Geophysical Drilling Project, University of Hawaii/U.S. Department of Interior." Several sets of muddy, red dirt tire tracks exited the barely-there road, headed downhill.

"Those weren't there when we passed this spot going uphill," said Dick.

Ace felt her eyebrows tilt inward as she stared at her partner. "You remember whether random tire tracks appear on every road you drive?" She tried to parse it out for a moment. "You one of those super-memory people? You know, the ones who remember everything that ever happened to them?" Now Dick's eyebrows were tilting inward as she rattled on. "Quick. What were the major news stories on ... October 13, 2003?"

Dick shook his head, as if she were a mirage he was trying to make disappear. "Who knows and who the hell cares?" He pointed out the windshield. "Look at the big chunks of mud that caked off those tires. I probably would have noticed that, being an attentive driver and all. But, more importantly, those tracks are fresh. Oncoming traffic hasn't crossed over them and spread the mud out. Somebody left here after the tsunami was triggered."

"Okay," Ace replied. "Is that important? I mean, we're kinda close to the epicenter, but what makes you think this is related?"

He nodded toward the sign. "Apparently there's a drilling project down this dirt path. And the quake started two and a half miles underground ..."

"Oh ... I get it now." She shook her head. "Fuck."

Dick shook his head. "No ... frack."

Ace screwed up her face. She recognized the euphemism, but since when had Dick gotten squeamish about language? I mean, he'd made it abundantly clear he didn't want to engage in a recreational fuck, but it didn't mean he couldn't—didn't occasionally—use the word. Before she could ask about his odd language choice, though, he'd turned down the road. He piloted the car with his left hand, creeping along at less than five miles per hour, as he simultaneously pulled his gun and checked the clip.

She decided to shut up for now and just follow his lead, but her fingers boogied over the keyboard of her laptop, looking for details on the drilling project. *Ježiši!* Dick was right to be worried. She nudged him and tilted her head toward the laptop screen. "Says here, this is the deepest hole ever drilled on a volcanic island. A press clipping from last year has them bringing up volcanic cores from more than twelve thousand feet down, headed for the Earth's crust at nineteen thousand feet."

155

Dick nodded. "Sounds like we turned off the road at the right place."

The jungle canopy soon swallowed the road and the vehicle. Ace closed her eyes for a few moments to speed their adjustment to the dim light. She needn't have rushed. The Range Rover trundled along for almost ten minutes through the foliage before the road opened up into a sizeable clearing along the shore of a small lake. The clearing was filled with a variety of construction trailers, trucks, tanks, and building materials, as well as a large derrick of the style typically depicted in pictures of oil drilling rigs—though, of course, she knew the islands had no gas or oil deposits. Several large hoses snaked from the equipment through an open entrenchment into the lake.

Dick kept the Range Rover moving, circling the site—no doubt to maintain a sheltered position for as long as possible while he confirmed there were no hostiles. They were only about a third of the way around counter-clockwise when Ace saw the first body face down in the grass and mud near one of the trailers. Then she noticed the blood spatter on the window of the trailer and a blood trail down the steps and past the first body, headed toward the derrick. She followed the trail with her gaze and saw a pair of legs poking out from the knee-high grass. She pivoted her look left and higher and saw more bodies scattered in the grass and on the platform at the bottom of the derrick. None of them held weapons; many looked like they had been shot from behind as they ran for cover.

Dick completed his circuit, driving the Range Rover over a metal plate covering the entrenchment with the tubing running into the lake. He squeezed the vehicle between stacks of metal piping of some kind.

"Nobody home," said Dick as he rolled the vehicle to a stop and shoved the gear shift into park. She noticed he left the engine running. "Still, weapons out, eyes and ears open while we have a look-see."

Ace shifted into combat mode, her thoughts flitting from confusion to high alert to being creeped out in a continual loop, as they inspected the bodies—all an hour or so dead—and poked around the equipment and the construction trailers. She stood lookout as Dick ducked inside the main trailer and crashed around for a while, flinging papers and clipboards about during his apparent search for clues. Finally, he came out, a neon pink clipboard in one hand and his automatic pistol still in the other.

"Pretty high body count just to drop a bomb down a hole," she prompted him. "I mean, I know ski masks must be tough to find in Hawaii, but a bandana and a ball cap and these innocent workers would never have been able to identify the bad guys who surprised them this morning."

Dick shook his head. "I don't think they're innocent—or, at least, uninvolved. This wasn't an ambush; this was clean-up at the completion of a project."

The math didn't make sense to Ace. "You mean all fifteen or so guys drilling the hole knew a bomb was going to be dropped down it? That's a fucking hell of a thing."

"No, that's a hell of a fracking thing." There he went again.

"You a big Battlestar Galactica fan or something?"

Dick stared at her as if she was deranged. "What? That some computer game or something? My kid, Seth, plays some of those, but not me. And what's that got to do with the price of tea in China?"

Tea in China? *Kurva!* She hated idioms. "It's a television show ... or at least it used to be. They say "frak" as a euphemism for "fuck" because ... because Americans love violence, but they don't allow tits or swear words on television ... unless it's cable."

Dick shook his head, as if weary beyond words. "Good to know, I guess. But when I say 'frack,' I mean ... well ... frack." He bounced his head in the direction of the tubing and the lake. "Oil companies force water and chemicals down a depleting or underperforming well to fracture the sedimentary strata holding the oil—especially shales, which break up fairly easily—and then pump out the additional oil and gas released."

He waved the clipboard toward the derrick. "It's North America's answer to dependency on Middle East oil. Or, at least, it used to be. The eco-freaks, they hate the whole process. Say it contaminates the ground water."

"Good to know, I guess," Ace mimicked him. "But there's no oil or gas in Hawaii to drill. Hell, there's no sedimentary rock. So what's that got to do with tea in China or bodies scattered about the fracking, fucking jungle?"

"I was getting to that. The environmentalists also say fracking increases the frequency and intensity of earthquakes. Evidence backs that up, big time. And Hansebi, he mentioned that an unusual amount of rainfall penetrated into the island and caused a section of the volcano to slide a few years back. So, I figure the bad guys used the cover of some geophysical drilling program to drill down and then inject a massive amount of water into the hole." Once again, he bounced his head toward the lake. "Notice the grass ends well short of the shoreline? The lake's low, really low, and the mud near the shore hasn't even had enough time to dry and crack. Somebody pumped a shitload of water out of the lake and not so long ago."

Ace took a deep breath and closed her eyes for a moment to think it all through. Guess she'd better add common engineering methods to the list of things she needed to know as a spy. Of course, she didn't have any expertise on any of this, but what Dick said made sense. "So," she said, "you think the PPIPF put together a crew to do this, then offed them to cover their tracks when the plan went forward?"

"Nah," replied Dick. "Some of these guys are native, but not most. Besides, why off your own guys? No, I think the PPIPF guys ... the whole Great Crack thing ... is just a cover for what's really going on. Hell, the sumo wrestlers in the PPIPF probably think the bombs in the Crack worked as intended. They're probably taking credit for the whole thing, scaring the tourists and *haoles* from ever coming back to the Kingdom of Hawaii. But the natives, they're just patsies ... fall guys for whoever is really in charge. And that guy doesn't want to leave any loose ends. Hence the clean-up squad right on the heels of success."

"What makes you so sure?"

Dick held up the clipboard. "Regular phone calls overseas. Plus, a note scribbled in the margin: 'The Great Crested Canary will soon sing.'"

"Obviously a code phrase of some kind," Ace replied. "Or they have a hard-on for birds, like you."

Dick said nothing for almost a minute. "I've heard of Crested Canaries, for sure. Gloster and Norwich Crested's have mop-tops, like the haircuts for the Beatles when they first started. And some people refer to Yellow Crested Canaries or even Giant Crested Canaries, especially when they're bred for color or size. They're tough to breed because the gene for the crest is dominant, but if you breed two crested birds, it's fatal to the offspring, so you always have to breed a crested to a non-crested."

Sakra! Why had she ever brought up birding?

Dick continued. "But I've never heard of a Great Crested Canary."

"Like I said, obviously a code phrase," replied Ace, desperate to get the conversation off of Dick's birding fetish and back on the business at hand.

"Maybe, but maybe not."

159

"Those are the choices," she snapped. When Dick threw her a sharp look, she softened her tone. "Let's focus on the phone for now. Give me the number and I'll get the techs at the Subsidiary to trace it, even though I'd bet money it's an untraceable burner."

"Yeah, sure, but I can already tell you for a fact this operation wasn't reporting in to some high muckety-muck at the PPIPF. The number begins with '41.'"

"So?" Why did she have the feeling Dick was treating this entire discussion like she was still an agent in training, rather than a partner?

"That's the country code for Switzerland. It's not only *not* Pan-Pacific, it doesn't even border on a damn ocean."

Chapter 20

Long ago, Dick had noticed Glenn Swynton's voice dropped lower and lower in octave the more irritated he became. At this point, Dick figured the man could sing bass for a heavy metal band ... or one of those a cappella groups Dick's kid listened to on YouTube.

"The Quartermaster says you are being both demanding and unreasonable, Agent Thornby. Why am I not surprised?"

"Well, Director of *Operations*, Swynton. I happen to be in the middle of an *operation*. And I, and my youthful and exuberant partner, need transportation as soon as humanly possible to continue that *operation*."

There was a pause Dick guessed was long enough for his boss to both roll his eyes and clench his teeth while he mentally conjured up an image of Dick in front of a firing squad. "Well, *Dick*, due to the lack of success of your efforts in Hawaii, no flights in or out are taking place at the moment. As you might recall, all of the airports are on the coast ... barely above sea level. While I understand most of the runways are high enough to be dry, important infrastructure components were still inundated, debris and pools of water have yet to be cleared, and all commercial flights are on hold both at Hilo International Airport and Kona International."

"Yeah, Glenn, I know. But according to the headlines on my phone's browser, TMZ says Hugh Jackman is already headed back to L.A. He was doing some eco-lodge thing in yurts or something on the Kohala Coast."

Dick heard a deep sigh before Swynton continued, his voice practically vibrating in *basso profundo*. "You're not Hugh Jackman ..."

"You're right," interrupted Dick. "I couldn't take him in a fair fight, not that I'd have any interest in fighting fair if I was up against that hunk of beef. But it means a private jet from Nine to Five Charters can get in and out of Upolu Airport, on the north tip of the Kohala

Peninsula. Ninety-six feet above sea level. Not much in the way of infrastructure to damage, even if it got wet in the wave. Quartermaster admits as much, but he won't spring for the ride. What's the use of the Subsidiary having a false front air charter service if it doesn't use it for its agents when they are on ... an *operation*."

"It's not a taxi service. Besides, your mission is done, complete. A failure, as I recall. Repositioning idle assets is not a top priority when scheduling or budgeting resources."

"We're not idle. Or at least we wouldn't be if you would get us a plane. Have you forgotten about the intercepts talking about some big 'east coast action?'

"But which east coast? Japan's? Australia's? The east coast of the island you're already on?"

"Not here. This scenario is played out. Now that people are spooked, the smallest tremor will send everyone running for the hills. No, the Big Island was just a warm-up, a test run for something much, much bigger, impacting a much more populous east coast, like the one where your offices are located."

Dick knew Glenn didn't frighten easily, but he imagined the Brit's forehead wrinkling as he recalculated the cost/benefit analysis of the charter given this new variable.

"Fine. I'll tell the Quartermaster to send a charter from the west coast. What's your destination?"

"We'll have that figured out by the time he gets here."

"See that you do or I'll have to turn this over to Internal Audit."

The very last thing Dick needed was to get in the crosshairs of Pyotr Nerevsky and his ilk. Hiding things from the Subsidiary was hard enough when you weren't getting the evil eye of the rat squad; it was nigh unto impossible if they decided to take a good hard look. Almost any response he made would increase the chances of getting their attention. Instead, he simply thumbed off the connection and pocketed his cell phone.

"So," said Ace, "sounds like you got the plane. You got a destination in mind?"

"Yeah," said Dick, "but I wanted to mull it over, then walk through it with you, before I tried to sell it to HQ. Buckle up."

#

Ace stared out the window as Dick headed back uphill, taking the road across the saddle between Mauna Kea and Mauna Loa, the shortest and, fortunately, highest road to get from the Hilo on the southeast side of the Big Island to the west. The western side of the island held the popular tourist beaches of Kailua/Kona, along with the tonier mega-resorts on the northwest, heading toward the Kohala shore. Once away from the outskirts of Hilo, the wide, paved road climbed with few distractions or interruptions. As she rode in silence, waiting for Dick to gather his thoughts and explain his theory to her, she had nothing to do but look out over the largely treeless expanses of jumbled lava. Two plumes of gray smoke from the far side of Mauna Loa mixed together and snaked into the pass, then got sucked westward, plunging into the Kailua/Kona coast and filling it with a miasma of vog.

Finally, after they'd passed the turn-off up to the summit of Mauna Kea, where big telescopes tracked the stars from the deep dark of the mid-Pacific, she couldn't stand the silence any longer. "You ready yet to tell me where we're going and why? Or are you going to continue to be the dick you clearly are?"

Her partner harrumphed, then glanced over to her. "I was waiting til we got someplace with good wireless reception for your laptop."

Ace pulled out her cell phone. "I can create a hot spot for the laptop with my phone or even use the com gear in my glasses if I don't need too much bandwidth."

"Good to know. So, you got any bars on your cell?"

She thumbed her phone and looked at the glowing screen. "Reception's fine. The phone companies usually do a pretty good job of coverage along major roads." She looked up as Dick overtook a large semi. "Truckers seem to like this road."

Dick shrugged. "Big island, but not many big roads. You can circle the island or go over the middle. This baby's got wider lanes and less tight turns than the belt road."

"So, you need me to call up a navigation app to find Upolu Airport?"

"Nah. Not yet, anyhow." He pulled back into the right lane after having passed the truck. "Just thought I'd try a little experiment. So, what do we know about the perp behind this whole damn mess?"

Ace started to answer, but he cut her off.

"Rhetorical question." He exhaled and cricked his neck as he drove; she heard it crack. "We know he ... she ... they ... whatever ... likes to cause tsunamis. We also know they've talked about some big 'east coast action' and used the phrase 'Great Crested Canary.'"

"Yeah. So?"

"So, I want you to Google the word "canary," along with the word "tsunami."

She wrinkled her nose as she opened up her laptop. "That's your idea of top secret spy research? A Google search?"

"As you may recall from just a few moments ago, I'm not exactly tech savvy. Just do it."

She wanted to answer back, but held her tongue. Instead, she looked down at the screen and felt her eyes widen and her head jerk back in surprise. She swiped the screen to scroll down. "*Ježiši!* There's over a hundred thousand hits, including bunches of YouTube videos, with headings like 'Canary Island Mega-Tsunami' and 'Scientists Warn of Massive Tidal Wave from Canary Island Volcano.'" She looked at him, her eyes narrowing. "Did you do a Google search back on the drill site when I wasn't looking?"

Dick smiled. "Nope."

Ace shook her head and gestured at her screen. "Then how could you possibly know this shit existed? Forget that, how do bad guys come up with this shit?"

"I tumbled upon it last night when I was Googling the Great Crack conspiracy stuff Hansebi mentioned. There's a bunch of pirate YouTubes of a program that was originally broadcast years ago on the Discovery Channel—whose mission seems to be scaring the crap out of people at every opportunity."

"They do love natural disasters."

"And what you can't get from science, you can always get from fiction. Nobody talks about it, but the whole time right after 9/11 happened, when all the anchormen were droning on and on about how nobody ever imagined such a thing, I kept thinking, I guess nobody in news ever reads any thrillers. I mean, Tom Clancy dropped a jumbo jet on the Capitol Building during a joint session with the President, for Christ's sake."

"You read techno-thrillers? Spy work not exciting enough for you, big boy? You got a Jason Bourne complex?"

Dick fluttered his right hand, apparently waving off her question. "The thing I wonder about is why is it that the United States has set up a panel of science fiction authors to come up with scenarios the government should be worried about, but they pay no attention to the plots of spy thrillers. I mean, isn't that what Robert Redford did for a living in *Three Days of the Condor*?"

"Is that a movie?"

Dick let out a huff. "Yeah. Of course, it pre-dates *Harry Potter and the* ... whatever it was."

"*Philosopher's Stone ... Goblet of Fire ... Order of the Phoenix ...*"

"Yeah, yeah," Dick growled. "I read thrillers. I also watch a lot of educational channels when I have down time on a mission. National Geographic, Animal Channel, NASA ..."

"Makes you a smart guy, I guess."

"Not so smart. I think I actually saw the Discovery program on the Canary Islands volcano years ago, back when it first came out. But it was so hyperactive and sensationalist I switched channels and forgot all about it." He shook his head. "I can't believe I didn't make the connection when Hansebi was ranting about conspiracy theories and tsunamis. Getting old, I guess."

"Not to mention, that was before the 'Great Crested Canary' reference at the drilling site."

"Still ..."

Ace didn't know what to say. More macho bullshit, more evidence her dickhead partner insisted upon carrying the weight of the world on his shoulders. She scrolled back toward the top of the search screen. "Here it is. A link to the show on the Discovery Channel." She stared at her mentor. "I can't believe you spend your downtime watching educational programs on television."

"Why? What do you watch?"

"Talk shows during the day. You know, Oprah, Ellen ... pretty anybody but Maury Povich or Jerry Springer. It doesn't require much energy, plus I can improve my language skills."

"Let me guess. Action adventure and police procedural shows at night ... *Criminal Minds, Quantico*, etc. ... to improve your spy skills."

She wrinkled her nose. "Fuck that shit. If it's bedtime, I just dial up some porn. You know, to ..."

Dick threw her a startled glance and held up a hand. "Stop right there. I get the picture."

"Oh, you do, do you?"

Her partner turned his full attention back to the road. "You've got more than an hour until we get to the airport. Read up on Cumbre Vieja, the volcano on La Palma in the Canary Islands. It's got a crack along the summit ... you know on a great, crested Canary ... and they say when that breaks off, the massive landslide will take out the whole east coast of the United States. Which, right now, seems kind of important, so get to it. This isn't down time."

"Yes, sir," she replied.

She started to scroll through the items and click on the more substantive links. But she'd only gone through a couple when she noted movement out of the corner of her left eye and looked up to see a military plane take off from a runway on the north side of the road. "I thought you said we had more than an hour to the airport."

"We do. Upolu's on the north edge of the Kohala coast."

She nodded toward a small control tower where the plane had taken off. "And why aren't we connecting to our flight there? Much higher elevation. Dry as a bone up here."

"Military base. Bradshaw Army Airfield. Getting Nine-to-Five Charters clearance to land at a military field is much more complicated and much higher profile." He sighed. "It would be nice if you occasionally assumed I knew what I was doing."

#

Wet Work

Taren Sykes didn't bother to duck as he alighted from the helicopter. He knew the machine's specs, including the flex in the blades and the power of their rotation when idling; he also knew his height and weight with precision. He had nothing to fear and, unlike most of mankind, he didn't flinch when something merely *appeared* to be dangerous.

He strode across the dedicated helicopter pad and into the nearby communications center, where his foreman, Chad Hanson, waited. The blue collar roustabout had a soda can in one hand, accompanied by what was clearly a chaw of tobacco in his cheek. A practiced squirt of spit connected the two disgusting items mere moments before Chad offered Taren his calloused, stained hand to shake in ritual camaraderie.

Taren didn't bother to take it. "Is everything ready?"

Chad grunted. "Sure. Told you that on the sat-phone. Didn't need to fly your whirlybird all the way out here for that."

"I like to see things firsthand. And you know I don't like streaming confidential information over data lines when it can be avoided. Show me the most recent reports. Now that the final push of the plan is in motion, I don't want to miss the optimal window for consummation."

Chapter 21

Dick took the turn-off toward Waimea when the opportunity arose, continuing toward their destination on high ground, rather than dropping down to the more crowded and, no doubt, devastated coast. Traffic tightened up as the road traveled through Parker Ranch into town. Not surprisingly, the gas stations, hardware stores, and grocery marts in town were all mobbed. The Hawaiian Islands weren't self-sustaining at the best of times—with significant destruction from the tsunami affecting residential, commercial, and agricultural areas, he had no doubt supplies of pretty much everything had plummeted just as demand was skyrocketing due to heightened needs for reconstruction. Good thing he didn't need to gas up to get to their destination.

They stopped at a local diner—no sense beating the plane to the airport. Service was slow and the food mediocre, though the portions were surprisingly hefty. Apparently no one had given the short-order cook the memo about supplies being short going forward. Dick focused on his food; Ace focused on her research. Dick didn't mind. A good spy, like a good soldier, doesn't need chit-chat. He eats, sleeps, and loads his weapon whenever given the opportunity.

The meal completed, they returned to the vehicle and Dick wound his way through the rest of the small town. Finally, he headed out along the ridge road to the Kohala Coast and pulled onto the beltway road. All the while, Ace continued her web surfing, earbuds in, eyes glued to the screen of her laptop. Finally, she looked up and pulled on the white cord until her earbuds fell into her lap.

"Okay, let me make sure I've got this. There's a three-mile-long, up to fifteen foot wide crack on La Palma in the Canary Islands, along the flank of the Cumbre Veija volcano. If the volcano splits apart at the crack, a chunk of the volcano up to ten miles long and a mile thick could let loose. And if all of this slides six thousand feet down the mountain, picking up speed the whole way on one of the steepest places on Earth, and continues all the way to the sea floor thousands and thousands of feet below sea level—an event which releases, according to the more sensationalist posts, up to seven thousand megatons—that would create a tsunami more than two thousand feet high locally."

"That's what they say."

"And this tsunami would propagate at the speed of a jet liner to the coasts of Africa, Europe, and eventually the east coast of the United States, Mexico, and South America. Africa gets the worst of it, with at least a three hundred foot inundation, but only eight to ten hours later the entire east coast gets hit with, not just one, but up to twenty waves spaced ten to thirty minutes apart, anywhere from thirty to several hundred feet high."

Dick nodded. "You can quibble all you want about the size calculations and about how remote the possibility of this type of an event occurring is, but the fact is the geologic evidence shows such collapses have happened before, and tsunamis of that size have hit land with devastating effect." He wrinkled his nose. "Not just the Alika events Hansebi talked about in Hawaii, but slides at …"

Ace waved her hand dismissively. "Yeah, yeah, I get all that. But, you know, after reading all this stuff, I can't help but think this Canary Islands thing is just like the Great Crack."

Dick tossed her a sideways glance. "Duh. That's why I told you to look at it. You got a short term memory problem?"

"No. I mean it's *just like* the Great Crack. You get a bunch of YouTube videos and half-baked, self-published thrillers all hyperactive and breathless about how some chunk of land is going to fall off an island and create a killer mega-tsunami, but when you push through and get to some actual science—you know, PDFs of academic papers and shit, it pretty much all gets debunked. Actual scientific studies say the whole scenario is predicated on a huge chunk of land releasing at great speed all at once, but the historical evidence of prior flank collapses on the sea floor near La Palma suggests they all occurred in smaller sub-units incapable of creating the type of mega-tsunami all the scaremongers talk about."

"So? Hansebi said the whole Great Crack thing was bunk, too, yet we just had a devastating tsunami which will affect the whole island chain, including everything from real estate prices to the tourist industry, for years and years to come. And the evidence is that the Aliki events were huge."

Ace shrugged. "I'm just saying the Canary Island event—even if it happens—might not be as big a deal as the programming guys at the Discovery Channel make out."

"So what? In some ways it doesn't matter what actually happens. If all goes according to plan, tens of millions of people die, coastal infrastructure is destroyed on at least four continents, and chaos and misery reigns over a large chunk of the Earth, with disease, starvation, and revolution as byproducts. If things don't turn out as well as the bad guy's wet dreams, then fewer people die, less infrastructure is destroyed, and there's a diminished quantum of chaos, riots, and misery, but there's still plenty of death and destruction."

He focused on the road as he ranted, looking for a sign for his turn-off. "Let's assume whoever is behind this is an anarchist. He doesn't have a specialized agenda, like the PPIPF. He probably doesn't even care much whether this works well because he's an anarchist, not a terrorist. He wants to create confusion, panic, and turmoil."

"Nothing like threatened disaster to breed panic," Ace admitted.

171

Wet Work

"He wants the governments of the world to look incompetent because they couldn't stop his plan. The partially failed Hawaiian attempt doesn't hurt him much in terms of those goals. Let's say he first sets off a landslide of some type, like in Hawaii."

"I'd say he's been there and done that."

"Then he moves on to the next stage, with a much bigger potential for devastation. If a warning is given and is taken seriously, but not much happens, trust in government goes down. If the warning is *not* given, or is given and not taken seriously because the damage wasn't overwhelming here in Hawaii, *and the plot works*, there is massive disruption to the economic and structural underpinnings of civilized society. Today was a success for our guy—whoever he may be—as part of the total plan. I'd bet money the PPIPF is boasting about how they caused all this by fracturing the Great Crack and that it's getting a lot of air time."

Ace closed her laptop and began idly rolling up the cord for her ear buds. "Sure, but today's event wasn't really from the Great Crack. It was from something else—fracking a completely different rift line. The Great Crack was just cover."

She was beginning to piss Dick off. "What's your point? You don't think we should go to the Canary Islands and check out the big crack there? We should just trust that nobody's trying to break off a giant slab of earth to kill millions of people because someone wrote a *paper* which says it might not be as big a deal as he hopes?"

Ace looked out the window. "No. We go to the Canaries, for sure. We just need to focus on how the Cumbre Vieja crack could be a cover for a more ... dependable ... means of generating a mega-tsunami."

Dick turned off the main road onto a single lane, paved roadway heading straight for the ocean. "Roger that."

As Ace's attention drifted away from her research and their operational conversation, Dick watched her head swivel back and forth, taking in the tall weeds and unadorned, narrow asphalt strip leading them downslope toward the drop-off to the ocean. Finally, she spoke. "You sure we're on the right road? This doesn't look like the entrance to an airport."

"It's a small, private airport used by the ultra-rich and famous to fly in and out to their private pieces of paradise without having to put up with riff-raff."

She looked at him and frowned. "So the ultra-rich and famous like six foot tall grassy weeds and no shoulders on a one lane road?"

Dick pursed his lips. "Back in the fifties, when a lot of the national laboratories were established, did you know the United States government planted lots of evergreens around the perimeter of the properties?"

"*Kurva!* Do you know the landscape design practices for government installations in Czechoslovakia forty years before you were born?"

"The thought was that when the trees grew up, they would keep spies with binoculars from looking in at what was going on. Of course, by the time the trees were full grown, the enemy had satellites and Wikileaks working for them."

"A fascinating bit of trivia I'll be sure to remember for the rest of my life—assuming I kill myself immediately. Why do I care?"

"Limited access. Not much signage. Tall grass. All impediments to *paparazzi.*"

The air strip didn't have much more to it than the access road. A single runway paralleled the coastline; a chain link fence protected the far side of the strip or, perhaps, the drop-off to the ocean beyond. As they approached, a lone attendant meandered out of a small terminal

173

to the left of where the access road teed into the crushed gravel surrounding the runway. Dick stopped the car and the two of them got out to meet their greeter halfway.

"Aloha," he muttered, bringing up a clipboard. "You here for the ..." He glanced down at a printout, "... Nine to Five Charters flight?"

"That would be us."

"Both of you?"

Ace spoke up. "Yeah. Is there a problem with that?"

The attendant nodded toward the car. "Can't park here."

Before Ace could reply, Dick took charge. "Somebody will be by to pick up the car," he lied. "Surprised they're not here yet."

"Yeah, well not a lot is running on schedule today. My name is Vince Sklar. C'mon, you can wait inside, out of the sun. Plane will pull up right to the tarmac on the other side of the building." He turned and headed back to the terminal, then stopped and twisted his shoulders back toward them. "Oh, gotta do an agricultural screening on your bags, too, so you might as well fetch 'em now."

"Don't have any luggage," replied Dick.

Ace piped in. "Lost our luggage in the tsunami. Oceanside resort and all."

Vince shrugged. "Well, if you can afford a charter flight, I expect you can afford new clothes."

They entered the empty, but tastefully decorated, terminal. Ace headed straight for the women's restroom, while Vince sauntered toward a counter.

"Speaking of lost items," I need a phone. Is there a pay telephone I could use here?"

"Nah," replied Vince. "What with minimal traffic and everyone using their cell phones, the phone company pulled it out a while back."

174

Dick frowned, pushing out his lower lip for emphasis. "Need to let someone know I'm headed back and connecting up through the cockpit of the plane is always a hassle." Dick pulled a twenty out of his pocket. "You don't think I could borrow ..."

Vince reached into his front pocket and pulled out an Android, handing it to Dick with one hand while he snatched up the twenty with his other. Dick took it and turned away, walking toward the far corner of the mid-sized room as he dialed.

"Don't forget to give that back," Vince called after him. "I'm loaning it to you, not selling it."

Dick flashed him a thumbs up as he put the phone to his ear.

"Hello?" Seth's voice was sleepy and uncertain. Jeez, it was evening back home already.

"Seth, buddy. It's Dad. Just checking in from ... uh ... Seoul to see how you were doing."

"Pretty much the same. Doc says I may get out in a few days—start doing my physical therapy on an out-patient basis. Of course, that's going to mean a lot of driving for Mom."

"I'm sure she won't mind. And, I'll pick up my share of the back and forth once I get home."

"So, how's South Korea?"

"C'mon, Seth. You know all of my business trips are literally to the shittiest places in the world. That's the job. Besides, you know what the biggest problem is with South Korea? It's right next to North Korea. I'm told they still squat in the bushes there. Hell, when I've got this place humming again, the North may invade just so their shoes aren't as full of shit as their Supreme Leader."

Seth chuckled. Damn, it was good to hear his kid laugh again, after all the pain and rehabilitation he had been through. "Hang on a sec, Mom wants to talk to you."

Uh-oh. "Hey, Melanie. I was about to ask Seth if you were around."

"Really?" his wife replied, her voice cold. "You didn't take my call earlier."

"I'm not always at liberty to take personal calls. Sometimes I am, you know, legitimately busy."

"Yeah, you seemed to be getting pretty busy the last time we talked." When Dick didn't immediately respond, Melanie continued, her tone harsh, but hushed. "And you didn't call me back for hours. Even now, you called Seth, not me. I was worried. With everything going on, I was worried."

"Watch what you say," Dick snapped, his voice sounding angrier to his own ears than he intended. "We can't have this conversation now, not with Seth in the same room. Nothing is 'going on' in Seoul, and Seth doesn't know where I'm actually calling from."

Her voice dropped to a whisper, echoing as if she had cupped her hand over her mouth and the receiver. "There were tsunami warnings for the whole Pacific basin."

"Seoul's not on the coast and the closest saltwater is west, not east of it. Seth is smart enough to know that." He let out a sigh and softened his words. "I'm fine, though. Thanks for your concern."

"I'm glad to hear that. I worry about you ... now more than before, even more than when you were a cop. It's like you're in the Army again and deployed in a combat zone."

"One of the many reasons why the Subsidiary doesn't want spouses to know what's really going on. Look, I just wanted to check in. I'm getting on a plane in a few minutes, so I'll be completely unreachable for a while"

Melanie's tone perked up, no doubt for Seth's benefit. "Well, Seth and I are both looking forward to your return."

"Me, too, but I'm not on my way home yet."

"Oh?"

"I'm headed to the Canary Islands. I'll wave from the plane as we go past, assuming we fly that way around the world."

"A tropical island." Melanie's tone was once again flat and louder than he liked. He started to hush her, but she continued. "Work takes you to some nice places."

Crap. He heard Seth in the background. "Dad's going to a tropical island?" This was one of the many other reasons the Subsidiary didn't allow spies to let their spouses know what, where, who, and why they were doing. His mind raced for a way to fix this, but he wasn't in control of the situation. Melanie had the phone; he couldn't even lie to his own kid to fix this because Seth couldn't hear him.

He heard Melanie talking, but not into the phone. "Your dad has to stop in Hawaii when he finishes up in Seoul. Apparently the tsunami did a lot of damage to the wastewater treatment infrastructure there."

Nice save. Who knew Melanie could be such a glib and effective liar? For the briefest moment he was pleased. Then he realized what that ability might portend. He lived a lie at work; he hoped she hadn't been living a lie at home.

"Let me know when you can what your schedule will be," she said to Dick.

"Will do," he replied. "Love you."

"Love you, too."

He thumbed up the phone and turned around to see Ace leaning against a counter less than twenty feet away, staring out toward the Pacific and Maui. Fuck. How long had she been there? How much had she heard? Fuck. Fuck. Fuck.

He padded toward her, veering to the right a few steps only to hand Vince back his cell phone. "Figured I should call my kid in the hospital while I had a chance, you know."

177

"Of course," said Ace, without looking at him. "What else could you possibly be doing?"

Chapter 22

Dee Tamany sat at the head of the table in the conference room used for virtual meetings. Glenn Swynton sat next to her, quite literally her right-hand man. The huge screen opposite them added their virtual avatars to the array of avatars of the ten-nation oversight board for the Subsidiary. Those for Brazil, France, Germany, India, Russia, and the United Kingdom were already on-screen. The United States followed. Australia and Japan joined within a few seconds of the appointed time. China logged on exactly two minutes late, a habit which had begun after Thornby's previous mission.

At first, Dee had attributed China's recurring, intentional tardiness as a passive-aggressive rebuke for the Subsidiary's refusal to turn over Luke Calloway to them for interrogation in connection with the Reality 2 Be matter. But as the rude behavior persisted, she saw it for what it truly was ... yet another of their many ways of saying they didn't like meetings run by women, especially strong, confident women like Deirdre Tammany, Director of the Subsidiary. One didn't have to hold a double major in communications and psychology to see the Chinese felt threatened by women in power.

She decided to gently tweak them about their petty behavior. "This meeting is convened, *all* members finally being present." The sophisticated real-time audio synthesizer electronically modulated voice communications during these meetings. Though the representatives all knew who the Subsidiary personnel were, the automatic modulation meant each of the national representatives was anonymous from each of the others—the flag of the appropriate nation (or, in the case of the Subsidiary officials, their title within the organization) glowed to cue who was talking. The flat electronic voices produced by such modulation, however, also meant any sarcasm in Dee's tone was stripped out, which was probably for the best.

Dee continued, without waiting for any response from the others. She liked to control not only the presentation of information at these gatherings, but the flow of discussions. "Although the Pan-Pacific Indigenous People's Front has claimed responsibility for the tsunami which inundated the coast of the Hawaiian Islands, with its residual ripples affecting low-lying areas along islands and coastlines of the entire Pacific basin, we do not believe that to be true. Even though the PPIPF was clearly behind a series of explosions along a volcanic crack on the Big Island of Hawaii, the tsunami was triggered by movement along a fault line in a completely different rift zone."

The Japanese flag glowed. "Our scientists interpret the seismic activity similarly, Director. But how do you know the PPIPF didn't use additional explosives along this other rift line, too? Perhaps they simply want to claim credit without giving away the actual details of action in order to hide such mechanisms against possible future use."

"While that is, to be sure, a possibility, we have found no evidence of PPIPF personnel or activity at the locus of the disruption to the predicate fault line."

"Despite that," interrupted the Australian representative, "both we and our Kiwi friends intend to continue to investigate and interrogate known PPIPF operatives, just to be sure."

"Agreed," said the Japanese representative, his avatar giving a curt nod.

China chimed in. "We have already begun rounding up PPIPF thugs, who are, of course, under the corrupting influence of foreign agents."

Dee knew anyone "rounded up" by the Chinese government would probably never see their compatriots or the Pacific Ocean again—but the internal politics of the nations overseeing the Subsidiary was not within her or the Subsidiary's purview.

180

The Stars and Stripes glowed brightly. "That's all well and good, but if those assholes at the PPIPF aren't behind this ... this ... act of war on U.S. soil, then we need to know who the hell is. Do your operatives have anyone in custody? Because we're happy to help with some ... enhanced interrogation techniques if need be."

Glenn Swynton spoke up. "We handle our own interrogation, sir, as you know. Besides, we have no one is custody right now."

"No? What the hell kind of sloppy operation are you running down there? You say the PPIPF isn't behind this. Well, who is?"

"That remains to be seen," Glenn reported. "The operation on the Big Island left no survivors behind to question, but we are following up on electronic leads."

"Electronic leads to whom?" demanded the U.S. delegate.

Dee stepped in. "We have no information on who, but we do have a lead as to a possible next action. Our agents are currently *en route* to the Canary Islands on the slim ... let me emphasize that ... *slim* ... possibility whoever is behind this may attempt a similar seismic action on La Palma. They should be landing there any minute."

"La Palma?" queried the French representative. "*Mon Dieux!* Please tell me you are not suggesting someone is attempting to unleash a tsunami by destabilizing Cumbre Vieja."

Dee could almost visualize the various aides sitting behind the delegates scrambling on their portable devices to look up "Cumbre Vieja" so their principals could appear informed as the virtual conference call continued.

"That scenario is being investigated as a possible follow-up to the Hawaiian tsunami," Dee admitted. She had to tread carefully here. Even the overseers of an international spy agency could panic. "But all of our scientific information suggests that, like the Great Crack scenario on Hawaii, popular theories about such an event are over-hyped and the cataclysmic damage scenarios theorized by some are way out of proportion to what might potentially occur, even if the effort was successful."

The Russian representative spoke. "The Discovery program was quite convincing to the contrary, Director Tammany."

Uncle Sam broke in. "Somebody gonna tell me what in God's sake we're talking about here?" Apparently the U.S. delegate didn't have a subordinate surfing for information for him during the call.

Glenn spoke up and recited the basics, mentioning the worst case scenarios offered up by reality television and YouTube panic-mongers, but emphasizing the difficulty in triggering any landslide and the unlikelihood of significant waves emanating therefrom. That set off a hubbub of comments of alarm and concern which she let work itself out for several minutes, contenting herself with the show of flags blinking and strobing as the various delegates tried to dominate the conversation.

Finally, the French delegate asked her a direct question. "How many agents have you assigned to preventing this looming disaster?"

"Two," she replied. The automatic audio modulation did nothing to mask the gasp she heard from the avatar beneath the French flag. "This possibility ... this remote possibility ... was developed during the course of the Hawaiian operation and is being pursued by the same team with, of course, the full support of our team here at headquarters in Philadelphia, with any needed assistance from our various field offices throughout the world."

The Union Jack glowed bright. "I don't recall the Subsidiary has any local field office in the Canary Islands ... or anywhere in close proximity, if my memory serves."

"Your memory serves you well, as always," replied Dee. "Our closest full field office is ..." She snapped her fingers twice and Glenn turned the screen of his tablet for her to read. "... in Barcelona, Spain. Director of Operations Swynton will be briefing them as soon as this call ends."

"But ... but ... that is hours away from the scene by helicopter or even private jet," said the French representative. "Why hasn't a Lightning Team already been dispatched?"

Glenn spoke up. Since he was Director of Operations, Dee knew it was appropriate for him to do so. "Lightning Teams are not investigative forces. They have neither the training nor the subtlety required to ferret out information without attracting attention, especially in a setting as bucolic and uncrowded as the Canary Islands. Their strong suit is quick, decisive, military action. Their presence ... even their approach ... would be noticed by any capable opponent, driving them underground or, perhaps, accelerating their timetable for whatever nefarious conduct they have in mind. Lightning Teams are used only as a last resort to protect the anonymity and the activity of the Subsidiary in keeping the world safe. They are generally only brought in if requested by the agents in the field in charge of the operation."

The American flag lit up. "And who might those be?"

Dee answered. "Agents Dick Thornby and Acacia Zyreb."

"Thornby," mused the United States delegate. "I don't usually pay much attention to who's doing what where, but isn't he the guy who was running around under the Denver airport a while ago? The agent who triggered our recent review of the organization's nuclear protocols?"

"And," added Japan, "the man who destroyed the harbor facilities in Dunedin, New Zealand?"

Australia joined in. "Not really fond of ports, is he?"

"He is a very dangerous and impetuous agent," interjected China. "We continue to be mystified why this man has not been eliminated from the Subsidiary. He adds nothing but chaos and destruction to Subsidiary affairs."

"Mr. Thornby's continued employment is an operational matter outside of your concern, representatives. And I am quite certain China is not nearly as mystified as to what Thornby's contributions are or have been as you assert." Dee paused and calmed herself before continuing. "In any event, this Canary Island possibility would not even be the subject of an ongoing investigation if not for Mr. Thornby's instincts, actions, analysis, and persistence. We stand by our man." The sentiment was correct, but she regretted the phrase as soon as she'd said it. Now she'd have Tammy Wynette running through her head for the rest of the day. She'd better ask Mitzi to put on some more contemporary hits when she got home or she'd fall asleep to the country western tune. She had enough cowboys to deal with in real life; she didn't need to dream about them.

"Still," offered up Brazil, traditionally the most reticent of the national representatives, "as a nation with a significant Atlantic coastline—albeit it far distant from La Palma—might it not be best if a Lightning Team was standing a bit closer to your man than in Barcelona?"

Glenn answered without bothering to glance at Dee for permission. "I will look into forward staging possibilities right away, sir."

"We'd best get to it, then," added Dee. "This meeting is concluded." She pressed a button, terminating the feeds. Only after she was sure they were all off did she turn to Glenn Swynton. "Not long ago we were undecided about Thornby's continued utility to the Subsidiary, so we assigned him a low-level nuisance investigation with a new recruit. Now I'm betting both our jobs are riding on him not screwing up."

184

Glenn sniffed, his lip twitching, but his face conveyed no emotion. "It could be worse."

"How's that?"

"We could have given him explosives."

"I wouldn't count on that," replied Dee, her voice weary from the stress of the meeting. "He had only minimal explosives in Dunedin and that fire took days to put out."

Chapter 23

Charter jets are nicer for flying long distances than coach in a commercial jetliner, but twenty-odd hours in the air (plus, stops to refuel) still made for a grueling trek. Sure, it wasn't like spending a year traversing the Oregon Trail, braving dysentery and, well, Indian braves, but you couldn't really stretch your legs, and Dick worried about deep-vein thrombosis when he spent too much time sitting. How people handled desk jobs, he never could understand.

Not surprisingly, the airport on La Palma was on the shore—typical of island airports—but it was larger and much busier than Upolu. The ledge of volcanic rocks holding the single runway jutted out marginally from the east coast of the island, meaning either end of the runway was over water. Oddly, the taxiway and the terminal were both on the ocean side of the runway. Coming in for a landing, Dick saw jets and propeller planes with logos for Condor, AirBerlin, Binter Canarias, and CanaryFly, among others.

The pilot of their Nine-to-Five Charter taxied the private jet to the main terminal and dropped them off without shutting down the engines, then headed away for refueling. They didn't know how long they'd be here; the jet wasn't going to hang around waiting for them. Nine to Five had arranged for them to be pre-cleared by Customs, so there was no need to wait in line with passports in hand and no need to worry about getting the matching weaponry they'd been supplied on board through inspection. And, since the Quartermaster had included backpacks to carry their requested equipment and necessities, it was an easy hike to the main terminal, which featured clean, but modest facilities typical of tourist destinations. Apparently, a lot of Europeans vacationed in the Canary Islands—no doubt due to the year-long temperatures in the 60s and 70s and the abundance of sunshine.

Given the snatches of conversation Dick heard as he passed other passengers, Germans seemed especially predominant among the visitors, although the locals, of course, spoke Spanish.

Fortunately, Dick knew all of the airport vendors likely spoke English, so he would have no trouble picking up the vehicle the pilots had called ahead to reserve, assuming he could find the right counter. He stopped for a moment next to an array of brightly colored seats for waiting travelers, the bold primary colors (blue, red, purple, and lime green) of the chairs competing for his attention with the directional placards and advertising within the terminal.

Ace didn't stop, instead elbowing him as she passed and nodding ahead and to the left. "Rental cars are down here."

Dick looked where she pointed, but didn't see any obvious sign. "You sure?"

"Vacationed here once for ..." She pursed her lips, then continued, "... what I think you would call 'Spring Break' during my training classes. Trust me, if you grew up in Prague, you'd go someplace sunny every chance you got, too. Italy's nearer, but La Palma is less crowded than most of the Mediterranean playgrounds. Cheaper, too. Cloudier than the rest of the Canaries—I guess because it's the farthest west and gets the moist marine winds before the others. Certainly the west side is cloudier than the east. Fair-skinned northern Europeans don't mind a bit of cloud cover. Especially on the nude beaches."

"I'm glad you have fond memories of your youth ... a couple years back, but I don't really need the tourist pitch," growled Dick.

Ace slitted her eyes. "Fine. Let's just get our four-wheel drive and head out for the Route of the Volcanoes and we can repeat our Hawaiian hike down a volcanic crack full of sharp rocks and occasional explosives."

Dick nodded. "Vehicle, yes." He shook his head. "Hiking *La Grieta*—the crack—no. I don't really see the point."

"We found explosives the last time."

"Sure, superficial devices whose only purpose was to get the PPIPF to take credit for the tsunami, shifting investigatory attention away from the real assholes behind the fracking of the other rift."

"Maybe the same thing's happening here. There's a small group of activists who want the Canary Islands to be entirely free of Spanish control. They don't have much political clout and their history of violence has been pretty minimal, but almost every place has some kind of secessionist movement."

"Maybe," mused Dick. "Of course, from what I understand, some people say Morocco's behind the whole secessionist brouhaha for its own purposes."

"Support from a bigger player like Morocco might mean they actually have the wherewithal to pull off some kind of explosion."

"Yeah, but what's the end game?"

Ace frowned at him. "What do you mean? Secessionist movement causes explosion, kills innocent people, gets attention for their cause even though it really doesn't change anything. *Kurva.* It's a pretty standard terrorist routine."

They arrived at the rental desk. "Maybe," said Dick. "But I think you're missing a big problem with how that routine would play out here." He pulled out his wallet and waved for the attention of a clerk. "Think it over. We'll talk more in the car."

#

Ace went to the combination gift shop and souvenir stand nearby and snagged a couple of maps, including one with hiking trails just in case they did head out to search *La Grieta* despite her partner's sudden,

188

maddening reservations. Sure, the long flight made her crabby, but what really infuriated her was the whole "quiz show" routine Dick was constantly pulling, hinting he had already figured things out and goading her until she stumbled upon whatever he wanted her to say, as if that made the analysis correct. She was younger and less experienced, sure, but she wasn't stupid. And, she had knowledge and skills he didn't. Dick wasn't just a dick, he was a dinosaur. And she was the pesky little mammal scurrying around the dinosaur's massive feet—just staying out of its way long enough for it to go extinct and for her kind to take over the fucking planet.

She finished her shopping and caught back up with the big guy as he strode toward the parking lot for the rental company while twirling a key chain around one finger of his beefy paw. She clambered in the passenger seat as he adjusted the rearview mirrors to his liking.

"Figure it out yet?" he asked.

"*Kurva to hovno.* I'm not going to play 'tell me what I'm thinking' with you."

"Suit yourself, but your analytical skills only get better if you exercise them from time to time."

She didn't respond. In fact, she made a point of staring out the passenger window as Dick navigated out of the airport and headed south.

"The PPIPF mooks, they wanted a moderate-sized tsunami because, well, they all lived *mauka* and the wave would mostly hurt the *haoles* and tourists they despise. And even if they believed, against the scientific evidence, the Great Crack explosions would result in a tsunami, they were smart enough to know it wouldn't be a big one— not like the Aliki tsunamis."

"Why's that?"

189

"Because the volcanic slope on that flank of Mauna Loa's just not as steep as the other sides. Even a big landslide there is only gonna move so fast."

"So?"

"So, the cracked slope on Cumbre Vieja is much steeper and, according to some of the reports I was reading during the flight from hell, the inferred slope which the debris field of the western slope rests on is even steeper. So, if you presume it gives way—or you take some kind of action to make sure it does—chances are whatever you dislodge makes its way all the way to the ocean floor, which makes a hell of a big splash."

Her brow knitted. "So, now you agree with Ward & Day's original paper suggesting a mega-tsunami is possible? Even though all of the smart, scientific papers since say they're full of crap?"

"Longshots do win sometimes. You can't look at recent events in U.S. politics and deny that basic truth." She started to reply, but he just kept on rolling along, like he did at the last stop sign. "But what I'm saying is slightly different. I'm saying that if someone is trying to trigger a collapse at Cumbre Vieja, *they* believe it's going to work and if it does work, it's going to do so big time."

Realization flooded her mind like an engulfing tsunami. "Which means the waves which hit locally could be two thousand or more feet high, which means almost no place—at least no place regularly inhabited on the island—will be safe. So the bad guys won't be here when things happen."

"Bingo," said Dick. "Not only won't the bad guys be on-island when things go down, no one from here is likely to buy into this plan in order to promote secession or independence or any of that shit, 'cause there won't be anyone or anything of importance left locally if this plan works."

190

"That makes sense," Ace admitted. Why hadn't she figured that out? But now, even when she knew that searching *La Grieta* for explosives was likely a waste of time, she was at a loss as to what was the next step. There was only one way to find out.

She looked over a Dick. "What's the plan?"

Dick shrugged. "We drive up to the top of Cumbre Vieja and check out *La Grieta*."

"Screw you," snapped Ace. "Didn't you just go through a long explanation as to why some local terrorist group wouldn't be planting explosives in this crack?"

"Yeah."

"So why are we going up the volcano?"

Dick scrunched up his nose. "One, we could be wrong. We need to know for sure. Two, we need to see if anyone is drilling volcanic cores there for research, like in Hawaii. Three, it's got a helluva view."

#

Taren Sykes leaned back against the lush leather of the oversized seat in his private jet. Having finished off his most excellent meal with a dark chocolate mousse drizzled with raspberry compote, he had time for a short nap before he landed in Geneva in just over an hour. He had barely closed his eyes, however, when he sensed someone hovering over him. He arched his right eyebrow, the lid of his right eye following just enough to open sufficiently for him to see Savatini fidgeting and looking back and forth anxiously between his phone and Sykes.

"What?" Sykes murmured.

"There may be an issue."

"No," replied Sykes. "There may or may not be a problem. If there's something you need to report for me to discern that, then we already have an issue."

Savatini nodded. "We have an issue, sir."

Sykes sat up and rolled his shoulders after they left the comfort of the soft leather. Both eyes were open now. "What is it?"

Savatini cleared his throat. "As you know, sir, we've been monitoring the incoming flights to La ..."

Sykes cut him off with a sharp flick of his right wrist. "If I know something, don't waste time telling me what I already know." He sighed. "So, a flight landed on La Palma that triggered the protocols. What was the triggering factor? Military flight? One of my short-selling competitors?"

"No, sir. Flight plan. Although it stopped several times for refueling along the way, the overall flight plan filed shows the private jet left a private airfield on the Big Island of Hawaii and flew to La Palma, a combination of locations which we had flagged for obvious reasons, even though it was deemed unlikely anyone not associated with your enterprise would travel such an itinerary."

Any remnants of his incipient food coma fell away. "It appears we were ... and by 'we were' I mean 'I was' ... right to include the flight plan triggers in our protocol." He often marveled at how much detailed effort went into creating anarchy. "Let me see the particulars." Savatini turned his phone, holding it while Sykes read the details about departure time, arrival time, and flight path. He closed his eyes while he calculated a few things. "It appears not only was someone investigating our enterprise, but they were on the Big Island in advance of the seismic event *and* managed to secure a private flight out, more or less directly to La Palma, which means they've either stumbled onto or deduced the endgame."

192

"Yes, sir."

"Increase security on site."

"Of course, sir."

"And have our local intermediary detain these interlopers, if possible. Better yet, eliminate them."

Savatini paled. "We don't have any identification on the passengers yet, sir. We're pulling up airport security video, but that might take some time."

"So we've got nothing?"

"Uh, well, not quite, sir. We know a rental vehicle was reserved by the charter flight company when they landed."

"That will do. Get me Dian Nordando in the Philippines. I need him to do an encore performance."

#

Dee stuck her head inside Glenn Swynton's office. "Any word from Thornby or Zyreb?"

Glenn's eyes narrowed. "No. Getting Thornby to check in is problematic at the best of times. He prefers to ... what's the American expression? ... go rogue. I'm afraid Ms. Zyreb may be learning some bad habits from him."

Dee walked into the office and sat in one of the chairs on the opposite side of the desk from her Director of Operations. "I don't know about you, but if my job ... and possibly millions of lives and billions of dollars in infrastructure alone ... are on the line, I don't like sitting around reading reports about mundane things like who Wikileaks is going to out next or how the Russian mob is using Facebook quizzes to ferret out personal information so they can steal the identities of witless users. I want to do something to help stop the big bad." Mitzi had taught her that last phrase, explaining that fans of popular televisions shows from *Buffy* to *The Walking Dead* used it to describe the antagonist for season-long plot arcs. It was apt in the real world, too.

Glenn put down the paperwork he had been going through. "I concur. Let's talk it through. Step one. Who gains by causing a mega-tsunami?"

Dee took a deep breath. "Well, let's start with who loses. Owners of coastal real estate, for starters."

"Hard to capitalize on that directly," mused Glenn. "There are few ways to 'short' real estate, especially on a broad, multi-national basis. I suppose in developed markets like the United States and Britain, you might be able to short baskets of mortgage securities, betting they will go down because of increased default rates. But that market is much smaller and less fluid than it was before the 2008 housing crash, and the baskets don't differentiate based on coastal locations. So it's an imperfect match to boot."

"Someone could just bet on an overall market decline, perhaps leading to an economic crisis."

"True," said Glenn. "But also an imperfect match. No, I think a narrower focus is the right approach. We just need something with more liquidity and a broader array of players than baskets of mortgage securities."

"Insurance company stocks would likely plummet. Sure, there are some big mutuals which don't have shareholders. But any publicly-held company with a large exposure to the residential or commercial real estate markets in any of the affected areas would take a huge hit, even with a moderate-sized tsunami affecting such a broad area."

Glenn started to nod, then stopped and frowned. "But aren't terrorist acts excluded from most coverage?"

"Sure, but who's going to tell the world this is a terrorist act?" She shook her head. "Not me. Not any of the constituent members of the oversight panel. Sure, groups like the PPIPF might claim credit, but what sane government is going to confirm that? It's political suicide, not only because it amounts to telling a devastated citizenry that the government failed to stop terrorists from doing this to them, but because the admission would mean insurance companies don't have to chip in for the reconstruction. Leaders lie, sometimes for the good of their constituents, but dependably when it comes to saving themselves." She reflected on the issue. "Insurance companies should definitely be on the list of affected industries. But with someone this Machiavellian, we need to look deeper."

"Insurance won't cover everything, even if they don't go topsy-turvy. Those damaged by the inundation will bear plenty of expense themselves, plus loss of operating profits during the reconstruction."

She agreed. "Public owners of large port facilities on the Atlantic coast."

"Tourism industries," countered Glenn. "Beach vacations are popular on both sides of the pond."

Realization came over her. "Oh my God! Disney. Disney would take a huge hit."

Glenn canted his head to one side. "Orlando's hardly on the coast and Anaheim is high and dry on the opposite side of the country."

Dee waved off his objection. "You're forgetting the potential magnitude of the tsunami. The entire state of Florida is nothing but a huge sandbar, for God's sake. Haven't you seen the climate change maps? If sea levels go up just a couple hundred feet, Florida is all underwater. A tsunami a couple hundred feet high would wash across the whole peninsula." Unwanted images of Florida during trips from her youth flashed through her mind. *It's a Small World After All* started playing in her mind. The manatees would be wiped out. Cape Canaveral would simply be gone. Crap. "The space program would be toast," she muttered. "All the big aerospace companies would take a hit."

"True," said Glenn, unflappable as always. "And not just tech companies. Best add frozen orange juice futures to the list of potential financial manipulations, then."

"What else?"

"This is a good start and we've got an entire research department at our disposal. I'll get the computer jockeys churning out algorithms to search for industries and companies likely to be affected and how someone could gain a financial advantage from such effects. It will take some time, but we can then move to an investigation of who holds a panoply of positions which would, in aggregate, benefit. It could lead us to a suspect."

"Let's hope it's before the other shoe drops."

Glenn smiled. "You Americans are so colorful with your idioms, but you really should treat your footwear better."

Chapter 24

Ace stood near the crater of Cumbre Vieja and did a full circle turn. The island was lush at the lower elevations, with the roads, houses, and infrastructure all crowded near the coast. Above, the jumbled rocks of solidified lava and scrub brush surrounded the pockmarks of volcanic calderas, fumaroles, and vents. In the distance, the deep blue of the Atlantic glistened with diamond flashes under the glare of the sun. It was all beautiful and inspiring and life-affirming and not at all what she wanted to see.

She wanted—no, she and her partner, Dick, *needed*—to see some evidence of what the bad guys were going to do on this "Crested Canary" to cause more than a quarter of the seven hundred plus square kilometer island to crack off and slide rapidly into the ocean. It wasn't that she wanted the disaster to happen or come close to happening but for their interference; it was that she feared what might result if she and Dick couldn't tumble onto the exact plan and how the forces of darkness were endeavoring to make it come to fruition.

She dialed up the magnification on her special Subsidiary-supplied sunglasses and did yet another three-sixty, this time at a slower pace. She saw trees, cell phone towers (some disguised as trees), a lighthouse, and—also near the shore—a few construction cranes. Nothing resembled the type of tall drilling derrick they'd encountered on Hawaii.

Dick walked down from higher up, where he had been engaged in a similar routine, with special emphasis on the area around *La Grieta* and the older, but related, Cumbre Nueva fault lines. He headed toward her. "Well, that's a bust."

"Thanks for noticing," she quipped, drawing a scowl.

He didn't return her banter. "I also checked in with Swynton at the Subsidiary. The cyber-geeks tend to ignore my calls. Anyway, they haven't been able to track any permits for drilling volcanic cores and there aren't many water wells drilled on the island. Population is less than a hundred thousand. A bit closer to that if a couple of the bigger cruise ships happen to be in port. Apparently the volcanic rock lets the rain falling on the windward side seep into caves and tunnels and lava tubes which run through the mountains and deliver fresh water even on the leeward side of the island. Handy for them, I suppose, and interesting to know the entire volcanic substrata is probably soaked with water much of the time. Remember, Hansebi said that can help grease the skids for a low-friction slide of sizeable slabs of rock."

"Yeah," she answered, "but that doesn't get us any closer to what whoever was really behind the Hawaiian tsunami might be doing to get things sliding in the first place. Did you ask about oil drilling operations, too?"

"Nah. Volcanic island. Even Jed Clampett couldn't find any bubbling crude hereabouts."

Jed Clampett? Probably some famous oil explorer from Texas. Her partner watched way too much Discovery and History Channel. Add it to the facts she didn't care if she ever knew. "So, what next?"

Her partner squinted westward. "Still have a few hours of daylight left. Might as well drive around the island. Talk to a few locals. See if we get lucky."

They trekked to the four-wheel drive vehicle, a boxy jeep-like jalopy with a canvas top, and climbed in. It had been a bone-jarring ride up the Route of the Volcanoes. Ace wasn't looking forward to the jolts and jars of the trip back down. Dick had a heavy foot on the petrol in her opinion.

True to form, they hadn't traversed a couple hundred meters downslope when the Dickhead was already cruising faster than she liked, and they hadn't even gotten to the steep part of the route yet.

"Hey, you wanna slow down, big guy? We don't even have a firm destination in mind. I don't need to go nowhere fast."

Dick turned to look at her with narrowed eyes, failing to watch where he was going longer than made her comfortable. "This isn't fast." He grinned and turned to look at the road ahead. Suddenly the vehicle jolted forward. "This is fast."

Guys were assholes the world around when it came to cars, but American guys were the worst by far.

"Ha, ha," she growled. "Very funny. Now slow down before you hit a pothole and rip the transmission off this thing."

She saw Dick immediately take his foot off the gas pedal. The growl of the motor died down in quick response, but the car continued to accelerate because of the slope. Dick was a guy, though, not a psychopath. She saw him shift his foot to the brake pedal and press down. As soon as he did, she saw his upper teeth press onto his lower lip, his mouth forming the classic "F" position before the lower lip slipped forward and his jaw dropped. Anyone who ever watched censored movies on American TV could lip read his expression as he gripped the steering wheel white-knuckled with both beefy hands.

"Fuck!"

Dick's foot jabbed repeatedly at the brake, but nothing happened. The car kept picking up speed as it rapidly approached the steeper portion of the unimproved roadway leading hikers to the pathways at the south end of the Route of the Volcanoes.

"Pull the emergency brake," Dick yelled as he suddenly started yanking the wheel left and right in rapid succession, the car caroming from soft shoulder to soft shoulder, sending dirt and gravel flying.

Was he insane?

She grasped the center-mounted lever for the emergency brake on the second attempt and yanked awkwardly upward. There was no resistance; there was no effect. She stared at Dick in horror for a split second before his gaze shifted to the rock-strewn slope plummeting away on both sides of the steep crest roadway. Dick jerked the gear shift, dropping the transmission into a lower gear, causing the transmission to whine like a banshee. Their momentum slowed and her mood shifted just as rapidly. Then they tilted over to the steeper portion of the descent. In no time, they were plunging just as fast as before. To the right, on the wetter west slope, a tangle of bushes gave way to saplings and trees at lower elevations. Dick continued to slalom from side to side of the narrow roadway as his head jerked from side to side. Ace gritted her teeth as a huge pothole loomed.

Sakra!

Dick seemed to steer straight into it, twisting the steering wheel hard to the right, so the left front tire hit the far edge of the deep divot sideways. She heard an explosive pop as the left front tire burst. The car shuddered for a moment as the corner dipped, slowing the jalopy momentarily before it powered out of the hole, headed for the narrow right shoulder and the rocky slope beyond.

Kurva!

This time her partner didn't turn the wheel back to the left. Instead, they tilted over the edge and the car picked up even more speed. With the left rim slicing into the shallow volcanic grit, the rear of the vehicle slid faster downslope than the front. Dick once again wrenched the steering wheel hard left. Sharp, heavy volcanic rocks bumped against the bottom, tires, and side of the car.

If she hadn't belted in, Ace was sure she would have been thrown into the roll-bar and canvas top of the four-wheel drive, if not thrown out of the vehicle completely. As it was, she hung on for precious life, pressing herself against the seat back, bracing herself as best she could against the terrors of the inevitable, when the car would flip and roll topsy-turvy until it hit a tree or rock too big to dislodge.

Wham! Bam! It was if Dick was aiming for the largest rocks in their path. The car groaned and metal squealed as parts of the undercarriage—exhaust system, oil pan, rocker panels, transmission—were ripped away during their tumultuous descent. The shrubs and trees were coming up faster ... much faster ... than she liked. Seconds before they hit, Dick grabbed the gear shift again, this time forcefully ramming it into reverse. She heard a grinding sound as the car spasmed, a rapid series of jerks slowing the momentum, then a sudden bang as the transmission, no doubt, dropped off the vehicle.

The four-wheel drive jalopy jolted forward, unimpeded by the friction of the gears for a microsecond just as they got to the tree line. She threw her arms over her face to protect herself from being impaled when a branch thrust through the windscreen. She heard the shushing scrape of vegetation envelop the vehicle, then the scraping and snapping of splintering branches, as her body leaned forward from deceleration.

Then, the front of the car seemed to tilt upward and her head nearly bumped into the windshield before the airbags deployed as the jeep slammed to a sudden stop. The airbag thrust her arms hard into her face, which shoved her head into the headrest behind. Then the bag rapidly deflated.

When she lowered her arms and opened her eyes, she saw a miasma of white powder swirling in the air and coating both the car and her. She looked to her left and saw Dick, dusted in white and his face in a fierce expression, like some Kabuki Samurai. His arms were folded over his chest as he gulped in huge breaths of air. His demeanor and his breathing quickly calmed.

Finally, he looked toward her and spoke. "Well, that was interesting."

Kurva to hovno! "Interesting?" She vibrated in rage. "You almost fucking killed us!"

Dick tilted his head to one side. "How's that? I didn't make the brakes fail."

She desperately wanted to get out of the car and stomp away in anger, but a deflated airbag encumbered her movement and her door was pressed against a mass of broken and torn branches. Dick's door, upslope, looked clear.

"Maybe not," she muttered as she took out her knife, snicked it open, and started cutting the airbag away. When she finished, she handed the knife for Dick to follow suit with the driver's airbag as she looked around for a way to exit which didn't involve cowboying her partner. "But you did your best to flip us. Weaving all over the road, hitting every fucking pothole and rock you could, then sending us over the edge into these ..." She gritted her teeth as she gesticulated at the cracked windows to the front and right. "... fucking trees."

Dick's brow creased. "You're right. I slalomed the car from one side of the road to the other. That's how skiers slow down. You go more lateral distance for each foot you drop, which means more friction and marginally less speed. The loose gravel on the shoulders lets the wheels furrow in a bit, too, just like loose snow, and impede forward progress. I dropped into low gear to make the tranny absorb some of the kinetic energy. Every pothole I hit hard did the same thing. Forcing the left front tire to blow meant the rim would dig in to the surface for even more friction, as well as lower the undercarriage, making it closer to the uneven ground so it would bottom out more often. Every rock ripping away at the undercarriage meant more friction and less speed. With a bit of luck, we might have broken an axle and stopped at least one wheel from turning freely altogether. Then, it was just a matter of heading for the softest possible landing. Bushes are better than trees, saplings and scrub trees better than the stout ones. Then I made us hesitate right before impact by cramming the gearshift into reverse. After all, you don't want to stop with too big of a jerk."

She couldn't believe it. This ... this near disaster was just another day at the office for her partner, her supposed mentor.

"No," she said. "You don't want too big of a jerk. You want one that is just right." She shook her head. "Don't try to tell me you were in control the whole time. No one has that much control. That wasn't good driving; that was fucking luck."

She retrieved her knife from Dick and thrust it hard straight up, punching into the canvas above her head and cutting through the thick top. Once she had an opening, she sliced through her seatbelt and stood, clambering out of the car while Dick glowered at her. She trudged up the slope, waving off a few passersby who had started climbing downslope to offer assistance.

"We're not hurt," she yelled. "My dad just thinks he knows how to drive better than he really does."

#

Dick let her get a good head start on the climb back to the road. She needed to vent; she needed to let her anger work its way out of her system. But most of all, she needed to come around to understanding that as a spy, you control as much as you can of any situation and, when things go bad, rely on your training and instincts to control the uncontrollable as best you can. And, if you survive, you always have to believe you survived because of those things. A spy can't believe in luck and function effectively, because when you believe in something, you tend to rely on it.

And he'd rather rely on himself, or even an immature, inexperienced, and impetuous partner, than on luck any day.

Ace was sitting on the side of the road when he eventually made his way up. She had calmed down, but still threw him a nose-twitch and a scowl as he approached.

"Something's bothering me," she said.

"Besides my driving?"

She ignored the jibe. "Why didn't the emergency brake work? I thought they're separate from the main brakes—simply mechanical."

Dick sniffed. "They're used more for parking than actually stopping vehicles at speed. Tourists forget to fully release them and then try to drive all the time. And rental agencies don't check 'em much. Broken cable, probably. Unrelated to the hacking." He looked up and down the road, surprised no crowd of onlookers had surrounded the damsel in distress. "You chase away the Good Samaritans?"

"Somebody called for a tow truck," she offered, "though I can't imagine they have a winch long enough and strong enough to pull that jumbled mess of metal all the way back up here."

"Not our problem," replied Dick. "We just need to get someplace we can pick up a new ride." He dropped down to sit next to her and stared out at the western sky where the sun was dipping in a miasma of orange and purple streaks.

Ace sighed. "That could be a bigger problem than you think. The Good Samaritan said the towing guy told him we weren't the only ones to lose our brakes in the last hour. Same thing happened to a whole shitload of cars. All rentals, as far as he could tell."

Dick smiled. "Even better."

"Better? I just told you there are no cars to be had."

Dick fluttered his hand at her. "I can hotwire a local car when we get back to civilization, so that's not a problem. But the fact that a whole fleet of rental cars apparently got hacked—just like the ones back in Illinois—means several things as relates to our mission, all of them good."

Ace turned her head to look at him. "Lend me you wisdom, Obi-Wan Kenobi." He would have liked the reference, had there not been the hint of a sneer beneath the words. He shrugged it off.

"One, the fact someone tried to kill us means that, despite us running out of leads an hour ago, the bad guys still think we're hot on their trail."

Ace raised one eyebrow.

"Two, the fact they hacked a fleet of rentals to attempt to kill us means they probably don't know who ... or at least where ... we are, so we can sit here pleasantly silhouetted against the sunset without worrying too much there's a sniper lining up a shot as we wait for the green flash when the sun goes down."

Ace snorted. "Mythical."

"Snipers?"

"The green flash."

"Maybe," he replied. He let the subject drop, but as the sun got closer to being swallowed up by the distant horizon, he noticed her gaze lingered on the ocean, as if searching, hoping she was wrong.

"Three, the hacking and the tsunami plots are definitely connected."

"Yeah," she admitted. "But that doesn't get us any closer to figuring out how they're going to drop this ..." She patted the ground. "... into the ocean along with a big-ass chunk of the rest of the island."

Dick ran his tongue across his teeth before answering. "True."

Ace shrugged. "Maybe they got a nuke and they'll just drive a truck into the tunnel underneath Cumbre Vieja north of here—the one that connects the east and west sides of the island—and set it off down there. That would probably do the trick."

"I don't think so." When Ace's eyes flicked to him for a second, he continued. "You made the point with your last phrase: 'That would *probably* do the trick.'"

Ace was back to staring at the sun's glare. "What do you mean?"

"Nukes aren't that easy to get. Believe me, I had to fill out forms in triplicate to get even the low-yield neutron EMP device I used ... well, you know where. Dr. No, or whoever is behind this plot, doesn't have the resources or the access to the stockpiles of the Subsidiary's oversight nations who belong to the nuclear club."

"You can't know that. Hell, Putin might give someone like this a decommissioned nuke just to stir the pot. Russia doesn't have an Atlantic coast, after all, but a lot of its enemies do."

"Sure, but as you said, a nuke in the tunnel might not even do the trick. At best, it's a probability, not a guarantee. It might just release a hell of a geyser of lava; it could release pressure, not ramp it up. And, as we know from the various reports debunking the original Discovery program and the Ward & Day analysis, the landslide triggered might not be big enough or fast enough to cause a tsunami, and the mountain might just dampen the effect of the wave-generating potential of the nuke, itself."

"Maybe."

"That's just it. There's a lot of maybes." He sighed. "The point is that if you are a psychopath *and* you manage to score a nuke, you don't take any chance of wasting it. If I was a bad guy with an atomic bomb and I wanted to cause a shitload of destruction, I'd just detonate it in the middle of ... or just offshore of ... whatever place I hated most. Setting off a nuke in Central Park or New York harbor would screw over America big-time. Not just the death and destruction in New York, but electromagnetic pulse. The EMP fries the electronics of significant parts of the region. If you detonate slightly offshore, you get

206

a bit less direct blast in the populated area, but you get fallout from the water vaporized in the explosion, maybe even a tsunami effect which propagates out to other shores. I'm sure there's a simulation for that somewhere on YouTube."

"Maybe he doesn't hate New York."

"Washington, London, Rio ... same thing. Whatever gives him a hard-on, he can vape at will, with plenty of chaos, destruction, death, and economic devastation to make even the most wild-eyed anarchist or nihilistic financial manipulator overjoyed. Or put the nuke in a private plane and set if off at altitude above Ohio or Belgium or some shit. The EMP would zap everything within hundreds of miles. Now, that's anarchy. Why chance wasting a nuke and getting nothing but fireworks at an out-of-the-way tourist destination? Why use it to set up a line of dominoes that may or may not fall when pushed? No, whoever this ..."

Suddenly, she jumped up, pointing at the horizon, just as the last sliver of light disappeared beneath the waves. "What the fuck was that?"

Had she caught the green flash? Had he missed it? He followed her arm, which was pointing a few degrees north of where the sun had set. Backlit by the gloaming, he saw the large ship in outline. Holy crap! The oranges and purples of the darkening sky poked through the superstructure of a massive drilling derrick.

Chapter 25

Ace was content to wait right where they were for a ride down the volcano to civilization, but Dick insisted they start walking down the slope in the dark because ... well, because those are the kinds of things macho spies do, she guessed. Fortunately for her aching calves and her attitude toward her partner, a convoy of tourist jalopies headed downhill stopped for them. That might have had something to do with the fact Ace insisted on walking down the middle of the narrow roadway, forcing them to halt. Her subsequent plea to the driver to give her and her dad a lift after Dad wrecked the car sealed the deal.

Ace settled in, attempting to get in a comfy position so she could nap on the long drive. Dick, on the other hand, seemed keyed up. He sat by a window and stared out at the passing shops and cars as they made their way back up the coast. Ace would also have been content to let the tourist caravan take them all the way to Santa Cruz de La Palma, or at least the airport, but as they trundled along the coast road Dick jumped from his seat and hollered "Here! We need to get off here."

She had no doubt her mentor needed to get off, but she had no idea why this particular section of mixed commercial and residential buildings along the waterfront was of particular interest. No doubt if she asked, she would get yet another of his teaching lectures. So she said nothing, got up from her seat, and trundled behind her lumbering leader as he exited their handy transport.

Without saying a word, Dick began hiking back along the road, passing three residences, one bed and breakfast with an inviting "vacancy" sign in the window, two bars, and a bodega, before arriving at yet a third bar—this one with a touristy beach theme. He tilted his head toward one of the several surfboards mounted over the doors and windows of the front of the open-air establishment. While the other surfboards were colorfully decorated, this one said *"No Petróleo en Canarias."*

Dick looked over his shoulder at her. "I figured somebody here would be able to tell us about the derrick we saw out to sea."

Ježíší! Didn't the guy ever just relax?

"Just one question before we go in," she said.

"What's that?"

"Daughter or date for this encounter? Don't want to confuse the two. Sure, it's a resort island, but the population is predominantly Catholic."

He stared at her for a beat, then glanced into the surf-themed bar and grill. "Date. No offense, but you're a sucky daughter."

"Okay, I'll do my best not to be a sucky date ... although ..."

"Shut up. Just let me do most of the talking." He walked in, snagging her hand and pulling her gently after him.

Spanish pop music eased out of a quartet of Bose speakers mounted on stripped log support beams. A bar with stools ran along the right side of the shack, perpendicular to the roadway. In the back corner, an old cathode ray tube television set showed a football game between Germany and Spain in progress, but with the sound muted. To the left, a bevy of tables and chairs were arranged haphazardly. Most of the tables were filled with half-empty drinks. Most of the chairs were occupied by tourists, most of them much closer to Ace's age than that of her "date."

Dick held up two fingers. *"Cerveza,"* he said, projecting above the noise of the music and the bawdy hubbub of the young, inebriated crowd. He laid a fifty euro note on the bar. "Let's run a tab." She watched as the bartender, who was closer to Dick's age than that of the crowd, pulled a handle marked "Tropical" and filled two frosted mugs. Dick sidled on to a stool and she did the same, grabbing her brew and downing it in one long, long draught. Light, refreshing, with just a hint of lime, but most importantly, cold. Truth told, she would have preferred a Cruzcampo, with its maltier and slightly hoppy flavor, or even a Dorada Especial, but she didn't think Dick was on a beer-tasting tour. And the most important thing right now wasn't the quality; it was the sheer cold quantity. She tapped the bar to indicate another and Dick looked over at her with a start; he'd barely slurped the meager foam off the top of his beer.

He said nothing to her, however. Instead, he turned his attention to the barkeep, who was already delivering Ace's second brew. Dick tapped his finger, as if absentmindedly, on the fifty euro note still on the bar. "I was hoping you could answer a question."

The bartender's right eyebrow shot up. "I don't sell weed. It hurts the liquor sales."

Dick smiled broadly. "Hah! No, nothing like that." He tilted his head vaguely northward. "When we were watching the sunset a while back, I ... we ... saw a big ship or platform of some type with what looked like it might be an oil derrick on it. What's that all about? I mean, it's a volcanic island, right?"

The bartender scowled. "The idiots in Spain, they pay no attention to the will of the people here. They want oil, they crave oil, so they risk everything ... *everything* ... here in the *Islas Canarias* to satisfy their craving. The fish, the water, the livelihoods of us all, stand in the balance."

"That sounds terrible," agreed Dick. Ace had to admit that, while his interrogation skills were not fancy, Dick knew who to talk to and when to shut up, which was more than half the battle.

"Ahh, we showed them." The bartender jerked his thumb toward the wall behind the bar, which had a photo of a bunch of protesters with signs. "They tried to let the big state petrol company drill east of the islands, in the Cap Juby fields that straddle the maritime border with Morocco, off of Tarfay. But we said, we have wind and sun and geothermal energy. We do not need the black death encircling our happy islands. And, so they have backed down, for now, but we are still on watch."

Ace interrupted. "So, if there is no drilling going on near the islands, why would there be a drilling rig out on the ocean?"

The bartender growled. "Even though no drilling can occur in our waters, the Moroccans, they still risk our homeland with their drilling. And the Mauritanians have rigs all over the Chinguetti oil fields well south. Even Western Sahara, as backward as it is, looks to the promise of oil to bring it wealth and power. Perhaps the rig, it is sent to explore the Boujdour Block between here and there. Sadly, many drilling ships and platforms stop in Santa Cruz de Tenerife for supplies or repairs, or simply to wait." His lip curled like that of a snarling dog. "It sickens me that some of my fellow islanders assist these evil projects."

Dick nodded. "I share your feelings, my good man. But, I'm still confused. We saw the derrick on the western horizon, north of the setting sun. Aren't all of the fields you're talking about east and south, in shallower water?"

"There are those who seek to develop the Agadir Basin, to our north and west. We can do little to stop those outside of our home waters. But, deeper waters require even larger platforms. More likely, the ship you saw simply circles *Carnarias* while it waits for a final destination. It can be cheaper than port fees for such a large structure."

Dick nursed his beer for another hour while Ace downed her second through fourth. Finally, they headed out the door into the night breeze.

"Now what?" she asked as she leaned out into the vacant roadway to look to the east. "I think that B&B still has a vacancy sign in the window."

Dick shook his head. "The Quartermaster's office booked us rooms in Santa Cruz de La Palma. Might as well use 'em. The fewer conversations I have with anyone from Internal Audit, the better, as far as I'm concerned."

"Well, then, we should have called a taxi before we left."

"Nah," said Dick. "We'll need a car in the morning." He strolled along the road, then walked up to a Range Rover Evoque, felt the hood, then went to the driver's side door and started working on the lock.

"So, you're just going to boost a car?" She looked both directions. "What if the owner sees you?"

"He won't. See the decal on the bumper? It's a rental ..."

"A rental? How do we know we can trust the brakes of a rental?"

"Sun's been down a while, but the hood's still warm. This was driven here after our incident this afternoon."

Ace looked up and down the roadway. "Okay, so what if the renter sees you?"

"He won't. I'm pretty sure the tall blond dude in the far left corner speaking German to a local *senorita* is the one who's renting it. Keys were on the table." He pulled the door open and leaned in to finish his work. "And he's way too drunk to drive." He slipped in behind the wheel and the motor turned over with a throaty road. "So, really, we're doing the guy a solid."

"A solid what?"

Dick sighed. "A favor."

Ace heard the lock click, so opened the passenger door and slid in. The rich leather seats were much nicer than the hot, dirty cloth seats of the tourist jalopy. As they turned out into the road, she closed her eyes for the nap which had been delayed by their stop. She knew Dick was paying attention, as always. Right now, she had a greater need to relax than he had a need for her.

#

Taren stared out over the twinkling lights of Geneva and the darkness of the lake beyond. The scene was serene, but his mind was awhirl with images of the chaos and destruction in the Hawaiian Islands and the lesser damage along the coastal areas of the Pacific Rim. Boats tumbled atop piers, bridges torn apart, debris floating in the water, the lights of emergency vehicles flashing. His eyes lingered on the shots of bodies—some in lines, shrouded by sheets, but others still floating amid the detritus of the tsunami. Some showed signs of having been thrown awkwardly in the surge and battered with flotsam. Others lay face down in the muddy water or hung haphazardly from trees denuded of their leaves.

Good times.

But tomorrow, tomorrow promised great times. With any luck, tomorrow's devastation would so dwarf the events in Hawaii that future historians would only reference the Big Island tsunami in obscure footnotes in scholarly theses.

Better times, at least for him, high and dry and rich beyond measure in safe, scenic Switzerland.

He pressed a button and Savatini entered. "Did Nordando deliver?" asked Taren.

"The disruption occurred as requested," answered Savatini. "We don't know if it eliminated the local threat on La Palma."

Taren took a deep breath and let it out slowly. "Elimination would be desirable, but disruption and delay are all we really need. After all, this is a local problem. First thing tomorrow, the Great Crested Canary, she will sing with the dawn chorus and nothing can stop the echoes of her *libretto* once sung. A few minutes later, there will be no opposition, no investigators, no agents … no one at all … in the Canary Islands left to disrupt the New World Disorder."

Chapter 26

Dick heard a knock and meandered to the hotel door, lazily checking the peephole, then opening it. He turned away and wandered back to the room service cart holding his usual travel breakfast: a three-egg ham and cheese omelet, crispy french fries in lieu of hash browns, wheat toast with butter and honey, orange juice, ice water, a pot of coffee, and a half-dozen extra orders of bacon.

"Asked Swynton to task some satellite surveillance to oil rigs near the island. I'm on hold while he flips through the pics with the analysts. Also asked him to get someone in the Dallas office with drilling expertise to link in." He picked up a piece of bacon and dipped one end into a single-serving plastic tub of honey. "Wanna bite?"

Ace shook her head. "I can't believe you're stuffing yourself with hog fat and honey at this hour. It's three in the morning. I've had all the breakfast I can stomach on less than four hours sleep. Tea, yogurt, and ibuprofen."

"Suit yourself." He took a bite of the gooey bacon, but had barely begun to chew when Glenn came back on the line. "Hang on," he mumbled, quickly masticating the salty, savory, crumble. "Acacia is here. I'm putting you on speaker." He thumbed the phone.

Glenn's voice rang out, a bit louder than necessary. "You know that speakerphone is bad protocol, Thornby."

"Yeah, well repeating everything you say to my partner is damn inefficient, so screw protocol."

Glenn sighed, somehow imbuing the susurrus with a British accent. "No F-bomb. Nice to know you are back to your normal level of curmudgeonly *insouciance*. Perhaps you should crash into a mountainside of trees more often."

"Somehow I have the feeling that if I ever crash into a mountainside of trees again, Pyotr Nerevsky and his goons will be behind it."

The silence which followed confirmed everything Dick had ever suspected about the Subsidiary's Internal Audit division. Not just that they dealt with ... troublesome ... agents in a permanent way, but that they listened in to all of the Subsidiary's communications equipment, as well as having most of the offices at HQ in Philadelphia bugged.

Delightful.

Finally, Glenn's voice emanated from the phone once more. "Sorry, did you say something? I was connecting up Agent Collingsworth of the Dallas field office. Chester Collingsworth has an extensive background with operations touching on petroleum producing trouble spots."

"Howdy," Dick drawled the word for the Texas boy's benefit. "So, here's how I figure it. The bad guys, they have this drilling rig circling the island, waiting to pounce. When they want to trigger the Ward & Day landslide scenario, they rush in close, start drilling, and pump in seawater the whole time, attempting, in essence, to frack the Cumbre Nueva fault line, sending the relatively loose debris field from Cumbre Vieja resting on that steep slope sliding down the mountain. Sound right?"

To Dick's surprise, an elite Boston accent emanated from the phone. "No, not in the slightest. I don't mean to be rude, but since you've asked my expert opinion, just let me say this about that. That scenario sounds positively stupid."

Dick glared at the phone.

"Let me explain why."

"Sure thing," drawled Dick, as he shot the screen a middle finger. There were reasons he tended to avoid speaking in FaceTime. "I always like to be told not only why I'm wrong, but why I'm stupid wrong."

Ace snorted. "If I'd only known."

216

Dick turned and flipped her the bird, too.

"Well, first of all, those rigs and their drilling operations require extensive set up. The notion of a free-floating platform, or even a drilling ship, rushing in and accomplishing anything substantive in terms of drilling in a matter of hours or even days is absurd."

Dick gritted his teeth and thought for a moment. "Sure, under normal circumstances, maybe that's true, given typical testing and safety precautions and all that crap, I can see that. But, given their plan in this case, maybe they've prepped all they need in advance and they don't give a shit about safety because they're pumping water, not oil. So they cruise in, drop pipe, and start drilling. I mean, nobody engages in foreplay with a Thai hooker, you know? They just drill hard and fast."

There was a momentary pause before Collingsworth responded. "That's ... uh ... that's a colorful analogy."

Glenn spoke. "Let's avoid the unprofessional analogies, please."

"Whatever," replied Dick. "The point is that since they're trying to frack a volcano, not pump oil, they don't have to worry about fires. And since they're fracking, they don't have to go super deep. They just prick the rocky core riding at the top of the magma chamber, pump in enough seawater to drown Moby Dick and crack the surface tension holding the magma back. It bursts like a balloon and *voila*, you get the wettest water-balloon fight ever."

"That's also quite ... colorful ... but I'm afraid it wouldn't work. First off, the magma chamber isn't just barely under the surface of the volcano."

"That's right," Ace chimed in. "Remember, there are those tunnels going through the mountain. We talked about them yesterday. You don't put in motorways close to the top of a magma chamber."

"Quite," added Glenn.

"The lady is most correct," enunciated Collingsworth. "Second, there is hydrological intrusion into the top of magma chambers all the time. Volcanic rock is quite permeable. Water seeps into the cracks and makes its way deeper and deeper until it gets to the rock which cooled and solidified at the top of the chamber. Those rocks are reasonably solid, but they're still damnably hot, so the water gets ever so hot, too. Soon, it's hot enough it gasifies. It turns to steam and, being lighter in its expanded gaseous form, it moves upward and out and away from the top of the mantle, eventually either cooling and condensing back to repeat the cycle or exiting the system through a fumarole, or steam vent."

"So you can't do this? Why did the drilling at the Hilo fault work then?"

"The what?"

Dick stuffed his face with bacon while Glenn brought Collingsworth up to speed.

"That sounds like it was a drilling operation which had considerable time to go deep. That's the key. Pouring water on the top of a superheated volcano just gets you a good sauna. If you want an explosive result from the sudden pressure of steam, it needs to come from beneath, with the steam expanding as it moves up, increasing the pressure of the chamber and forcing magma into the existing fault lines. That kind of drilling takes time."

Dick scratched his nose. "Okay, so maybe they've already got a rig ... or a ship ... close-in to shore already. We haven't circled the island to look. They may already be drilling someplace."

Glenn interjected. "Our satellite surveillance shows no rigs or drilling ships within the twenty kilometer—pardon me, the twelve mile—territorial limit."

Dick slumped down onto the bed, defeated. "Then what? The chatter suggests something is going down here." He jerked his thumb toward Ace, even though he knew they couldn't see either of them. "The attempt on both our lives yesterday suggests the bad guys are worried we're somehow going to stop them, but I don't know what to do to stop a plan I can't figure out."

"Maybe," suggested Collingsworth, "they're, as folks down here are fond of saying, all hat and no cattle."

"Pardon?" sniffed Glenn.

"Maybe they look the part, but don't have a ranch. Maybe this is all for show. Maybe they are just setting us up to think there's a plan to create a devastating tsunami so we sound an alarm or caution the world about the possibility of a tsunami. They still could be playing the financial markets in some way."

Glenn's voice broke in. "The detractors of the Ward & Day paper and the original show on Discovery have noted the show's sponsors included insurance conglomerates. Maybe we've got the insurance angle backwards. Fears, even unfounded ones, could significantly bolster purchases of catastrophic insurance." He paused. "It's a ponder, in any event."

Dick threw up his hands. "Better than anything I've got at this point. If they need to be close in and dig deep for a long time to make the cockamamie landslide-tsunami thing to work, I don't know how they're doing it. I mean, drilling twelve or more miles off shore isn't going to do diddley, from what you're saying."

"I concur," said Glenn. "Straight down from twelve miles offshore is well outside the magma chamber from what our experts are telling me."

"Down's the only direction to go," added Ace.

219

"More or less," agreed Collingsworth. "Unless ..." His voice trailed off, leaving Dick staring at his phone as if the connection had dropped. Then, Collingsworth voice rang out, louder than ever. "My goodness! Unless it's the Never-Ending Gusher all over again!"

There was a moment of stunned silence before Ace asked what they were all thinking. "I'm almost afraid to ask, but what the hell is the Never-Ending Gusher?"

Collingsworth tone took on a professorial tone; Dick could imagine the fellow teaching at one of the snooty, northeastern Ivy League institutions. "Back ... oh my ... many, many years ago. Late seventies or early eighties, I imagine. After the United States established the Strategic Petroleum Reserve in response to the Arab Oil Embargo, in any event. There was a driller here in Texas, I believe, who had a great deal of confidence that drilling deeper would unlock previously unknown reserves of petroleum, so they drilled down a considerable depth. Seven miles or more—deeper than pretty much anyone else at the time and, lo and behold, they struck a huge gusher, which, of course, they thought vindicated their theory."

"Thrilling," deadpanned Dick.

"Quite," replied Collingsworth, oblivious to Dick's sarcasm. "Now, I don't know exactly how much you know about the typical flow profiles of oil wells ..."

Glenn interjected. "Assume they're clueless."

Dick flipped off the phone again.

"Well, there's a huge spike at the outset, as the pressure from the oil deep—in this case extremely deep—underground finds an escape and tries to equalize with much lower surface pressures. But, as the oil gushes out, the pressure beneath goes down, so the flow rate diminishes. Now, even before the days of fracking, oil companies would often pump down fluids into the cavern holding the oil, so as to

220

attempt to maintain pressure despite the escaping oil. Even then, the flow rate declines, at first fairly rapidly, but then slower and slower until the well is tapped out."

Dick wanted to tap out of this conversation, but it was not wise to rush the egghead too much with his boss on the line.

The lecture continued. "But in this instance, the pressure and the flow rate—which were both quite high to start—barely budged. It wavered a tad, both down and, amazingly, up, but didn't drop off like every other well in history did. This led the experts at the driller to conclude they had tapped onto a reserve so huge that the large amounts of oil coming out were insignificant to the overall volume of crude in the chamber tapped, so there was still plenty to come. Sort of like the miraculous lamp oil which gave rise to Hanukkah, you might say, except lasting much longer than eight days."

Dick, a Methodist, knew for certain he would never say that.

"Eventually, they figured out that the drill pipe curved when going down and, for most of its length, it wasn't actually going down at all. Instead, it traveled lateral to the surface—horizontally—for miles and miles and ended up drilling into the Strategic Petroleum Reserve. The driller pumped it out, sold it to the SPR, which pumped it back down into the salt domes or whatever they were using to hold the reserves, where it gushed back up the driller's rig, only to be sold again in a never-ending cycle."

"Well, never-ending until the lawyers got involved," Ace said. "Americans love their lawyers."

"Quite," answered Collingsworth.

"Now that you mention it," said Glenn, "I seem to recall that Iraq accused Kuwait of what they called slant-drilling into the Iraqi's Rumaila oil field near the border. Same kind of thing, I guess, but perhaps not quite as lateral."

Dick had chomped down on another piece of honeyfied bacon, but stopped mid-chew. "I get it." He swallowed. "So, a rig outside the territorial limit could have been drilling for months or more, but if the pipe curved just the right way ..."

"... or they did something to make it curve," Ace suggested, "like getting a Filipino hacker to adjust the drilling software."

"... then they may have been drilling into the rock *beneath* the relatively big magma chamber sitting atop the relatively narrow magma tunnel coming up from beneath the earth's mantle. Sensors could probably tell them when they were close to the chamber or the tunnel just by measuring the heat at the end of the drill."

"Indeed," agreed Collingsworth, his professorial tone becoming more excited. "Then, they could suddenly attempt to frack the rock by sending massive quantities of cold seawater or some kind of mud slurry mix, rupturing the crust between the drill and the magma and injecting enormous amounts of water or volatile chemicals. The water or mixture, of course, immediately boils off into steam, with sufficient explosive force to keep the end of the drill pipe clear to expel more water, and creates a huge bubble of highly pressurized vapor within the magma, which moves upward and expands. More and more water keeps coming and the magma is forced up and out in an explosive surge, rupturing the magma chamber cap. Magma enters the existing fault lines at speed, shearing off the detritus on the southwest flank of Cumbre Vieja."

Even Glenn sounded animated when he chimed in. "When the steam eventually does escape, there could also be a large collapse of water into the ruptured magma chamber creating additional slides or underwater earthquakes."

"*Ježíši!*" whispered Ace. "The brake job hack isn't unrelated; it was probably a try-out for the drilling hack. Worse yet, the bad guys might have a plan that works."

Dick's brow knitted as he started grabbing his weaponry and equipment. "Not if I have anything to say about it," he growled. "Ace and I are headed to the southwest coast pronto to commandeer a boat while it's still dark outside. Glenn, you and Chester and the satellite and analyst guys need to put your heads together while we're *en route* to find us the target drilling platform to infiltrate so we can stop these assholes before they frack the volcano." Dick cut off the connection and continued to grab gear.

Ace turned for the door. "Well, if we're going to get wet, I'm going to need to wear something besides this t-shirt."

"Yep," said Dick without looking up. "A Kevlar vest is the clothes tip of the day."

"I know. Gotta keep the goats in check."

"Huh?"

"The goats. *Kozy*, which literally means female goats, is Czech slang for tits. Other languages have idioms, too, *pako*."

Chapter 27

Ace velcroed on her Kevlar vest, but she decided to keep only the plain gray T-shirt on underneath it. The investigation ... the operation ... was about to hit a critical juncture and she was ready to use whatever assets she had to make sure the bad guys didn't succeed. Dark slacks with lots of pockets, and comfortable, but sturdy canvas shoes with rubber soles, completed her ensemble, even though she knew Dick, as a former Ranger, preferred combat boots. She also loaded up every piece of equipment she'd gotten on the plane: the armaments included a new Glock 26 (the Quartermaster knew her preferences), four extra clips of ammo, three knives (one sheathed on her calf), two grenades, a garrote, and brass—actually aluminum— knuckles. Additional equipment included a set of lock picks, pliers with a wire cutter inset, waterproof matches, two flashlights, and a hundred feet of sturdy nylon rope with a collapsible aluminum grappling hook at one end.

By the time they were less than a mile from the hotel, headed up the twisty-turny roadway leading to the tunnels on LP-3 that crossed the island between Risco de La Concepción and El Paso, she'd wished she's swiped the air-sick bag from the plane. Dick was an aggressive driver at the best of times. This was the worst of times—the fate of millions of innocent people might rest in their hands—and Dick wasn't going to let speed limits, curves, hills, hairpin turns, no-passing lanes, or the meager pre-dawn traffic slow his mission a single second. She hung on to the handle above the passenger window and choked down her rising bile as Dick veered, cussed, swerved, and screamed down the road as if the psychopathic denizens of a *Mad Max* movie were on his tail.

After exiting the tunnels, Dick continued on LP-3, taking a sharp right on LP-2 toward Los Llanos and Tazacorte beyond. Once in

Tazacorte, he cursed the entire time the highway circled four-fifths of the way around the town before straightening and heading downhill where signage showed the way to the El Puerte de Tazacorte. As marinas went, it wasn't big. Ace worried it was farther north on the island than would be efficient for accessing an oil platform somewhere in the dark sea off the southwest coast of Cumbre Vieja. She perked up, however, when she saw the marina included several sizeable yachts among the sailboats, cruisers, and fishing boats crowding the marina's dozen piers.

Dick slammed the car to a stop in the parking area on the oceanside of the protected harbor near one of the larger yachts, grabbed his gear and power-walked toward the nearest pier. Ace scrambled to keep up as she saw him trigger the communications equipment in his sunglasses, perched atop his forehead. She linked in via her similarly positioned sunglasses, just as he reported: "Leaving El Puerto de Tazacorte in less than ten. Bearings, distance, and coordinates now."

Glenn's smooth voice responded. "We've identified two possibilities ..."

"Pick one," snarled Dick.

"Both have been operating ..."

"Pick one," repeated Dick as he headed toward the largest yacht on the pier.

Ace heard a sharp exhale over the comm. "RS147DW, bearing two-hundred thirty-two point four degrees southwest. Seventeen point two eight nautical miles. Texting coordinates."

"Roger that," said Dick, then reached up, clearly disconnecting the communications.

"I'm still on," volunteered Ace.

"Thank heavens for you, Ms. Zyreb. Agent Thornby can be ..."

"An asshole?"

"I was going to say abrupt and single-minded, but I believe you have encapsulated his dominant personality trait well."

"Roger that," said Ace. "Tell me what you were going to tell him. I'll try to work it in when he's in a better frame of mind."

"Yes, well the second—basically equally likely—prospect is about four nautical miles south-southeast of the first. We, quite frankly, are guessing which one may be behind the current plot, if, indeed, either of them are. Thus, your task is investigatory only. Find out if RS147DW is a normal operation or appears to be drilling laterally into Cumbre Vieja. I've got a Lightning Team hop-scotching down from Gibraltar right now. Once you've reconnoitered the target and find out what needs to be known, you can call in the Lightning Team while you escape to the open ocean. If RS147DW is not the target, you can move from it to the secondary location."

"In the daytime?" *Sakra!* Ace took a deep breath. "That'll be fun."

"Glad to hear you enjoy your work, Agent Zyreb. In the meanwhile, we'll be trying to discern which location, if either, is involved by electronic surveillance and intercepts. Those electronic chaps can be quite effective."

"I'm sure the 'ladies' in IT can be effective, too," she shot back without thinking who she was talking to. "Er, in any event, do me a favor and don't let the geek squad know Big Dick is on the case. I get the impression they don't much like him."

"Understood. Frankly, I don't much like him either, but he can be resourceful in tight situations."

"Roger that. Out."

She'd slowed during the conversation. Dick was already aboard the yacht, the *Killer App.* She quickstepped to catch up. "Nice ride."

Dick's eyebrows turned inward as he looked at her, but he said nothing. Instead, he merely strode down toward the stern and pulled at a nylon rope wrapped to a stanchion there.

"That's not connected to the pier," Ace pointed out as she clambered aboard.

"I know," Dick replied.

"Want me to untie us from the pier?"

"No." Dick finished unhitching the rope. "We're not taking the yacht."

"We're not?"

"Too big, too easy to spot." Dick took another step and started clambering down a ladder affixed to the stern. "We're taking the dinghy."

Ace followed him and looked down from the stern as Dick stepped off the ladder onto a roughly three meter long, inflated Zodiac boat with mounted outboard engine.

"Hurry up," commanded her partner. "We've got a lot of distance to cover before dawn."

Ace swung over the side and climbed down the ladder. *Kurva!* At least with a boat that small, it would be easy to heave over the side as they bounced their way across open ocean to an uncertain future. Life as a spy sure was glamorous.

#

Dick was in operational mode, which meant that although there was really nothing to do during the trip to their target except point the boat and endure the bucking jolts of the ride and the intermittent heaving of his partner, his concentration was focused as he sorted through the tactical permutations of their mission. Despite the fact that he hated to lose even a few minutes on their approach, once the lights of the rig were visible on the horizon, he shifted the Zodiac ever so slightly to pass well north of the platform. By circling back and approaching from the west—the direction much more unexpected for anyone to come from—they were less likely to be spied by the crew, assuming anyone wandered out to see the sunrise. And, they wouldn't be silhouetted by the pre-dawn glow of the eastern horizon. He wasn't too worried the crew would notice the noise of the outboard or pick up the craft on a radar scan. Floating oil rigs were huge behemoths; the bulk of the crew would be as high above the water as residents of a ten or twenty story apartment building were above the street. The Zodiac had a low profile compared to the size of the swells in the open ocean, and the radar and light absorbing black synthetic rubber of the raft blocked most of the flat edges of the outboard motor housing. Sure, the Zodiac was colder and less pleasant than a rigid hull yacht or cruiser, but he'd made the smart operational choice.

After all, that was his job.

Ace looked pale in the dim light. Part of that was no doubt due to urping up her meager early morning breakfast, whether impelled by seasickness or, perhaps, the beers she'd imbibed the night before on an empty stomach. Mostly though, he figured she was also contemplating the coming action in her own way. Dick had been through these kinds of surreptitious reconnaissance missions more times than he could count, and they had ended in firefights more times than his superiors liked. He was battle hardened. He guessed Ace, while tough and smart-alecky, was a bit more apprehensive about what might occur than he was.

Dick didn't fear fighting; he didn't fear death. But, he did fear failure. And there was a lot at stake if the Never-Ending Gusher theory was actually in play. Of course, they weren't even sure they were on target; between hurling sessions Ace had given him details on their secondary objective should the first not pan out.

Time to find out one way or another.

Dick throttled down the outboard and let the dinghy coast in the last forty feet before being swallowed up by the mammoth cavern formed by the stanchions of the floating rig. He avoided the cluster of piping dropping down from central sections of the platform far above and, instead, circled toward one of the thick pillars holding the superstructure high above the waves. As he suspected, fixed rungs spiraled up the pillar to the top and all the way down to below the water line. He cut the engine entirely, and reached out to catch a rung, then tied the boat to it and stepped off onto the ladder. The lack of ambient light underneath the superstructure and the shift from the sway of the boat to the stability of the stanchion affected his balance slightly, so he flipped down his "sunglasses" on low-light mode. He glanced back at Ace, ready to follow him up the ladder, and tapped at his glasses for her to follow suit.

He climbed as quickly as safety allowed. No one would see them here and he knew Ace would have plenty of time to catch up, if need be, when he stopped to get his bearings and listen for personnel at the lip of the lowest level of the multi-tiered oil drilling platform. Given it was just before dawn, all seemed quiet, except for the hum of equipment and the chug of gas generators. Sure, there'd be a night shift, but they'd happened to infiltrate the rig at an optimal time, well enough into the night for the shift on-duty to be tired, but sufficiently before a change of shift the day-workers probably weren't clamoring for breakfast yet.

Ace caught up while Dick was looking into the door of what appeared to be some kind of utility or generation shed. "Good place to blow up if we want to stop work," Dick mused.

Ace peeked past, looking under his arm, which was outstretched holding the door open. "Yeah, but that's not the drill. We don't know

229

this rig is up to anything nefarious and we don't exactly want a repeat of Deepwater Horizon on our hands by mucking up ... or blowing up ... an actual operating well."

Dick shrugged. "Assuming these guys are the real deal and not some bad guys fracking a volcano, the blow-out preventer down on the ocean floor should save the day if bad things happen up top."

"*Ježíši!* Your file was right about your hard-on for explosives."

Dick chuckled. "Yeah, I always thought Eisenhower had it right."

"The general from the war against the Nazis?"

"Yeah, but I was thinking about his military defense policy when he was President of the United States after the war: 'A bigger bang for a buck.'"

Ace frowned. "*Kecáš kraviny.* You're making that up."

"His Secretary of Defense believed building big bombs was a lot cheaper than relying on conventional forces to get your way while keeping the peace." Dick shrugged. "I told you I watch a lot of educational television."

"Yeah, well, before we blow something up, how do we make sure this rig is the one that needs blowing up?"

Dick frowned. "Unlikely all the rank and file know what's really going on. Why would they need to? And, if they did, why in the world would they stay on board knowing they're about to start a tsunami that will likely kill them and their families back home?"

Ace wrinkled her nose. "Maybe they're true believers. Maybe their families live inland or on a damn mountain."

"Unlikely. Deepwater rig workers' families always live near the coast. Too much hassle to get to and from for visits otherwise. And, I'm not sure there is enough of a cause here for there to be many true believers. Anarchy. What kind of cause is that? Helping some bad guy get rich is even worse. Might be able to persuade or con one or two underlings to stay on, but not a whole crew in-the-know."

"Fine," snapped Ace. "You're right, as always. So, if the rank and file don't know shit, then how do we get a handle on this?"

"Communications shack, off the heliport straight above us, above the crew quarters, mess, and recreation modules. If the head honcho from Switzerland is making satellite calls, there'll be a record, *especially* if the communication workers don't know they're involved in nefarious activities. It's standard procedure to log all communications."

"Can't the Subsidiary track that remotely?"

"Tough to track and intercept satellite calls unless you control the satellite. No, this is something we have to do by hand."

Ace smirked. "You should be used to that."

Chapter 28

Dee walked into Glenn's office and shut the door. She could have made him come to her, but she didn't play those kinds of games.

Glenn looked up from his computer screen and gave her a curt nod in greeting. "Nothing new from communications re which oil rig, if either, is part of the volcano fracking plan."

"What if both rigs are part of the plan, but only one is needed to execute it?"

"Then the Atlantic coast is in deep trouble." His eyes narrowed for a few moments before he continued. "But I don't think such a redundancy is likely. Doubles the cost; doubles the chances of what's really going on being leaked or found out. Doesn't seem like a good bet for either a financial manipulator or an anarchist. Of course, we don't even *know* there is a plan. This could be all smoke, mirrors, manipulation, and speculation."

"Everything points to a plan existing. We're just not sure what we have come up with is it."

"I've pushed the scientists on call. The scenario is fantastic, but feasible."

"Which is why we need to move on to the next question."

Dee guessed Glenn knew what she was about to say, but he was polite enough to play dumb. "Which is?"

"Do we dial up the Subsidiary's oversight board now and recommend that tsunami warnings go out and evacuation procedures commence?"

Glenn folded his arms and leaned back in his chair. "Premature. And, it could precipitate the kinds of panic and financial disruption those behind this entire plot crave without them actually having to successfully accomplish what they seem to threaten."

"True, but it could save a lot of lives."

Glenn leaned forward. "Not necessarily. A tsunami warning without some seismic event to back it up might not be taken seriously by the scientific community or the civil defense authorities. It would be difficult to get it taken seriously without a detailed explanation of how it could come to be, which could lead to scientific disagreement amongst the experts and confusion within the general public. It could also undercut any subsequent warning if a landslide is triggered which could generate a tsunami, due to confusion with the earlier, discredited warning or simply warning fatigue."

"I don't know," replied Dee, "the Hawaiian event gives any warning more credibility and newsworthiness than it would have had absent that event."

"Which may have been precisely the reason behind the Hawaiian event. It could have been precipitated not to test the fracking theory, but to spook the authorities and the population into overreacting to an Atlantic threat that, for all we know, may not really exist or may not be achieved even if attempted." Glenn formed his hands into a steeple. "Plus, we do have agents attempting to foil the scenario. I may not be fond of Agent Thornby and his incendiary ways, but he does tend to get the job done ... whatever the cost."

"He could fail." She considered her next words carefully; she didn't want to risk damaging her working relationship with her Director of Operations. "I know we've got plenty of resources backing him up here, but I have to admit to wondering whether we should have committed more agents on the ground."

"Nobody believed this threat was particularly credible until mere hours ago when Collingsworth postulated the lateral drilling scenario. Even now, it's all speculation. Besides, all Agent Thornby and Agent Zyreb have to do is identify the target." Glenn looked at the clock on his desk. "And, at this point a Lightning Team could raid the offending oil platform in just a matter of a couple hours."

"Assuming we have hours."

"It's not like there are a lot of friendly, out of the way places nearby to stage a tactical assault team without drawing attention. I'm not dropping a team down in the middle of the Moroccan desert to just sit around without support until needed. Besides, for all we know, we could have days or weeks. Even assuming everything we've theorized is correct, there's no indication of the timing of the event being triggered."

Dee sat in one of Glenn's client chairs. "True, but if it was me, I'd trigger the tsunami or at least instigate the threat of a tsunami within a reasonably short window after the Hawaiian event, while the markets are still skittish."

"That makes sense, but let's assume the worst for a moment and play it out. If a mega-tsunami is triggered, there will be some time to react, unless you're in the Canary Islands or the west coast of Morocco, Western Sahara, or Mauritania."

Dee scowled. "And no one cares about lives in Africa. Is that your point?"

A micro-expression of shock danced across Glenn's face. "Not at all. Those coasts are lightly populated and devoid of significant infrastructure improvements. My point is that even though the tsunami would propagate at considerable speed, major population centers in Europe, Africa, and the Americas would have hours of warning before disaster could strike. After all there are buoys set up to detect tsunamis that tell us one way or another whether an evacuation is warranted. Plus, their readings provide any warning given at that point the credibility it needs to be taken seriously."

Dee sighed. "Unfortunately, the computer skills demonstrated by the related car hacking event means our perpetrator probably has the ability to counteract the actual readings of tsunami detection buoys, showing one where none exists or eradicating the evidence of a real threat, as the 'big bad' decides." She continued to play Devil's Advocate. "Besides, if the tsunami was triggered when the most populous areas were asleep, any attempted evacuation would be considerably hampered. Beach dwellers understand what a tsunami siren is and most of them know what to do, but tsunami and hurricane evacuation plans only cover a fairly narrow band of very low-lying ground. With something of this potential magnitude, much of the population could literally sleep through most of the wave propagation time."

Glenn glanced at his clock again. "Thornby and Zyreb have been on the rig for twenty minutes already. At this point, there's no significant measure in making this decision until we get some kind of response from them."

"Let's make sure we have a keyhole satellite directed on that rig in the meantime. With Thornby, the first communication we might get could be a giant fireball blossoming off the coast of La Palma."

"Already done, Director."

Of course it was already done. Glenn was as meticulous about operational details as he was about his attire. It was after midnight, and his tie was still knotted as tightly as he was wound.

#

Ace had worried about how they could successfully maneuver around the oil rig without being seen, but, as always, her partner applied brute force to solve the problem. As soon as they moved up from the utility area to the lowest level of the crew quarters, Dick picked the lock on a room. She heard a brief kerfuffle, then a thump followed seconds later by a second thump. She was about to peek through the half-opened door when Dick grabbed her arm and pulled her in the darkened room. Two crewmen in t-shirts and shorts were on the floor, unconscious. Dick was wriggling the fingers of his left hand, no doubt having used it to knock the occupants senseless.

He stepped to a small built-in closet and snatched out a grimy, orange coverall, then he brushed past her to repeat the process on the opposite side of the room.

He held the smaller of the two onesie uniforms up to her torso. The pants draped over her shoes and onto the floor. It looked like an oversized prison jumpsuit, but with plenty of pockets.

"Yeah, I know you're not fat, but it leaves plenty of room for the Kevlar and your equipment underneath. You can roll up the sleeves and pants."

Ace started donning the outfit. "Won't they notice we're not someone they know?"

Dick shook his head as he put on the larger outfit. "Rig this size probably has a hundred or a hundred and fifty workers. And they come and go in varying combinations as workers rotate on or off every week or so, not to mention replacements for those who get sick or have vacation. Night shift, heavier manned day shift, plus consultants, vendors, experts, and company brass checking in from time to time, it all adds up to plausible anonymity. Besides, it's not like people can casually wander on to the work site."

"Yeah, but most of those aboard aren't gals, if any," Ace noted. "Blue collar job, far from wives and girlfriends, I guarantee every hetero guy on this rig can identify the tits and ass of every woman on board from across the room."

Dick gave her a once over. "Trust me, Ace, with the baggy coveralls, and Kevlar and equipment underneath, you won't be getting any ..."

She missed the rest as the background whine of miscellaneous equipment suddenly kicked up a notch as another generator or high speed pump joined in. *Ježíši!* How these guys slept in this racket, she had no clue. She pointed at her ear. "What did you say?"

Dick sighed and thrust a logoed ball cap at her. He leaned in and shouted in her ear. "Wear this low and put your sunglasses on. Sun's up and glaring low off the water. You'll be fine."

Dick, of course, was right, not that there were many people in the stairwells leading up from the lowest level of crew quarters to the heli-deck high above them. The sound of chugging, whining equipment was even louder in the stairwell than in the crew quarters, so they had no need to be stealthy. Dick climbed quickly and she did the same, her heart rate elevated because of the situation, not the exercise. When Dick got to the top, he marched across the pad like he belonged there and she followed right behind. He didn't slow when he reached the communications shed on the opposite side of the platform. He simply opened the door and entered.

Four crewmen were seated at counters of monitoring equipment along two sides of the room. A Scandinavian-looking man in uniform whites was near the middle of the room, talking with a chubby, swarthy man wearing a crumpled suit and tie—probably a consultant or vendor. Her partner didn't hesitate, walking to the two men in the middle of the room.

"Excuse me," he said as they looked up at him. "Your presence is required in ..." He threw his right elbow into the solar plexus of the man in whites, while kneeing the pudgy guy with his opposite leg. Both instinctively bent over at the waist, setting them up for two fast uppercuts which flung their heads up and back as their knees buckled and they fell to the floor.

Ace pulled her Glock 26 from an oversized pocket in her orange onesie and leveled it at the techs at the counter, slowly panning the gun back and forth to emphasize the ease and range of coverage.

"Don't be stupid," she hissed. "Hands up and away from the controls and nobody will get hurt."

As the four techs brought their hands away from the keyboards, knobs, buttons, and controls of the panels in front of them, the one farthest from the door brushed his hand over a bright orange button near the edge of the counter. Before she could swing her gun around and decide on the best response, Dick pulled his Glock and shot the tech, a single round entering the back of his head and bursting out the forehead, sending a hot red mist across the counter.

But even her partner's quick reaction was too late. A harsh buzzing rang out, like the growl of the buzzer on *Jeopardy* magnified a hundred times, followed quickly by what was obviously a prerecorded woman's voice, repeatedly declaring between continued buzzes: "*Piratas! Piratas! Estaciones de batalla. Se preparan para repeler a los huéspedes.*"

"There was no reason to shoot him," Ace hissed. "He'd already pressed the button. What's the point?"

The remaining three techs cowered in terror as Dick strode toward them. "I'm maintaining control of the room," he barked. "That's the point." The alarm continued to cycle. "What's the *senorita* saying?"

Ace shrugged, then yelled to be heard above the noise of the alarm. "My Spanish is only fair, but they think we're pirates. We *are* off the coast of Africa. I think they have a pre-packaged drill to repel pirates trying to take over the rig."

Her partner mumbled. It sounded something like "Pirates. Why the hell did it have to be pirates?" Then he raised his voice. "That gives us some time; they're probably manning water cannons and looking for people trying to board from a craft underneath the platform. All that *Captain Phillips* shit."

Sakra! There was no way their rubber dinghy was going to be there if they ever got back to it now.

Dick apparently didn't share her concerns. Maybe because he was too focused on the task at hand. He approached the techs and used the barrel of his pistol to nudge the one most covered in his departed fellow tech's blood. "Communications logs, now. Start with the sat phones."

When the tech hesitated, Ace spoke up. "He might not understand you."

"Nah," said Dick, "the communications guys always speak English. It's the language of commerce, and money talks." He turned back to the tech. "Right? You can't fool me, so don't think about trying. Just do as you're told and before you know it, we'll be gone."

The tech nodded, then inclined his head toward a desk on the adjoining wall. Dick and the tech got up, walking over in a half-crouch with his hands raised. The tech reached onto a shelf above the desk and pulled out a heavy book with a green cloth covering. A thin bookmark poked out from the top. Still cowering and shaking in fear, he offered the book up to Dick.

Dick grabbed the volume and looked over at Ace. "Position yourself so you can watch both the prisoners and the door," he ordered. She obliged, motioning for the techs to sit on the floor against the wall with the door to the helicopter landing. She glanced furtively over at her mentor, but he was already flipping open the heavy ledger.

Seconds stretched into minutes that seemed like hours.

She jumped when Dick slammed the ledger book down on the desk. "Bingo! Satellite phone calls to several numbers with the Swiss country code. I think one of them's the same as the one we saw in Hawaii." He tore out the relevant sheet from the log book and stuffed it in his pocket.

"You think? Isn't it kind of important to be sure?"

Ace glanced over her shoulder to see Dick glowering at her. "Fine. I'll have Swynton confirm it when we call this in." He reached up to his sunglasses. "Shit." He repeated the motion. "It fucking figures." He took off his shades, tucking them in the front pocket of his orange jumpsuit. "No comm. Try yours."

Ace did, but her luck was no better. "Imagine, crappy reception when you're far out to sea." She scanned the room, her eyes lighting on a microphone sticking up from the communications counter on a bendable arm. She pointed toward it with her off hand. "We are in a communications shack. Use that. Have the Canary Coast Guard or whoever patch you through."

Dick sneered. "Yeah. That ain't gonna happen. I don't really need some guy in a naval uniform listening in on both sides of the conversation while I check in with HQ. Besides, we don't have time for patches and bureaucrats. Sooner or later, somebody's gonna notice there aren't any *piratas* down below and come looking up here."

Her eyes lit on the desk behind Dick. A boxy, black sat phone was half-covered with papers. "Use the phone on the desk."

He went to pick it up, but as he did she saw him stop, then snatch up one of the papers sitting atop the phone. He spun and glared at the tech who had given him the log book earlier. "Has this been sent?"

The tech cowered, his face contorted in fear and confusion.

"This message, was it sent? When?"

The man cringed, but then leaned forward to look at the paper Dick held in his fist. "*Si, En la madrugada.*" The terrified tech closed his eyes for a moment, then opened them. "At dawn."

"Shit!" Dick wadded up the paper and threw it on the floor, then lunged for the sat phone and started pressing buttons.

Ace snapped her fingers to get the attention of the tech, then pointed at the balled up transmission form. "Open it up and give it to me," she said, keeping her Glock trained on the tech. He scrambled over to it, unfolded it on the floor, and reached it up to her, clearly trying to stay as far away from her as he could.

Ace glanced down at the form: "Hydrological fracking commenced at dawn. All systems functioning as planned."

Kurva to hovno! The rig had been fracking the volcano since ... when? ... since that extra pump kicked in while they were down in crew quarters?

Suddenly she was dizzy with questions. How long would it take for the flow to reach the end of the drill pipe? Did liquid start pouring out, converting to steam, at the instant the flow was turned on? Was a bubble coursing explosively through the magma chamber already? Had the shockwaves commenced? Was a wave the size of a major skyscraper already forming and sliding toward them?

Her reverie was broken when a burst of gunfire shattered the window of the communications shack facing the helicopter pad.

This day was just not going to get better.

Chapter 29

Glenn's phone rang. "Do you mind?" he asked Dee Tammany. "Not at all."

He lifted the receiver. "Director of Operations."

A tumult of gunshots, shouts, and screams assaulted his ears. He instinctively pulled the receiver away from his ear, then thumbed the button for speaker phone. A crackle of static punctuated by a burst of automatic weapons' fire and men screaming in Spanish flooded the office. He looked at Dee in confusion and she returned the gaze.

Suddenly, they heard a voice shouting in English. "Thornby. This is the rig. Repeat. We are on the correct platform. Confirm receipt." Glenn calmed a little. Of course there was gunplay. No doubt an explosion would follow. This was Thornby after all.

"Message received," he yelled back.

"Get the hell out of there," shouted Dee. "Your job is done. Retreat. Do you hear? Retreat. A Lightning Team will be there in ..." Dee snapped her fingers.

Glenn did his best to tamp down his irritation at her poor manners as he brought the necessary information up on his screen. "Ninety-two minutes."

"Ninety minutes," Dee shouted at the phone

Glenn toggled to a different screen and typed: "RS147DW. GO, GO, GO!"

"Too much time," Thornby shouted back as they heard the sound of more shots and breaking glass. "Fracking commenced at dawn local. We need to shut this down now."

Dee looked over at Glenn. "How long?"

He understood her meaning. His fingers flew across the keyboard. "Dawn in the Canaries was ..." He swallowed hard. "... thirty-six minutes ago." Glenn buzzed for his assistant, who was clearly startled by the noises emanating from the phone. "Get me Collingsworth, NOW!"

"SitRep," Dee barked out at the speakerphone.

"Outnumbered. Outgunned. Will attempt to cut power to pumps or do whatever damage we can."

"Roger that," replied Dee. "Keep informed." Her voice dropped in volume. "Get to it."

"Godspeed," added Glenn.

The connection dropped and the room fell into stunned silence.

Suddenly, the phone rang again. Glenn punched at the button.

"Chester Collingsworth reporting, at your service. What do you need?"

#

Dick stuffed the sat phone in his pocket, then looked up and absorbed the chaos of the communications room. The techs had crawled to the best shelter they could find, a closet near the desk. One brave soul had even snagged the legs of the men Dick had knocked out when he first arrived, whether to save them from the bullets and glass flying around them or to use them for cover, Dick couldn't be sure, but he didn't care. Ace was hunkered down behind a support, trading fire with several gunmen who had approached from the same stairwell they had used to get to the helipad. A few bodies strewn across the landing zone demonstrated the crew either took their pirate drills way too seriously or the son-of-a-bitch in charge of this evil enterprise had loaded up the rig with henchmen after the attempt on their lives via brake failure had not gone as planned.

"We need to get downstairs," Dick shouted, as he moved up to Ace's flank in support.

"You mean the staircase filled with an endless supply of bad guys shooting at us? *Kurva to hovno!* Not going to happen. No way, no how."

Dick snapped off a shot and the head of the lead shooter from the stairwell snapped back, showering his companions with blood and tissue. "It's a natural choke point. We just take 'em out one by one. How many of 'em can there be?"

Ace ducked as a burst of automatic weapons' fire riddled the flimsy wood siding of the shack and slammed across to the opposite side. "I believe you said upwards of a hundred. Of course, you also said they'd be oil rig workers, not a fucking assault team."

Dick checked his ammo and his watch. "Somebody must have gotten nervous when we showed up in the Canaries and hired a squad of thugs to protect the rig. You're right, though. Don't have the ordinance and sure as hell don't have the time to take out a squad of mercs one by one as they pop up. We've got to shut down that fracking pump, pronto."

"To hell with that," answered Ace. "Let the Lightning Team earn their pay for a change."

Dick shook his head. "Too far out. If we hunker down and conserve our ammo, we might hold out til they get here, but that means the fracking keeps pumping another hour and a half. Hell, if their plan actually works, a fucking wave might knock the Lightning Team's helicopter out of the sky on its way here." Dick scanned the platform. "Still got all your equipment?"

Ace fired off a short burst at the stairwell. "Everything but what I've shot at the bad guys. What are you thinking?"

"We jump."

She turned her head and looked at him as if he was crazed. "We jump? Assuming we don't hit anything on the way down, we survive hitting the water at terminal velocity, and the goons with guns still looking for pirate ships down below don't pick us off, what's the plan? Dive down and try to clog up the intake pipe with our quickly drowned, lifeless bodies?"

"Clogging the intake pipe ... Not a bad idea for down the road. But, for now, I was thinking more along the lines of fixing the grappling hook at the edge and running off the platform attached to the line, then swinging back ninety or so feet down and getting a quick detour around the guys on the stairs with guns."

"*Ježíší!* You are as crazy as your file said."

Dick shrugged. "You got a better idea?"

She looked out at the helipad. "We're going to die, you know. They'll cut us to pieces before we can get even halfway to the edge of the helipad."

"Not if we keep up a steady stream of suppressing fire."

"And how are we going to do that? There's only a hundred feet of rope and one grappling hook. We both need to run at the same time."

"Yeah," said Dick. "But I've got an idea."

#

"I've got an idea," said Glenn. "But, we've got to move fast."

"I'm listening." Dee was wary, but truth told she was fresh out of ideas, and Chester Collingsworth had just spent five minutes depressing the hell out of everyone by emphasizing how every minute the fracking continued increased the risk that a mega-tsunami would soon be surging across the ocean to take millions of innocent lives.

"Take out the whole platform." Glenn assaulted his keyboard as he continued to talk. "We'll need the help of one of the oversight nations, but with any luck, we can take out the platform with a cruise missile much quicker than the Lightning Team can arrive."

245

"Try the United Kingdom," said Dee. "The *HMS Queen Elizabeth* carrier group is doing its sea trials in the Atlantic somewhere southwest of Gibraltar. And, being closer to the Canaries than us, your countrymen have a lot at risk. No time to evacuate the coast if things go badly."

It took two agonizing minutes to get the United Kingdom's representative from the Subsidiary's oversight board by secure connection—actually quite speedy, but time was their enemy. Dee Tammany didn't waste time with formalities or explanations.

"Sir, I need your carrier group southwest of Gibraltar to launch a Tomahawk cruise missile—better yet two or three—at an oil platform off of the Canary Islands."

"Two or three? You know those things run well over a million euros apiece."

"Yes, sir. And it's the best money the Royal Navy will ever spend. Because if they don't fire in the next few minutes, the white cliffs of Dover could be underwater in less than two hours."

#

Ace stared at her crazed partner. "Why do I think this is going to be a very, very bad idea?" She'd wanted the adventure of being a spy; she just had hoped for a bit of life expectancy to go with it.

"Get out your rope, deploy the grappling hook, and tie a loop to wrap around me with the free end, one that won't slip and squeeze the life out of me when the rope stops my momentum."

"Your momentum? Where does that leave me?" She felt anger rising in her like bile in her throat as she shrugged off the pack one arm at a time and fished it out of her jumpsuit. "Grabbing you as you jump off a cliff wasn't so much fun last time that I'm looking for an encore. Or am

I just supposed to sit around providing covering fire while you save the day?"

"Yeah, but not from here. Not where you'll get overrun as soon as the bullets run out." Dick grabbed her pack away from her as she took out the rope, dumping the rest of the contents, then flipping open his knife and cutting out holes on either side of the bottom of the pack. "No, you'll be strapped to my back, facing the rear, providing covering fire while I make the dash for the edge."

Kurva! It was so crazy it might work. "Might" being the operative word. She readied the grappling hook. "That clinches it. You're completely mad. I was right before when I said we're going to die."

Dick shrugged. "Probably, but we've got to try. If we don't stop this, millions of people could die, all along the Atlantic coastline."

"Yeah, and if this is as big as the Discovery Channel said, I think the Subsidiary's going to need a new HQ."

Dick's face drained of color.

"They'll get out," she continued, assuming she'd read his thoughts. "They'll have more warning than anyone. They're probably the safest people on the whole Atlantic ..." Mother of God, she suddenly remembered Dick's family lived in New Jersey. She felt the blood drain from her face. "Your family will have time to evacuate, too. I'm sure."

Dick shook his head. "My kid, Seth, he's in the hospital, the opposite direction from home for any sensible evacuation route. Once this happens, Melanie's got no hope of getting to him. Traffic would be bad enough, but we've done the hurricane evacuation drill a few times ... you know, for Superstorm Sandy and shit. The first thing they do is reverse all the highway lanes so all traffic moves inland." Her partner reached into his pocket and held the phone in his beefy paw, just staring at it for a few seconds.

247

"Call," said Ace, as she continued to work on readying the hook and rope.

"It's against protocol," replied Dick, as if in a trance.

"Fuck protocol," growled Ace. "What good is saving the world if you can't save your own family?"

One thing about her partner, he was decisive. She hadn't even finished her sentence when he raised the bulky sat phone and started punching the keypad. She set the rope down a few moments to fire a short burst at the whack-a-mole bad guys in the stairwell to keep them at bay during the call.

She didn't mean to listen, but she couldn't help it.

"Melanie, it's Dick. Listen. *Just listen!* You have to go to the hospital now and get Seth, then head inland and uphill as fast as you can. Don't stop for anything. Keep moving. Get on I-76 and head towards Harrisburg, the farther west and the higher the better." He paused. "Then check him out against medical advice. Fucking kidnap him if you have to, but get him out and head for high ground."

Dick took the phone away from his mouth, then brought it back up. "One more thing. Whatever happens, you need to know you and Seth came first. Before my job, my mission, the whole damn world. We're a team; we always will be. Now MOVE!"

#

As soon as Dee got off the line with the United Kingdom, she dialed up the satellite phone Thornby had used to give him the news that he had less than fifteen minutes to get off the oil platform and make as much distance as possible before it was obliterated by two incoming cruise missiles launched by the United Kingdom. This was one explosion she didn't think he would be that fond of.

As the seconds ticked away while the connection was made, she mentally prepared what she would say, but she was totally unprepared for what happened next.

A busy signal. The sat phone was in use; she had no way to warn her agents they were about to be blown to United Kingdom come.

Chapter 30

Dick divvied up the ammo. There wasn't much left, but he gave the bulk of it to Ace, keeping only a partially empty clip for himself.

"You need to do one thing for me," he said, as Ace checked her weapon and got into the makeshift harness Dick would be strapping to his back before his mad dash across the helipad.

"Yeah, yeah," replied Ace. "I know, 'don't die.' I promise I'll do my best not to die."

"Screw that," said Dick. "I'm prepared to live with you dying. I've had partners die before. Hell, I've made my peace with me dying."

"Then what?"

"Don't you dare die with any bullets left in your gun."

"What?"

"Kill all the sons-of-bitches you can. That's what I'm going to do with what I've got left and I can't bear the thought of any ammo being wasted in the clip of a dead man."

"Dead woman."

"Yeah. That, too."

Ace stood on a chair to help Dick strap her on. Then he picked up the grappling hook and dropped the loop on the other end of the rope across his body, from his left shoulder to his right thigh. He leaned forward, hefted her up and off the chair and let out a blood-curling roar as he bolted for the southwest corner of the helipad.

What the fuck. She'd always wanted to die a hero.

Ace watched as the mouths of the latest bad guys to poke out of the stairwell in the northeast corner of the helipad gaped open, then she fired off a brief burst in their general direction to force them to scatter for cover. She couldn't hit shit, not bouncing along on the back of a beefy, middle-aged spy who was still yelling at the top of his lungs as he lugged her on his back as fast as his stocky linebacker legs could pump. She didn't even bother to gauge the distance to the jump — better not to know. Instead, she just did her best to steady her aim and pop off a few more rounds.

She heard a clang and glimpsed the grappling hook dropping to the side into the tangled superstructure at the edge of the helipad, then she abruptly tilted backward and seemed to float, weightless, as they plummeted to death or glory.

What the hell, she decided to bellow with her burdened beast as they fell off the edge of the world. Her final thought: There be dragons here.

#

Finally, on Dee's fifth attempt, the sat phone rang. She breathed a sigh of relief, but it was not long-lived. The phone rang and rang and rang, but Thornby didn't pick up. What the hell was he doing that he couldn't answer the phone so she could save his life?

#

Dick had always loved the sensation of freefall. And, for a moment, everything fell away. His mission. His job. The problems in his marriage. And then, with a wrenching jerk, the weight of the world returned. Not just his troubles, but a multiple of his body weight and the weight of his lithe partner as the rope tightened, the G-forces slammed into him, and the rope began to arc back toward the oil platform.

He desperately tried to twist himself to face the platform before he slammed against it. But he didn't have the same easy maneuverability as someone sky-diving. Still, at the last moment, he caught sight of a gangway along the edge of the lower platform coming up. He slid the edge of his knife blade out between his body and the nylon rope and began to cut, pushing the blade against the cord with every bit of force he could muster, slicing at it in a mad panic in time with a buzzing pulse from the sat phone in his pocket as the pendulum swung him and Ace inward, under the edge of the helipad toward the superstructure holding the crew quarters.

Just as they were nearing the end of their inward swing, the nylon parted and the two of them plunged toward the gangplank and its railed edging. He forced his legs together and angled them toward the crew quarters as best he could, then bent his knees and gritted his teeth.

This was going to hurt like hell. Thank God he wore good combat boots.

#

Melanie didn't like to drive fast, but Dick had scared the hell out of her. At least the light traffic this late at night meant she could do twenty or thirty miles over the posted speed limit without having to weave around traffic. She didn't worry about being stopped for speeding—not only were the police assigned highway patrol more likely to go after trucks and sport cars, but between Dick having been on the job as a cop and her being able to truthfully say she was rushing to the hospital because of her son, she figured she could talk her way out of a ticket if she had to. Of course, that would take time and she didn't know how much time she had. From the urgency in Dick's voice when he called, she wasn't sure how much time anyone had.

She pressed the accelerator to the floor and punched the button on the radio for the twenty-four hour news station, but all the stories were routine. Apparently no one else knew what she knew, and she didn't even know anything, except that something very, very bad was about to happen very, very soon.

#

Ace slammed against the wall of the utility module as Dick landed hard and did a half-somersault to lessen the shock of the drop. As soon as their roll stopped, Ace took out her knife and sliced through the straps holding her to Dick's back. The configuration of their intertwined bodies was awkward at best and, though they'd literally gotten the drop on their adversaries, she couldn't be sure a bevy of Mac-10 wielding thugs wasn't about to burst out of the stairway or come around the corner any second. She preferred to be ready to dodge, run, and charge as the developing situation warranted, not to be tied to the back of her partner, facing the wrong damn direction for whatever happened next.

Within seconds, she was loose and upright with Dick scrambling to his feet next to her. She flung open the door to the utility module and they both ducked quickly inside. She blocked the door with a loose piece of equipment, while Dick looked at the machinery.

"What the hell are you doing?" she yelled over the incessant whine of rotors.

Dick shot her an angry look. "Trying to figure out what does what, so I know what to turn off."

"*Kurva to hovno!* Screw that, big guy." She reached down and grabbed both of the grenades she'd brought along, tossing him one. "I say we just blow the fuckers up."

Dick responded with a curt nod, then ran to the door on the opposite side and looked through the square pane of glass in the middle. "Coast is clear." He motioned toward a large tank against the far wall. "You hit the spare fuel; I'll dump mine in the electronic controls. One or the other should do the trick."

Ace pulled the pin, but held the handle tight while Dick did the same with his grenade. He glanced out the door again. "Go! Go! Go!"

Ace tossed her grenade over the equipment toward the tank and took off at a run for the door without waiting to see where it landed. About two steps into her dash, Dick lobbed his under the control area and opened the door, stepping back to let her exit at speed. He followed quickly behind, shutting the door. They raced along on open gangway past another, shorter module above which loomed a crane. Ahead and to the left, the tall derrick of the main rig pierced the clear morning sky.

Then a tremendous explosion, followed quickly by a second, lesser explosion threw them up and forward as the utility module pulsed outward, then blew open in a burst of orange and black. The screech of wrenching metal and shouts and screams of dying men called out as Ace was flung down on the gangway and Dick fell atop her legs. She looked back to see Dick already getting up. In the background, the crew quarters listed heavily to the southeast, flame licking at the lower levels. Then the support beam on the southeast corner bent and finally gave way and the multi-level module and the helipad atop it wrenched down, hanging for a few seconds before it plunged into the sea.

Ace smiled—not at the destruction or the certain loss of life that accompanied it—but with the glow of a mission successfully accomplished.

"Uh-oh," said Dick as he looked in the opposite direction, past her. She stopped smiling.

#

Dick looked past Ace and scowled at the sight before him. Lights were still on up the derrick on the workover rig and in both of the modules to its right and behind it.

Modules. That was it. Fucking modules.

They'd blown up the utility module for the crew quarters and communications shack. What hadn't fallen into the ocean was burning, thick black smoke roiling off, with secondary explosions shooting orange and yellow flames through the dark soot. But, the power, drilling, and wellbay modules were distinct, discrete entities. They still had power, the pumps still whined, and the fracking probably still continued.

Oh, and they'd used all their grenades. He was patting himself down to confirm the lack of additional explosives when his hand lit upon the brick-like sat phone in his pocket, which was vibrating. He wrenched it out of his pocket and shoved it toward his face, thumbing the controls as he did so.

"What?"

Director Tammany's voice crackled from the tiny speaker. "Agent Thornby. So glad I finally ..."

"I'm busy," Dick growled. He thrust the phone toward his partner. "Talk to Ace."

As Ace took the phone, he brushed past her and took a few steps forward, then leaned out to get a better angle on the area below the derrick. Several workers were scrambling about, but none of these crewmen seemed to be carrying guns, so there was still hope they could finish their mission.

Ten seconds later, Ace was at his side. "We need to leave. We're done here and we've got two incoming Tomahawks ten, maybe twelve, minutes out."

Dick tilted his head toward an enclosed emergency lifeboat off the gangway about thirty feet ahead. "You go. I'm staying here." He pointed up at the lights on the derrick. "Power's not down over here. They're probably still fracking Cumbre Vieja."

Ace sighed. "Fuck." She pursed her lips, then shook her head. "Doesn't matter. We've got orders. Besides, the Tomahawks will vaporize everything in ten minutes anyhow."

"And in nine minutes, the whole side of the volcano might slide into the sea and the wave generated might swallow up the Tomahawks *en route*, then swallow up my house, my wife, and my kid—my entire life—along with a whole lotta other people's lives six hours later. Do what you want; I'm stopping that pump before I leave." He turned and double-timed down the gangway.

He heard Ace swearing behind him in Czech as she followed him toward the wellbay rig.

It was nice to know he wasn't the only one who did what needed to be done.

#

Ace had to triple-time to keep up with her partner, especially since she stopped for a few seconds along the way at each of the three different lifeboats they passed to grab the top item in the emergency supply kit. She also watched their six, stopping to pick off a crewman armed with an AK-47 who was following their trail at a distance. After that, she stopped looking for trouble from behind. They were both dead in ten minutes anyhow. What was the fucking point?

Dick rushed ahead at full speed, taking the stairway up from the lower level to the next three at a time, yelling *"Salida! Salida!"* the entire time. The old-timer might not know how to say "abandon ship" in Spanish—she sure as hell didn't—but he remembered the extra word plastered on every "exit" sign on their commercial flights.

Workers were taking Dick's advice, even if they never heard him. By the time they'd reached the main platform of the wellbay module, all the workers looked to be gone. Ace had seen several of the emergency boats deploy and depart and for good reason. The conflagration on the south side of the massive platform was spreading, just not fast enough to please her partner.

The mud room under the derrick in the workover rig was so loud she could barely think. Drilling pipes came down from the derrick above and disappeared into a large, center gap in the floor, but everything was so solid, so massive, she didn't see any way to disrupt it. Apparently, Dick didn't either, because he didn't slow, instead loping up more stairs to a roof platform directly below the massive derrick. He swung his head from side to side as he continued his desperate search. Then she saw it stop and followed his gaze. The roof overlooked yet another equipment module from which emanated a loud whine. The doorway, which was swinging in the gusty air high above the ocean read "Compression Room." The volume of the keening whine ebbed and flowed with the swinging of the door. Ace didn't know squat about oil drilling, but her guess was the pump for the fracking fluid was in that room.

Dick must have had the same thought because he fired into the room on full auto. Unfortunately, he had less than two seconds of ammo, which seemed to have no effect.

"Shit!" he yelled, flinging the gun away. Ace nudged his arm and handed him one of the flare guns she had retrieved from the lifeboats they had passed. "Try this."

Dick snatched up the gun and Ace readied one of her own. "Through the open door." They both aimed at the doorway, where the module door swung erratically on its hinges in the gusting breeze. "NOW!"

Just as they both fired, the wind shifted and the door swung mostly shut. The flares hit the door and ricocheted, sending sparks flying and the red flaming cartridges skittering along the gangway spewing smoke and fire.

"Damn!" yelled Dick.

Ace handed him another flare gun. "Last one." As Dick readied it, Ace checked the ammo left in her gun. One round left. At least she wasn't going to die with any ammo left. She aimed at the module door, which was once again banging open and shut. "On my signal," she hollered, as she again aimed and tried to calculate the rhythm of the irritating door. The door hit the outside wall and started to swing back toward closed.

"Now," she yelled as she fired. Dick's flare gun blazed an instant after her own and she watched as her round hit the door at supersonic speed, puncturing it, but nevertheless slamming it back against the wall just as the flare arrived, flying through the open doorway into the room beyond.

They both dropped their weapons.

Three long seconds later, the wail of the machinery cut off as the walls of the Compression Room bulged out. Ace flung herself back and down as a large orange fireball erupted, flattening the module and bathing everything in a roar of flame and destruction, burning her eyelashes off as it thundered past her, before abating into a raging inferno tearing at the sky less than thirty feet away.

#

"We've confirmed missiles are launched," said Glenn. "Five minutes out. Let's hope they get there in time to stop the tsunami."

Dee stared out the window. "Let's hope our agents get off the rig in time."

Chester Collingsworth's voice broke in from the speakerphone. "Seismic activity at Cumbre Vieja!"

Dee slammed her hand down on the desk. "Damn. Prepare to begin emergency evacuation protocols."

#

Melanie ran past Ornell at the third floor nurses' station, straight into Seth's room, flicking on the lights as she did. "Seth, wake up. Now." He opened his eyes as she reached to shake him awake. "We're leaving now. C'mon. Move."

He blinked at the bright lights. "Wha ... It's the middle of ..."

She lowered the pitch of her voice to full-on Mom voice. "NOW, mister."

"Okay, okay. Just let me get dressed."

"No time for that." She pulled him up from the bed, grabbing at the intravenous tubes snaking into his arm and yanking them out. "Move."

"Oww, Jesus, Mom. I don't understand."

Ornell skidded into the room. "What the hell?"

Melanie leaned toward Seth. "Your father says we have to leave here NOW."

"Holy crap," said Seth, suddenly shifting into gear. Melanie grabbed his arm as he got up and the two of them rushed for the door, Seth grabbing his cell phone off the bed's tray table as they left.

"Sorry, Ornell," yelled Seth as Melanie ran past the startled nurse.

"You can't leave," muttered Ornell. "You haven't been discharged."

Melanie and Seth ran down the hallway. "Family emergency!" Melanie called back as they hit the panic handle for the stairs down to the parking garage.

Melanie wasn't even sure exactly was going on; all she knew was she was running for her life. All because her husband was a spy.

Chapter 31

Dick scrambled back up to a standing position as Ace did the same. "Nice move," he grunted, "pinning the door back with a round. I wouldn't have thought of that."

"Let's not get gushy now," she replied and pointed to the west. "Lifeboat. We still have five minutes."

They lunged toward the stairs that would take them to an escape vehicle, two floors down, but before they'd even gone twenty feet, Dick was stopped cold by a blood-curdling scream. Looking back, he saw a man emerge from the burning wreckage of the Compression Room, his uniform aflame, his hair smoking.

"*Ježiši!*" whispered Ace.

"Go," replied Dick as he turned and took a step toward the human torch. He had seen what burns had done to Seth. He couldn't let another human being die like that, not if he could help it. "Get the boat ready. We'll meet you there."

She grabbed his arm as if to stop him. "He's dead in four minutes. We're dead in four minutes. It's not like we haven't been killing people here."

Dick shook her off. "People shooting at us, sure. The rest deserve a chance to get out of here alive, if they can." He started running toward the screaming man.

"This is macho bullshit nonsense," she called after him. "You're not a hero, you know. You're just a spy."

"Spies are heroes," he muttered to himself as he leaped off the roof of the workover rig onto the flaming gangplank outside the burning remains of the Compression Room, tackling the man afire and smothering the flames with his rolling embrace.

#

"*Ježiši! Do prdele! Káĉa pitomá!* Ace's anger burned away her pain as she marched to the western edge of the room and did a navy handrail slide down two flights toward the waiting emergency lifeboat. *Ty jseš debil!* Her partner wasn't just an asshole; he was bound and determined to be a flaming asshole. *To jsou žvásty!*

She didn't know how things worked in America, but where she came from, once you finished the job, you stopped working.

She reached the lifeboat, opened it, and unclipped the safety from the lever that would jettison the boat by letting it slide down and drop into the water. She had no doubt plunging into the water from this height, even in a closed boat that probably wouldn't sink if fully flooded, was going to be a bitch, but it was better than waiting on a flaming oil platform for two Tomahawks to obliterate you.

Two fucking minutes.

She looked toward the stairwell and the gangway along the lower level, searching through the swirling gray and black smoke for any sign of her idiot partner, but saw nothing.

To hell with him.

She turned to close the hatch and shove the lever, when she heard a muffled shout. She turned back to see Dick, with a smoldering body draped across his back in a fireman's carry, lumbering toward her.

Sakra!

She ran to him and together they managed to shove Dick's unconscious burden into the lifeboat and slam the hatch shut.

Less than one minute.

She strapped in and grabbed the lever, but Dick's strong hand gripped her arm and kept it from pulling down.

"What the fuck are you doing?"

Dick pointed through the thick windshield of the lifeboat. Even with the distortion and the swirling smoke, two pinpoints of flame were rapidly rocketing toward the platform.

Kurva! What was he waiting for?

The Tomahawks sped toward them impossibly fast. Just as Ace tensed for the impact she knew would end her life, Dick slammed the lever down and the craft slid, then suddenly lurched off the skid, plummeting toward the blue water below, accelerating downward, hitting the surface of the ocean and plunging into its sapphire depths just an instant before two flashes of light from above illuminated the water around them with a yellow-white glow that dwarfed the light from the morning sky.

A shockwave hit the craft from behind and starboard, sending it yet deeper in a jerky, sideswiping motion, as if buffeted by big surf. A spray of water burst from a seam along the side of the windshield, then another from the door jamb. The flash of light subsided and darkness flooded the cabin. Then, slowly, the pitch of the boat evened out, then tilted upward. The boat gathered speed and the jets of water leaking in lost pressure as the pitch grew more severe and the water around them brightened once more.

The lifeboat popped to the surface, leaping out of the water for a second before crashing heavily back down. Above and around them debris fell from the sky amid flames and smoke, but whatever direction Ace looked, she couldn't see the oil rig any more.

Dick unstrapped from his seatbelt and stood to start up and pilot the boat.

Once they were far enough away they were no longer surrounded by smoke and debris, Dick turned to look at Ace. "Thanks for waiting. When we do up our after-action reports, though, I need you to do me one favor."

Ace harrumphed at her big, old, wet, dirty, burly partner. "Let me guess. You don't want me to tell them you went back to save some random guy."

Dick harrumphed right back at her. "Nah. Who cares about that? I just want you to make it abundantly clear that last explosion ... that wasn't my doing."

#

"Missile strike confirmed," intoned Glenn. "Rig is demolished."

Dee waved him off without looking up. "That part was never in doubt." Her focus was riveted to the speakerphone, as it had been since Collingsworth had reported seismic activity.

Finally, she heard his voice. "Tremors on La Palma peaked at four point three on the Richter scale and appear to be subsiding. A few aftershocks in the two point eight range, all with epicenters approximately two miles below the seabed underneath the southwestern edge of Cumbre Vieja. A minor slide of loose debris on the southwest flank, but it never made the shore. No tsunami warning warranted."

"Good news, as far as it goes," she intoned.

Glenn raised an eyebrow. "That seems a tad pessimistic given the fact the Subsidiary may have saved millions of lives and trillions in infrastructure."

Dee shrugged. "A good day's—night's—work, but the Royal Navy just vaporized almost every possible lead we might have had as to who's behind this. And, tomorrow is another day."

#

Melanie drove on in the dark. Seth had peppered her with questions for the first few miles, but had fallen silent as the news radio droned on, repeating the same banal headlines every seven minutes, none of which had anything to do with the Canary Islands, tsunami warnings, or imminent threats to the state of New Jersey. She didn't know when she would hear from Dick. She didn't know if she would ever hear from Dick.

Was this what it was going to be like, now that she not only knew he was a spy, but knew where he was? A constant series of questions about what he was doing and whether he was safe, but no answers.

Seth's cellphone pinged.

"What's that?" asked Melanie. "Anything important?"

Seth looked at his phone. "Nah, just a routine notice from one of my apps."

Melanie wobbled her head. "You mean it isn't a real person? Your apps just contact you on their own?"

"Sure. This one notifies you about earthquakes around the world. Brian had it and it looked kinda cool, so I downloaded it, too. Of course, earthquakes happen *all* the time, so it was pinging like crazy at first. I bumped it up to trigger at four point two now, which is at the lower range for damage, but it still goes off way too often. Just told me there was a quake in the Canary Islands. Big whoop."

Suddenly, Melanie was awake again. "The Canary Islands? Couldn't that be dangerous? You know, like the Hawaii quake?"

"Nah," said Seth. "Not at four point three. Nothing much happens at that size. Nobody dies, that's for sure."

She could only hope he was right. She drove through the night, reaching and passing Harrisburg before dawn, then climbing into the Appalachians north and west until she was too tired to go on, the surge of adrenaline from her earlier panicked flight now leaving her tired, irritable, and with a tinge of metallic taste in her mouth.

#

High above the glittering lights of Geneva, Taren Sykes read between the lines as he went through the end-of-quarter after-action reports from the Canary Islands. News sources had consistently reported that an oil rig west of La Palma had exploded due to an accident precipitated by "human error." While the media reported there were no survivors among the workers, no oil was spilled. Still, local groups in the Canaries opposed to ocean-based drilling were marching both locally and at the headquarters of the Spanish oil company behind such drilling efforts. Good thing he'd shorted the drilling company; he'd at least offset some of his expenses.

Hmmm. Maybe he could purchase the oil rig four miles further south for a good price given their awkward PR situation. After all, just because a plan fails doesn't mean you don't fix the mistakes and try again. That's the problem with most anarchists; they don't really work at their craft.

He'd think about it. Right now he had to see a man about a bomb.

The world was so fragile. There were so many ways to break it. And he wanted to try them all.

He pressed a button and asked for his car to be brought around, not bothering to wait for any response from his underling. But as he strode toward the door, it opened and a young woman stepped in wearing an evening gown—something red and flowing, with a full skirt and a plunging neckline. Her dark hair was a bob cut and her body lithe and toned; her features seemed vaguely Eastern European.

"I think you've gotten lost," Sykes said, stepping toward her. "The U.N.'s charity fundraiser is five floors below in the reception area for the hosting law firm."

"Silly me," she replied. "I just was looking for a place to check my lipstick away from the crowd. Women's restrooms ... there's always a line. I just want to look perfect."

"Let me see," said Sykes, stepping close and reaching out to lift her chin up and look into her face. Obviously, the fates were with him tonight.

Suddenly, he felt a sharp pain between the bottom two ribs on his left side, followed in quick succession by ten or twelve more in just a few short seconds, the last piercing pain reaching up into the center of his chest cavity. Then everything began to fade as he fell onto the plush, ash-and-charcoal patterned sofa opposite his desk. Oddly, the tony sofa was sporting maroon accents he didn't remember.

The last thing he saw was the woman in red walking out his office door, motioning for his assistant. "Pardon me, but Mr. Sykes asked for his car to be waiting for me. Is it ready?"

Epilogue

Dick knew that he couldn't complain. Six weeks off after a mission was well above-average, even with the few burns and scrapes he had incurred. Seth was back at home and Melanie somehow understood that making her drive into the mountains in the middle of the night was his way of showing he cared. Her one-dimple smile had even crept onto her face when he had returned to their cozy ... and unflooded ... home.

And even if he could complain, Dick knew he shouldn't, at least not out loud. Not given the source of his summons to the Subsidiary's offices in downtown Philadelphia: Internal Audit.

Instead of heading to the upper floors of the Casualty Crisis Consulting high-rise, he parked his car and headed to the Accounting Department, down in the basement. As always, it was chilly there. If you asked, they said it was because of the cooling needed for the computer servers housed there, but he knew better. The cold made people uncomfortable and that was how Internal Audit liked their guests, even if they were only there to discuss excess charges for rental vehicles and losing track of explosive devices while in the middle of an op. Pyotr Nerevsky's minions were made in his image: cold and unforgiving.

He checked in and was escorted to a windowless, featureless conference room, then left to ponder his situation for a good half hour. He knew this drill, too. Irritate the guest and make them more pliable before any inquiry, no matter how minor.

Finally, the door opened. Dick looked up to see what underling was going to read him the riot act about procedures and expenses this time.

Shit. It was all he could do to stifle an audible gasp when Pyotr Nerevsky entered the room, his balding head glaring under the harsh blue light of the LED fixtures.

"Agent Thornby. I'm here to discuss your phone habits."

"Did I go over my allotted minutes?" asked Dick, doing his best to keep his tone light. "You should really look into those unlimited plans."

"Yes," replied Nerevsky without smiling. "I'll do that. But right now, I'm more interested in the content of your calls, than their duration."

Dick's mind raced. Could Internal Audit know about his calls to Melanie, letting her know where he was? No, that was impossible. He never used his Subsidiary provided cell or his sunglass communication features for those calls. That's why he'd been buying crappy burners, searching out pay phones, and borrowing strangers' cells whenever he had to touch base with family since Denver. Had he messed up? He went back over the calls in his mind, flipping forward from Singapore to Chicago to Hawaii to the Canary Islands. He'd been careful, hadn't he?

Then it hit him. He'd used the room phone at the hotel in Hawaii. No way it was monitored in real time, but his home number would have been on the hotel bill if anyone from Accounting had checked when his work credit card was charged. "Oh, sorry. Checked in with my sick kid using the hotel's phone. Probably a big long-distance surcharge. Not supposed to do that, huh?"

"No," said Nerevsky, his eyes as cold as the metal table in the conference room.

Dick's mind idly meandered into thinking about why the tables in Internal Audit were stainless steel. Easier to clean the blood off?

"Sorry," said Dick. He put his hands on the armrests of his chair to push up and leave. "That it?"

"No."

Dick shrugged and relaxed back into the chair.

"I'm especially interested in your satellite call from the rig on the Canary Islands."

Dick tried not to let his confusion show. Satellite phones were a bitch to monitor; that's why he had needed the communications logs to confirm the rig's connection to the bad guy in Switzerland. Maybe the tech guys in the office had followed up on that lead and also found Melanie's cell number in the sat phone records. "Oh," he said, as casually as possible. "Yeah, called to check on my family using the bad guy's phone, too. Probably made the electronic techs waste time on a false lead. Shouldn't have done that."

"Definitely not."

There was no way even Internal Audit had monitored his conversation with that satellite phone. He just had to play it cool. "Look, just a month or so ago, I was trading gunfire with a bunch of goons on an oil rig to stop a major disaster. I not only did so, I returned with a phone number for the megalomaniacal madman behind the curtain and with one of his henchmen—who from what I understand hasn't *stopped* talking since he regained consciousness. Apparently he's pretty pissed the helicopter his boss promised would pluck him off the rig at the last minute never showed. Look, I did my job. Are you really telling me your job is to nickel and dime me about what phones I use to check up on my wife and kid while I'm out saving the world?"

Nerevsky gave him a Mona Lisa smile, then folded his hands and leaned forward. "As I said, I'm actually more interested in the content—the precise content—of your calls home than in what phones you use to make them. Exactly what you say and to whom."

Crap! Ace hadn't snitched on him, had she? She could have. She'd certainly heard the satellite call from the drilling rig and she'd probably heard at least parts of one or two of his calls from Hawaii.

Maybe that's why he hadn't heard from her since they'd arrived back. She'd sold him out and couldn't bear to talk to him again.

"Like I said. Checking in on my sick kid. You know, 'How are you feeling? What's the doc say about a release date? I care about you.' Shit like that." He decided to test his concerns about Ace, even though he could scarcely believe he had them. "Ace was there. She can confirm."

"Oh, she did, which is why she's been re-assigned back to the Eastern European field office, at least temporarily. Lying to Internal Audit is never appreciated."

"What makes you think she was lying?"

Nerevsky glanced over his left shoulder at a small, dark panel in the corner of the room. "The high resolution cameras covering this room are very good at recording micro-expressions." His beady, ferret eyes zeroed in on Dick once more. "Besides, don't you think catching a Chinese assassin trying to kill your son warrants Internal Audit focusing extra attention on you and your family?" Nerevsky folded his hands together. "For your protection ... and ours."

Damn. That's when Dick remembered that not only did Pyotr Nerevsky have a reputation for not asking questions in interrogations he didn't already know the answers to, but that he had a background in the KGB, an organization that never gave a second thought to tapping every wire they could find. Ace hadn't sold him out, but he was still busted, even though Internal Audit couldn't possibly have monitored the satellite phone on the oil rig or the switchboard at the hotel in Hawaii or some random guy's cell phone at Upolu airport. They didn't have that reach.

But an asshole like Nerevsky, he would absolutely monitor everything the Subsidiary could reach. Nerevsky knew exactly what Dick had said on all those calls because Internal Audit had bugged every phone Dick regularly called. Not just his home phone, but his wife's phone, his kid's phone, the damn land line in his kid's hospital room, and who knew what else.

Suddenly, it seemed very warm in the conference room. Still, he had no regrets. He'd saved the world. He'd done his job. He'd done his best to keep his marriage alive and save his family. And, he'd even taught the new kid, Ace, a thing or two.

He always did what needed to be done.

The End

Dick Thornby will return in *Flash Drive*.

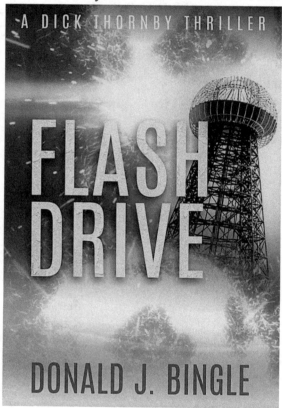

Dick Thornby Thriller #3

AFTERWORD / ACKNOWLEDGEMENTS

Like *Net Impact,* much of this book is based on real things rabidly discussed on the internet. Even the most rudimentary search will locate plenty of websites and YouTube videos on mega-tsunamis, including the possibility of tsunamis being triggered in the Hawaiian Islands or by the Cumbre Valeja volcano on La Palma in the Canary Islands. The Ward & Day paper and the television show about how a landslide on La Palma could create a mega-tsunami which would devastate a large swath of the Atlantic coastline exist. And, of course, so do sites debunking such doomsday scenarios. It's also true that fracking has been linked to increased seismic activity and that cars can be hacked, including while on the road. That said, this book is fiction, not science. My job as a thriller writer is simply to link together bits of fact with bits of fiction to give the reader an entertaining experience. If I succeeded, I hope you'll take a few minutes to tell a friend or post a review on your favorite book seller website, social media platform, or review blog.

A number of people helped me with advice, information, comments, or suggestions on the book, the cover, and other aspects of its publication (including my crowdfunding effort on Kickstarter to bankroll its publication), along with much encouragement and support. Thank you all. Special thanks to Christine Redford, Jean Rabe, Lori Swan, Mary Konczyk, Joni Holderman, John Helfers, Richard Lee Byers, Kelly Swails, William Pack, Brent Meske, Juan Villar Padron, Marianne Nowicki, Christine Verstraete, Paul Genesse, Richard Bingle, the St. Charles Writing Group, everyone who read and reviewed *Net Impact* (the first book in the Dick Thornby Thriller series), and especially my wife, Linda, who puts up with my constant complaints about my computer, my interminable struggles with formatting software, and my rants on marketing frustrations.

Thanks to all who supported the *Wet Work* Kickstarter campaign. Listing all of you would have delayed publication, so I'm not doing that here, but please know that each and every one of you have my personal, heartfelt gratitude.

Please go to my website at www.donaldjbingle.com to find out more about my writing or follow me on Facebook, Twitter, and Goodreads @donaldjbingle to hear my latest announcements. I've begun plotting and research on the next Dick Thornby Thriller, *Flash Drive*. When and whether that book comes out depends entirely on the sales of *Net Impact* and *Wet Work*. Dick's future is in your hands.

Donald J. Bingle
Writer on Demand ™
St. Charles, Illinois

ABOUT THE AUTHOR

Best known as the world's top-ranked player of classic role-playing games for the last fifteen years of the last century, Donald J. Bingle is an oft-published author in the science fiction, fantasy, horror, thriller, steampunk, romance, and comedy genres, with a half dozen published novels (Forced Conversion, GREENSWORD, Net Impact, Frame Shop, The Love-Haight Case Files, and Wet Work) and about fifty stories, many in DAW themed anthologies and tie-in anthologies, including stories in The Crimson Pact, Steampunk'd, Imaginary Friends, Fellowship Fantastic, Zombie Raccoons and Killer Bunnies, Time Twisters, Front Lines, Slipstreams, Gamer Fantastic, Transformers Legends, Search for Magic (Dragonlance), If I Were An Evil Overlord, Blue Kingdoms: Mages & Magic, Civil War Fantastic, Future Americas, All Hell Breaking Loose, The Dimension Next Door, Sol's Children, Historical Hauntings, and Fantasy Gone Wrong. A number of his stories have been collected in his Writer on Demand™ Series, including Tales of Gamers and Gaming, Tales of Humorous Horror, Tales Out of Time, Grim, Fair e-Tales, Tales of an Altered Past Powered by Romance, Horror, and Steam, Not-So-Heroic Fantasy, and Shadow Realities.

Donald J. Bingle is a member of the International Thriller Writers, Science Fiction and Fantasy Writers of America, Horror Writers Association, International Association of Media Tie-In Writers, and Origins Game Fair Library. More on Don and his writing can be found at www.donaldjbingle.com.

Dick Thornby Thrillers by Donald J. Bingle:

Net Impact
Wet Work
Flash Drive (forthcoming)

Other Books by Donald J. Bingle:

Forced Conversion
GREENSWORD: A Tale of Extreme Global Warming
Frame Shop: Critiquing Another Writer Can Be Murder
The Love-Haight Case Files (with Jean Rabe)

Stories and Story Collections by Donald J. Bingle

Writer on Demand™ Vol. 1, Tales of Gamers and
Gaming
Writer on Demand™ Vol. 2, Tales of Humorous Horror
Writer on Demand™ Vol. 3, Tales Out of Time
Writer on Demand™ Vol. 4, Grim, Fair e-Tales
Writer on Demand™ Vol. 5, Tales of an Altered Past
Powered by Romance, Horror, and Steam
Writer on Demand™ Vol. 6, Not-So-Heroic Fantasy
Writer on Demand™ Vol. 7, Shadow Realities
Crimson Life/Crimson Death
Season's Critiquings

Merry Mark-Up
Holiday Workshopping
Santa Clauses and Phrases
Gentlemanly Horrors of Mine Alone
Running Free: A Tale Inspired by Patsy Ann
Father's Day Deluxe 3-Pack

Also from 54°40' Orphyte, Inc.

Familiar Spirits Edited by Donald J. Bingle
Ratfish by Buck Hanno
Surrounded by Love: A Story of Orphans and Family
by Marjorie L. Bingle

**Semi-Finalist in 2015
Soon-to-be-Famous
Illinois Author Competition**

From its lurid, over-the-top prologue to its quirky addendum, *Frame Shop* mixes violence, humor, and occasional writing advice in a format that will keep mystery lovers, aspiring authors, NaNoWriMo participants, and established writers turning the pages.

Harold J. Ackerman thinks his latest cat mystery proves he is the best writer in the Pleasant Meadows Writers' Guild and Critiquing Society, not that the motley assortment of poets, poseurs, and wannabe writers in the PMWGCS provides much competition. But then Gantry Ellis, the NYT best-selling author of the Danger McAdams mystery thrillers, joins the group and wows everyone. Still, Harold hopes to leverage his connection to the famous author into a big break, but soon his efforts lead to murder ... and then more murder.

Visit **donaldjbingle.com** for more information.

Love-Haight is a comedy, locked within a mystery, hidden in a horror story...
Wonderfully clever, stylish, and ghoulish. Delightfully twisted fun!
William C. Dietz, New York Times bestselling author

A seamless blend of horror, romance, and legal intrigue that makes for an urban
fantasy-laced cocktail of literary delights sure to thrill readers of all stripes.
Matt Forbeck, New York Times bestselling author

Part fantasy noir, part supernatural legal thriller, Love-Haight sparkles with wit and
originality.
Troy Denning, New York Times bestselling author

You have to enjoy a book where they kill the lawyer and he still defends his undead
clients.
Jody Lynn Nye, New York Times bestselling author

Visit **donaldjbingle.com** for more information.